ENCLAVE

ANN AGUIRRE

FEIWEL AND FRIENDS
NEW YORK

A FEIWEL AND FRIENDS BOOK
An Imprint of Macmillan

ENCLAVE. Copyright © 2011 by Ann Aguirre. All rights reserved.
Distributed in Canada by H.B. Fenn and Company Ltd. Printed in March 2011 in
the United States of America by R. R. Donnelley & Sons Company, Harrisonburg,
Virginia. For information, address Feiwel and Friends, 175 Fifth Avenue,
New York, N.Y. 10010.

Library of Congress Cataloging-in-Publication Data

Aguirre, Ann.
Enclave / Ann Aguirre. — 1st ed.
p. cm.
Summary: In a post-apocalyptic future, fifteen-year-old Deuce, a loyal
Huntress, brings back meat while avoiding the Freaks outside her enclave, but
when she is partnered with the mysterious outsider, Fade, she begins to see
that the strict ways of the elders may be wrong—and dangerous.
ISBN: 978-0-312-65008-7
[1. Science fiction.]   I. Title.
PZ7.A26877Raz 2011   [Fic]—dc22   2010031039

Book design by Susan Walsh

Feiwel and Friends logo designed by Filomena Tuosto

First Edition: 2011

10 9 8 7 6 5 4 3 2 1

macteenbooks.com

For Andres, always. Though the path was sometimes strewn with thorns, you were always there to hold my hand, or catch me when I stumbled.

one

down below

In the windowless tomb of a blind mother, in the dead of night, under the feeble rays of a lamp in an alabaster globe, a girl came into the darkness with a wail.

—George MacDonald, *The Day Boy and the Night Girl*

Deuce

I was born during the second holocaust. People had told us legends of a time when human beings lived longer. I thought they were just stories. Nobody even lived to see forty in my world.

Today was my birthday. Each one added a layer of fear, and this year, it was worse. I lived in an enclave in which our oldest had seen twenty-five years. His face was withered, and his fingers shook when he attempted the smallest tasks. Some whispered it would be a kindness to kill him, but they meant they didn't want to see their futures written in his skin.

"Are you ready?" Twist stood waiting for me in the darkness.

He already wore his marks; he was two years older than me, and if he'd survived the ritual, I could. Twist was small and frail by any standards; privation had cut runnels into his cheeks, aging him. I studied the pallor of my forearms and then nodded. It was time for me to become a woman.

The tunnels were wide and laid with metal bars. We had found remnants of what might've been transportation, but they lay on their sides like great, dead beasts. We used them for emergency shelters sometimes. If a hunting party was attacked before it reached sanctuary, a heavy metal wall between them and hungry enemies made the difference between life and death.

I had never been outside the enclave, of course. This space comprised the only world I'd ever known, cast in darkness and curling smoke. The walls were old, built of rectangular blocks. Once they had borne color but the years had worn them gray. Splashes of brightness came from items we scavenged from deeper in the warren.

I followed Twist through the maze, my gaze touching on familiar objects. My favorite item was a picture of a girl on a white cloud. I couldn't make out what she was holding; that part had worn away. But the words in bright red, HEAVENLY HAM, looked wonderful to me. I wasn't sure what that was, but by her expression, it must have been very good.

The enclave assembled on naming day, everyone who had survived to be named. We lost so many when they were young that we just called all the brats Boy or Girl, along with a number. Since our enclave was small—and dwindling—I recognized each face shadowed by the half-light. It was hard not to let the expectation of pain knot my stomach, along with the fear I would wind up with a terrible name that would cling to me until I died.

Please let it be something good.

The oldest, who carried the burden of the name Whitewall, walked to the center of the circle. He stopped before the fire, and its licking flame painted his skin in terrifying shades. With one hand, he beckoned me forward.

Once I joined him, he spoke. "Let each Hunter bring forth his gift."

The others carried their tokens and piled them at my feet. A mound of interesting items grew—and a few of them, I had no idea what purpose they might've served. *Decoration, perhaps?*

People in the world before seemed obsessed with objects that existed simply to look pretty. I couldn't imagine such a thing.

After they finished, Whitewall turned to me. "It's time."

Silence fell. Cries echoed through the tunnels. Somewhere close by, somebody was suffering, but he wasn't old enough to attend my naming. We might lose another citizen before we finished here. Sickness and fever devastated us and our medicine man did more harm than good, it seemed to me. But I'd learned not to question his treatments. Here in the enclave, one didn't prosper by demonstrating too much independent thought.

These rules permit us to survive, Whitewall would say. *If you cannot abide by them, then you are free to see how you fare Topside.* The eldest had a mean streak; I didn't know if he had always been that way, or if age had made him so. And now, he stood before me, ready to take my blood.

Though I had never witnessed the ritual before, I knew what to expect. I extended my arms. The razor glinted in the firelight. It was our prized possession, and the oldest kept it clean and sharp. He made three jagged cuts on my left arm, and I held my pain until it coiled into a silent cry within me. I would not shame the enclave by weeping. He slashed my right arm before I could do more than brace. I clenched my teeth as hot blood trickled downward. Not too much. The cuts were shallow, symbolic.

"Close your eyes," he said.

I obeyed. He bent, spreading the gifts before me, and then grabbed my hand. His fingers were cold and thin. From whatever my blood struck, so would I take my name. With my eyes closed, I could hear the others breathing, but they were still and reverent. Movement rustled nearby.

"Open your eyes and greet the world, Huntress. From this day forward, you will be called Deuce."

I saw the oldest held a card. It was torn and stained, yellow with age. The back had a pretty red pattern and the front had what looked like a black shovel blade on it, along with the number two. It was also speckled with my blood, which meant I must keep it with me at all times. I took it from him with a murmur of thanks.

Strange. No longer would I be known as Girl15. My new name would take some getting used to.

The enclave dispersed. People offered me nods of respect as they went about their business. Now that the naming day ceremony was complete, there was still food to be hunted and supplies to be scavenged. Our work never ended.

"You were very brave," Twist said. "Now let's take care of your arms."

It was just as well we had no audience for this part because my courage failed. I wept when he put the hot metal to my skin. Six scars to prove I was tough enough to call myself Huntress. Other citizens received less; Builders got three scars. Breeders took only one. For as long as anyone could remember, the number of marks on the arms identified what role a citizen played.

We could not permit the cuts to heal naturally for two reasons: They would not scar properly and infection might set in. Over the years, we had lost too many to the naming day ritual because they cried and begged; they couldn't bear the white-hot conclusion. Now Twist no longer paused at the sight of tears, and I was glad he didn't acknowledge them.

I am Deuce.

Tears spilled down my cheeks as the nerve endings died, but the scars appeared one by one, proclaiming my strength and my ability to weather whatever I found out in the tunnels. I had been training for this day my whole life; I could wield a knife or a club with equal proficiency. Every bite of food I ate that had been supplied by someone else, I consumed with the understanding it would be my turn someday to provide for the brats.

That day had come. Girl15 was dead.

Long live Deuce.

After the naming, two friends held a party for me. I found them both waiting in the common area. We'd come up together as brats, though our personalities and physical skills put us on different paths. Still, Thimble and Stone were my two closest companions. Of the three, I was the youngest, and they'd taken pleasure in calling me Girl15 after they both got their names.

Thimble was a small girl a little older than me, who served as a Builder. She had dark hair and brown eyes. Because of her pointed chin and wide gaze, people sometimes questioned if she was old enough to be out of brat training. She hated that; there was no surer way to rouse her temper.

Grime often stained her fingers because she worked with her hands, and it found its way onto her clothing and smudged her face. We'd gotten used to seeing her scratch her cheek and leave a dark streak behind. But I didn't tease her anymore because she was sensitive. One of her legs was a touch shorter than the other, and she walked with a whisper of a limp, not from injury, but that small defect. Otherwise, she might easily have become a Breeder.

Because he was strong and handsome, but not especially bright, Stone landed as a Breeder. Whitewall figured he had good material in him, and if matched with a clever female, he should sire good, solid offspring. Only citizens with traits worth passing on were allowed to contribute to the next generation, and the elders monitored births carefully. We couldn't allow more brats than we could provide for.

Thimble rushed up to examine my forearms. "How much did it hurt?"

"A lot," I said. "Twice as much as yours." I gave Stone a pointed look. "*Six* times as much as yours."

He always joked he had the easiest job in the enclave, and maybe that was true, but I wouldn't want the burden of making sure our people survived to the next generation. On top of siring the young, he also shared the responsibility of looking after them. I didn't think I could deal with so much death. Brats were unbelievably fragile. This year, he'd sired one male, and I didn't know how he dealt with the fear. I could barely remember my dam; she'd died young even by our standards. When she was eighteen, a sickness swept through the enclave, likely carried by the trading party from Nassau. It took a lot of our people that year.

Some citizens thought the offspring of Breeders should stay in that role. There was a quiet movement among the Hunters to take their number from their own—that once a Hunter got too old for patrols, he or she could sire the next crop of Hunters. I'd fought my whole life against that thinking. From the time I could walk, I'd watched the Hunters going off into the tunnels and known it for my destiny.

"It's not my fault I'm handsome," he said, grinning.

"Stop, you two." Thimble got out a present wrapped in faded cloth. "Here."

I hadn't expected this. Brow raised, I took the parcel from her, hefted it, and said, "You made me new daggers."

She glared. "I hate when you do that."

To appease her, I unfolded the fabric. "They're *beautiful*."

And they were. Only a Builder could do such fine work. She'd poured these just for me. I imagined the long hours over the fire and the time in the mold and the tempering and the polishing and sharpening afterward. They gleamed in the torchlight. I tested them and found them perfectly balanced. I executed a couple of moves to show her how much I liked them, and Stone jumped as if I might hit him on accident. He could be such an idiot. A Huntress never stabbed anything she didn't intend to.

"I wanted you to have the best out there."

"Me too," Stone said.

He hadn't bothered to wrap his gift; it was simply too big. The club wasn't Builder quality work, but Stone had a fair hand with carving, and he'd taken a solid scrap of wood for the core. I suspected Thimble must've helped him with the banded metal along the top and bottom, but the fanciful figures cut into the wood came from him, no mistake. I didn't recognize all of the animals, but it was lovely and solid, and I would feel safer with it on my back. He'd rubbed the carvings with some kind of dye, so they stood out from the grain. The decorations would actually make it harder for me to keep the weapon clean, but Stone was a Breeder, and he couldn't be expected to think of things like that.

I smiled in appreciation. "This is wonderful."

They both hugged me and then produced a treat we'd been saving for my naming day. Thimble had traded for this tin long ago—in anticipation of the occasion. The container itself offered unusual pleasure in that it shone bright red and white, brighter than most things we found down here. We didn't know what was inside it; only that it had been sealed so thoroughly that we needed tools to pry it open.

A lovely scent drifted out. I had never smelled anything like it, but it was fresh and sweet. Inside, I saw nothing but colored dust. Impossible to tell what it might have once been, but the aroma alone made my naming day special.

"What is it?" Thimble asked.

Hesitantly, I touched a fingertip to the pink dust. "I think it might be to make us smell better."

"Do we put it on our clothes?" Stone leaned in and gave a sniff.

Thimble considered. "Only for special occasions."

"Anything in there?" I stirred, until I touched bottom. "There is!"

Elated, I drew out a square of stiff paper. It was white with gold letters, but they had a funny shape and I couldn't read them. Some of them looked like they were supposed to; others didn't. They looped and dropped and curled in ways that made them confusing to my eye.

"Put it back," she said. "It might be important."

It *was* important, if only for being one of the few complete documents we had from the time before. "We should take it to the Wordkeeper."

Even though we'd traded for this tin fair and square, if it yielded a valuable enclave resource and we tried to keep it for ourselves, we could wind up in serious trouble. Trouble led to exile, and exile to unspeakable things. By mutual agreement, we replaced the paper and closed the tin. We shared a sober look, aware of the potential consequences. None of us wanted to be accused of hoarding.

"Let's take care of it now," Stone said. "I have to get back to the brats soon."

"Give me a bit."

Moving at a run, I headed to look for Twist. I found him in the kitchens, not surprisingly. I still hadn't been assigned a private living space. Now that I'd been named, I could have a room of my own. No more brat dorm.

"What do you want?" he demanded.

I tried not to take offense. Just because I'd been named didn't mean his treatment of me would improve overnight. To some, I'd be little more than a brat for a couple of years. Until I started edging toward elder territory.

"Just tell me where my space is?"

Twist sighed, but obligingly he led the way through the maze. Along the way, we dodged many bodies and wound through the layers of partitions and makeshift shelters. Mine sat in between two others, but it was four feet to call my own.

My room had three crude walls, constructed of old metal, and a ragged length of cloth for an illusion of privacy. Everyone had more or less the same; it only varied in terms of what trinkets people kept. I had a secret weakness for shiny things. I was always trading for something that glittered when I held it to the light.

"That all?"

Before I could answer, he went back toward the kitchen. Taking a deep breath, I pushed through the curtain. I had a rag pallet and a crate for my meager belongings. But nobody else had the right to come in here without my invitation. I'd earned my place.

Despite my worry, I smiled while I stowed my new weapons. Nobody would touch anything in here, and it was best not to visit the Wordkeeper armed to the teeth. Like Whitewall, he was getting on in years, and tended to be strange.

I didn't look forward to this interrogation at all.

Trial

I t didn't take long to spill our story and show him the tin. He reached inside, letting the pink dust trail through his fingers. The card he handled carefully.

"You say you've had this item for some time?" The Wordkeeper glared at the three of us, as if we were guilty of stupidity at least.

Stone explained, "We traded for it together and agreed we'd open it on Fifteen's . . . er, Deuce's naming day."

"So you had no idea of the contents before now?"

"No, sir," I said.

Thimble added a timid nod. Her limp made her self-conscious, as the enclave seldom permitted such imperfections. But hers was minor and didn't impede her performance as a Builder. In fact, I'd say she worked twice as hard, not wanting anyone to feel they'd made a mistake about her.

"Are you willing to swear?" the Wordkeeper asked.

"Yes," Thimble said. "None of us had any idea what it held."

They fetched Copper from the kitchens and she witnessed. The Wordkeeper growled as he took the document into evidence. "Get out, all of you. I'll let you know of my decision in due time."

I felt sick as we went back to my room. I wanted to show them where it was, anyway. Stone could enter with Thimble present as a chaperone. Like in the old days, in the brat dorm, we flopped onto the pallet together. Stone sat between us and wrapped an arm around each of us. He felt warm and familiar, and I leaned my head against his shoulder. I wouldn't let anybody else touch me like this, but he was different. We were bratmates, practically related.

"It'll be fine," he said. "They can't punish us for something we didn't do."

Looking at the pleasure in Thimble's face as she nestled against him, I wondered if she might do better as a Breeder. But the elders wouldn't let her, even if she'd preferred it. Nobody wanted imperfections passed on, even the small, harmless ones.

"He's right," she agreed.

I nodded. The elders looked after us. Certainly, they had to consider the matter, but once they'd studied all the facts, no harm would come to us. We'd done the right thing and turned the paper over as soon as we found it.

Absently, Stone played with my hair; for him, it was a simple instinct. Touching wasn't forbidden to Breeders. They hugged and patted so easily it alarmed me. Builders and Hunters had to take such care not to be accused of wrongdoing.

"I have to go," Stone said regretfully.

"To make some brats or look after them?" Thimble asked with a flash of ire.

For a moment, I felt so sorry for her. To me, it was painfully obvious she wanted something she could never have. Unlike me. I had *exactly* what I wanted. I couldn't wait to start work.

He grinned, taking the question at face value. "If you must know—"

"Never mind," I said hastily.

Her face fell. "I should go too. Hope you had a good naming day, Deuce."

"Apart from seeing the Wordkeeper, it was fine." I smiled as they both left and fell back on my pallet to think about my future as a Huntress.

The first time I saw Fade, he frightened me. He had a lean, sharp face and shaggy dark hair that fell over his forehead into the blackest eyes, like a bottomless pit. And he bore so many scars, as if he'd lived through battles the rest of us couldn't imagine. Hard as life had been here, his silent rage said he'd seen worse.

Unlike most, he hadn't been born in the enclave. He came in through the tunnels, half grown when we found him, half starved and more than half feral. He didn't have a number designation, or even any concept of how to behave. Still, the older citizens voted to let him stay.

"Anybody who can survive out in the tunnels on his own has to be strong," Whitewall had said. "We can use him."

"If he doesn't kill us all first," Copper had muttered back.

Copper was second oldest at twenty-four, and she served as mate to Whitewall, though it was a fluid arrangement. She was also the only one who dared to back-talk him, even a little bit. The rest of us had learned to mind. I'd seen people exiled because they refused to obey the rules.

So when Whitewall decreed the stranger stayed, we had to make it work. It was a long while before I actually set eyes on him. They tried to teach him our ways, and he spent long hours with the Wordkeeper. He already knew how to fight; he didn't seem to know how to live with other people, or at least, he found *our* laws confusing.

I was just a brat at the time, so I wasn't involved in his assimilation. I was training to become a Huntress. Since I wanted to prove myself with blade and boot, I worked tirelessly. When the strange boy got his name, I wasn't there. He didn't know how old he was, so they guessed when to christen him.

After that, I saw him around, but I certainly never spoke to him. Brats and Hunters didn't mix, unless lessons were involved. Those earmarked for combat and patrol duties studied under the veteran Hunters. I'd spent most of my time training with Silk, but a few others had schooled me over the years as well. I formally met Fade much later, after my own naming. He was teaching the fundamentals of knife work when Twist delivered me to his class.

"That's all," Fade said, as we joined them.

The brats dispersed with quiet grumbling. I remembered how sore my muscles had been when I started training. Now I took pleasure in the hardness of my arms and legs. I wanted to test myself against the dangers beyond our makeshift walls.

Twist tilted his head at me. "This is your new partner. Silk ranked her as the best in her group."

"Did she?" Fade's voice sounded odd.

I met his black eyes with a lift of my chin. *Can't let him think he intimidates me.* "Yes. I scored ten out of ten in throws."

He raked me with a scathing look. "You're puny."

"And you're quick to judge."

"What's your name?"

I had to think; I almost said Girl15. I fingered the card in my pocket, finding comfort in its edges. It was my talisman now. "Deuce."

"I'll leave you two to talk," Twist said. "I have other things to do."

He did, of course. Since he was small and fragile, he couldn't hunt. He served as a second to Whitewall, running errands for him and taking care of administrative tasks. I couldn't remember ever seeing him just sitting still, not even at night. I lifted my hand as he went around the jagged metal partition to another section of the settlement.

"I'm Fade," he told me.

"I know. Everyone knows you."

"Because I'm not one of you."

"You said it, not me."

His head jerked in a nod that said he didn't want to answer any questions. Since I refused to be like everyone else, I swallowed my curiosity. If he didn't want to talk, I didn't care. Everyone wondered about his story, but only Whitewall had ever heard it—and maybe *he* didn't even know the truth. But I was only interested in Fade as the one who guarded my back, so it didn't matter.

He changed the subject. "Silk assigns hunting parties daily. We join the rotation tomorrow. I hope you're as good as she claims."

"What happened to your last partner?"

Fade smiled. "He wasn't as good as Silk claimed."

"You want to find out?" I lifted my brow in a challenge.

The space had cleared of brats, so he shrugged and took a position in the center. "Show me what you've got."

It was a clever tactic, but I wasn't that green. The offensive fighter lost the chance to assess his opponent's style. I shook my head at him and curled my fingers. He almost smiled; I saw it start in his eyes, but then he focused on the fight.

We circled a few times. I leaned toward caution because I'd never seen him spar with anyone. I watched the Hunters every chance I got, but he didn't spend much time with them outside of patrols.

He lashed out with a quick left, followed by a right cross. I blocked one but not the other; kind of him not to use his full strength. Still, the blow rocked me. I used the new angle to sink a fist into his ribs and spin away. *He wasn't expecting me to recover so fast*, I thought.

Our sparring gathered an audience. I tried to ignore them, as I wanted to make a good showing. I went for his leg but he leaped and I recovered in a clumsy stumble while he pressed forward. When he swept, I didn't slide away in time and he took me down smoothly. I tried to roll out of the lock, but he had me. I glared up at him, but he held me until I tapped.

Fade offered me a hand up. "Not bad. You lasted a couple of minutes."

With a grin, I took it. I refused to make the excuse that my arms were sore. He could see that for himself. "You got lucky today. I'd like a rematch."

He walked away without giving me an answer. I'd take that as a maybe.

That night, I honed my blade. I double—and triple—checked my equipment. Even with all my training and my preparations, I found it hard to sleep. I lay and listened to the comforting sounds of life around me. A brat cried. Someone was breeding. Moans of pain mingled with softer sighs.

I must have dozed because Twist roused me with a foot in the ribs. "Get up and eat. You're due on patrol in a little while. And don't think I'll be bothering to wake you personally after today."

"I won't," I said.

It was a wonder I'd slept at all. *My first patrol.* Excitement warred with nerves. Using a touch of oil, I slicked my hair into an efficient tail and geared up. That meant looping my club across my back and sliding my blades into the thigh sheaths. I had made all of the equipment myself; Whitewall thought such self-sufficiency encouraged greater care, and maybe he was right.

As I approached the kitchen area, the smoke stung my eyes. Copper was roasting something on a spit, and the grease hissed as it dropped into the fire. She got out her dagger and cut me a hunk of meat. It burned my fingers as I took it and gobbled it down. I'd never eaten breakfast first; only Hunters did that. Pride blazed in me.

I watched the Hunters wolf down their portions, each larger than I'd ever received before. They all looked hard and ready, not nervous at all. I glanced around for Fade and found him eating alone. The others didn't talk to him. Even now, he was an outsider, still regarded with subtle suspicion.

As we finished our food, Silk stepped up onto a table. "There have been sightings closer to the enclave than we want."

A male Hunter whose name I didn't know asked, "Freaks?"

A shiver ran through me. Freaks looked almost human—and weren't. They had lesions on their skin, razor-sharp teeth, and claws instead of fingernails. I'd heard you could detect them by smell, though in the tunnels, that could be hard. It already smelled of a hundred things down here, only half of them good. But Twist had told me Freaks stank like carrion meat. They feasted on the dead, but they would eat fresh meat if they could get it. We had to make sure they didn't.

Silk nodded. "They're getting bolder. Kill any you come across." She held up a cloth sack. "Your goal today is to fill this bag with meat. As long as it's not Freak, I don't care what you put in it. Good hunting."

The others headed out. I cut through the throng and headed for Fade. He looked even scarier than he had the night before. He might not be more than a couple of seasons older than me, but it was a lifetime of hunting experience. His weapons shone, a reassuring sight. For all I wanted to prove myself, I also wanted a partner I could count on. I would be stupid not to worry that his last one had died out there. Maybe someday he'd tell me the circumstances.

"Let's do this," he said.

I followed him through the kitchen area and into an adjunct tunnel. Long ago, we'd erected barricades in key points, preventing an easy flow to our main settlement. We exited through the east blockade, and it required me to scramble using my hands and knees before I got past the rubble. To my eyes, it needed shoring up again with new salvage, but that was Builder work.

Beyond the light of the enclave, it was dark, darker than I'd ever seen. It took my eyes long moments to adjust. Fade waited while I made the shift.

"We hunt like this?" Nobody ever told me. Primitive fear scuttled up my spine.

"Light attracts Freaks. We don't want them to see us first."

Reflexively, I checked my weapons as if mentioning the monsters could bring them slavering out of the murk. My club slid free cleanly. I put it back. Likewise, my knives found my palms in a smooth motion.

As we moved, my other senses compensated. I had done visual deprivation as part of my training, but I hadn't understood just how much I would need that skill out here. Now I was glad I could hear him moving ahead of me because I could make out only vague shadows. No wonder Hunters died.

Ahead of me, Fade checked the various snares. A couple yielded meat. Another partner might've put me at ease; he left me trailing in the darkness and the silence. Fine, I could handle myself. I wasn't scared.

I told myself that right up until we made a left turn and I heard noises in the distance. Wet, sucking sounds echoed, so I had no idea how close they really were. The ground roughened beneath my feet, broken metal and chunks of stone. Fade melted into the dark, going *toward* danger.

Because it was my job, I followed.

We came to a crossing, where four tunnels connected. Above, the ceiling had cracked and fallen, leaving debris everywhere. Sickly light trickled in from a great distance, speckling everything with a peculiar glow, and I spotted my first Freak.

Because we moved as silently as twin knives, the monster hadn't seen or heard us yet. It crouched over a dead thing, tearing raw flesh with its teeth. There would be more nearby. In my lore classes, they'd told us Freaks ran in packs.

Fade made a silent gesture, telling me he would take this one. I should watch for the rest. A lift of my head confirmed my understanding of the plan. He went in, lean and deadly, and ended the creature with a lightning-fast spike of his blade. It shrieked, likely alerting the rest. The death call carried like a mournful song.

Movement to the north drew my eye. We had two more incoming at a dead run. Instinct kicked in, leaving me no space for fear. My knives slipped into my hands—unlike most Hunters, I could fight with two at the same time.

Silk didn't lie. I am the best of my group.

I told myself that as the first Freak slammed into me. But I greeted it with an upward slash and an outward thrust with my left hand. *Hit the vitals. Go for the kill shot.* I heard Silk's voice in my head, telling me, *Every moment you spend fighting this thing drains energy you won't have later, when you need it most.*

My blade bit into rank, spongy flesh and slammed through bone. I shook my head mentally. Too high. I didn't want the rib cage. It howled in pain and raked its filthy claws toward my shoulder. This wasn't like training; this thing didn't use moves I knew.

Grimly, I countered with my right hand. I wished I had the leisure to watch Fade, assess his style, but this was my first real fight, and I didn't want to come out of it looking worse than an untrained brat. It mattered that I earned my partner's respect.

My leg lashed out, and I combined the kick with an angled knife thrust. Both connected, and the Freak went down, gushing foul blood. It didn't look like ours, darker, thick and fetid. I popped it in the heart with my left hand and danced back to avoid getting clawed while it was in its death throes.

Fade finished faster than me. To be expected, I supposed, given his greater experience. I cleaned my knives on the rags the Freak wore and slid them back into their sheaths. Now I understood on a visceral level why the Hunters spent so much time caring for their weapons. I felt like I might never get the stain off the metal.

"Not bad," he said at last.

"Thanks."

I'd done it. I was officially blooded. As much as the new scars on my arms, that marked me as a Huntress. My shoulders squared.

We left the three corpses. Horrible as it sounded, other Freaks would eat them. They had no care for their dead. They did not attack each other, but otherwise, anything in the tunnels—living or dead—offered fuel for their endless appetites.

By comparison the rest of our patrol passed with relative ease. Half the traps yielded meat. A number of animals lived down here with us; four-legged furry creatures we called food. I killed a wounded one, where the snare hadn't broken its neck clean, and that bothered me more than killing the Freak. I held its warm body in my hands and bowed my head over it. Wordless, Fade took it from me and dropped it in the sack with the others. We had brats to feed.

I didn't know how he marked the time, but eventually he said, "We should head back."

On the return, I tried to memorize our route. Though no one had stated it, one day Fade would expect me to lead. He wouldn't accept excuses, any more than I was inclined to offer them. So on our way, I counted our steps and turns and committed them to memory.

By the time we reached the enclave, other Hunters had already begun reporting in. Twist took charge of the bags, weighing the meat and either commending or berating the team. We heard "nice job" while the pair after us got "thanks to you, the brats go hungry in the morning."

"I'll see you tomorrow," I said to Fade.

He inclined his head and circled around the fire. Without meaning to, I found myself watching the lean, muscular lines of his back and the way his hair fell against the nape of his neck. Fade moved like he fought, economically and without wasted effort.

"What do you think of him?" Silk asked. At twenty, she stood a little taller than me with fair hair she wore shorn close to her head. Her toughness made her an ideal leader. But her face contorted with contempt as she gazed at Fade. She didn't like what he stood for and that he didn't accept his orders with the same zeal as everyone else.

My opinions about Fade were far too tangled to talk about, so I murmured, "Too soon to say."

"A lot of citizens fear him. They say he must be part Freak or he'd have been eaten out there."

"People say a lot of things," I muttered.

Silk took it as a tacit defense of my new partner and her mouth twisted. "That they do. *Some* say you should be a Breeder like your dam."

I set my teeth and strode out of the kitchen, determined to find a partner and do a little extra training. Nobody would dismiss me as unfit to be a Huntress. Nobody.

Wordkeeper

Two days later, they called Stone, Thimble, and me before the Wordkeeper. He'd had time to consider the matter of the white card. Though I knew we hadn't done anything wrong, my stomach still tightened with dread.

He wasn't quite as old as Whitewall, but he had an air about him that made me nervous. The Wordkeeper was tall and thin with arms like bone. He sat before us wearing a heavy look.

"After examining the tin, I have determined you had no fore-knowledge of its contents. I judge you all innocent." Relief spilled through me as he went on. "You did well in bringing me the document. I will add it to our archives." He referred to a gray metal box in which he stored all of our important papers. "But as a reward for your honesty, I have decided to read this to you. Make yourselves comfortable."

That was new. Most of us could read enough to make out warning signs, but not a lot more. Our training focused on other areas, those more valuable to the whole. At his invitation I sat, folding my legs before me. Thimble and Stone did likewise on either side of me.

The Wordkeeper cleared this throat. "'You are cordially in-vited to the wedding of Anthony P. Cicero and Jennifer L. Grant on Tuesday, June the Second, year of Our Lord 2009 at four o'clock. Thirty-five East Olivet Avenue. RSVP enclosed. Reception to follow.'"

It all sounded very mysterious. I wanted to ask some questions, but he'd already granted us a favor. The Wordkeeper made it clear we were dismissed once he finished, so I led the way to the common area.

Thimble looked thoughtful. "What do you think a wedding is?"

"Some kind of party? Maybe like we have after naming day." I did wonder why the paper had been sealed in a box full of sweet-smelling powder, but I had long since accepted that I'd never understand everything. In the enclave, it mattered more that we performed well in our allotted roles. Life didn't permit extensive curiosity; there was no time for it.

"Do you have any other contraband?" Stone joked. "We could take a look at it before we have to go back to work."

Thimble leveled a stern gaze at him. "That's not funny. They're going to be watching us for weeks now, just to be sure . . ." She trailed off, not wanting to voice the possible offense.

To be sure we're not hoarding. Last year, a boy named Skittle had been discovered with old documents and technology in his living space, some hidden beneath his pallet, other things concealed in hollow objects. Hunters had taken his whole collection to Whitewall and the Wordkeeper for examination and judgment. Most of it was judged significant to our cultural development, and they exiled him. Apart from Fade, I'd never heard of anyone surviving outside a settlement.

There were others down here, of course. We weren't alone. Sometimes we traded with the closest enclave, but that required a three-day hike through dangerous territory. Natural resources didn't permit large groups to live in the same area. Coming up as brats, each elder drummed it into our heads how without proper balance, we were doomed. And we believed it because it was true.

We had heard stories about other enclaves; they'd died out because they didn't enforce the rules. They overbred and starved, or they didn't follow hygiene procedures and they perished of the dirty disease. Here, the rules existed for a purpose. They saved our lives.

So I agreed with Thimble, shaking my head at Stone. "If you're going to be like that, I don't want you hanging around us."

His good-natured face fell. "I didn't mean it."

"I know you didn't," Thimble said gently. "But other people might not understand."

Likely not. They didn't know Stone like we did. He sometimes spoke before he thought, but there was no harm in him. He'd never do anything to hurt the rest of the enclave. You only had to see him with a brat in each arm to understand that, but Whitewall and the Wordkeeper had to err on the side of cruelty, if it came down to the greater good. I didn't want my friend sent on the long walk.

"I'll be more careful." He looked truly chastened.

Shortly thereafter, we split, going our separate ways for work. Part of me knew our friendship couldn't hold its close ties. Over time, Thimble would bond with other Builders; they had more in common, things to talk about. Stone would stay with the Breeders, and I'd find myself more at home with the Hunters. I didn't like thinking about the inevitable because it reminded me how soon our lives would change forever.

I arrived in the staging ground just as Silk began to speak. She cut me a sharp look, but she didn't dress me down in front of the others. I sent a silent thanks. Hopefully she knew I wouldn't make a habit of being late; any other day I would be among the first to assemble. I was so proud to wear the Hunter marks on my arms.

Silk ran down the day's priorities. "I don't know where their numbers are coming from, but even after stepping up patrols, we have more Freaks in the area."

I didn't know all of the Hunters' names yet, but a short boy said, "Maybe one of the nearby settlements has turned."

A rumble went through the group and Silk fixed a fierce glare on the worst offenders. Rumors had long circulated that Freaks could be made, not just born, and if something happened— the *wrong* something—we could all end up like that. I tended to think that was superstitious junk. We'd had Hunters bitten before, and if the bites didn't go septic, they went back out into the tunnels with no problems. They didn't change into slavering fiends.

"Enough," Silk snapped. "If you're going to turn into scared little brats, why don't you go join the Breeders?"

"They don't want his ugly face," one girl joked.

We all laughed nervously, while the short Hunter flushed bright red. He wasn't ugly, but he didn't have the qualities the elders sought in Breeders, either. They chose attractive or intelligent citizens, no exceptions. So far, their schedule seemed to work well enough. I had no complaints anyway.

Silk stared until everyone quieted. Satisfied she'd cowed us, she went on. "Find the source of the Freak incursion. Something in the tunnels is driving them our way." She turned to Fade and me. "I'm taking the two of you off meat duty. Someone else will take care of your route. Instead, I want you to check out the back ways."

And there it was, my punishment for being late. Silk didn't like Fade much at the best of times—then again, nobody did. He kept to himself. He'd never fully become part of the enclave, even after being named and marked.

"Is everyone clear on their jobs today?"

I nodded miserably. It was impossible for me to judge this as anything but a reprimand. The back ways were filthy, some flooded, and others defied description. I'd never seen them my-self, but as a brat, I'd made a habit of sitting within earshot of the Hunters. I'd lived through their stories, tried to imagine things they'd seen and done.

"Then good hunting." Silk hopped off the crate she carried with her for the briefings. She didn't like looking up to people.

Fade found me as the meeting broke up. "You had something more important to do today?"

So he was blaming me for our new assignment—and maybe he was right. "I couldn't ignore a summons from the Word-keeper."

That would earn me worse than a day's patrol in the back ways. We could survive it, right? Other Hunters had. They came back filthy and disheartened, but it wasn't a death sentence.

"I guess not. Let's get this over with."

"So we're looking for signs of what's sending the Freaks our way?"

"Hunger," he said. "We're not going to find any other an-swers out there. But I'm a good boy and I do as I'm told." His tone sounded mocking, like he thought that was a *bad* thing.

I started to explain, and then stopped myself. Instead I fol-lowed him in silence. There was no point in trying to make him understand, if he didn't already. He'd never belong with us with that attitude. He only cared about himself and his own selfish will.

Before I went over the barricade, I checked my weapons. We kept guards posted here at all times in case enemies slipped past our traps; they were Hunters who had committed some minor infraction, and so were punished with such a boring assignment. Freak incursion hadn't occurred since I'd been born, but people told stories about how in the old days, they used to raid regularly.

Fade's crazy, I thought, scowling at his back. The rules worked to protect us all, and people following orders made life better and safer for everyone.

Instead of following our usual patrol route, which I'd committed to memory, he broke left and went down a half-flooded tunnel. Like the one where we found the Freaks, it had cracked up top and water cascaded in a dirty stream. He skirted the edge of it, so I stepped where he did. There was a stone lip along the edges raised higher than the rest of the tunnel. If I stayed on it, I could avoid stepping in muck up to my waist.

It smelled disgusting and I averted my eyes from the stuff floating in it—even worse, the stuff *swimming* in it. As the tunnel sloped up, the water levels decreased until it was merely damp. The light was dim here, but it wasn't as dark as some of the other tunnels. A faded sign on the block wall read, AC ESS T MAI T ANCE S AFF ONLY. Since reading wasn't my strong point, I didn't know what the missing letters might be.

Ahead of me, Fade paused, listening. I didn't hear anything. But I didn't speak. A good Huntress respected her partner's instincts, even if he was socially ignorant.

I stilled my other senses—and then I picked up on it too, a

faint sound in the distance, like something drumming on metal. Fade loped off in that direction, weapons in hand. I drew my daggers and followed, slip-sliding in the muck.

"What is it?"

He flashed a look over his shoulder. "A distress call."

Now that he'd mentioned it, I heard a pattern in the repetition. Noise carried in a deceptive manner down here, so it took us longer than I would've believed to reach it, even going at a full run. Good thing I had been training or I would've fallen behind. As it was, I kept up with him. The pace he set carried us a long distance, out of the back ways and into a wider tunnel. I'd lost my sense of how far we were from the settlement, because of the way we'd looped.

We rounded a bend and saw one of those giant metal boxes, flipped on its side. The sound came from there. Fade waved me around to the far end. We would come in from different angles, so if this was a trap, it shouldn't catch us both.

I scrambled up over crashed metal and broken glass, being careful where I set my hands and feet. When we were both in position, we dropped down into the darkness of the compartment. It smelled of old blood and feces. My eyes adjusted to the dark, a valuable trait in a Hunter; I had been practicing since our last patrol, doing more visual deprivation, and it paid off.

I scanned the interior. I'd never been inside one of these emergency shelters. They were braced with metal poles and had seating bolted to the floor. No monsters here, only one small, emaciated human boy. A brat like this would never be allowed outside the enclave; I couldn't imagine what he was doing here. He couldn't possibly know how to hunt yet. In one hand, he held a length of metal, both a potential weapon and a signaling device. With what was obviously his last strength, he lay on one side, tapping it against the floor in a repeating pattern. At first he didn't even seem aware of us.

I knelt on his other side, away from the jagged shard he held. He reacted then, lashing out wildly.

His aim was so poor I didn't even need to dodge. "We're not going to hurt you. We've come to help."

He turned his face toward my voice. Even in the dark I could see his eyes shone an eerie white. This brat was completely blind. A shudder went through me. In our enclave, he wouldn't have survived infancy. The elders didn't waste resources on those who couldn't someday pull their own weight.

"You're human," he breathed.

"Yes. You're not far from College, that's our enclave."

The brat put his head down in relief and dropped his weapon. "I have to talk to your elders."

I wasn't sure they'd like us disobeying orders, leaving the back ways, and bringing in a stray, especially one like him. But I couldn't leave him here to die either. Fade watched me in silence, as if testing me somehow. I made my decision, knowing I'd probably face worse than a day patrolling the back ways over it.

"Can you carry him? I don't think he can walk."

"He won't weigh much. I can, but if we run into trouble you'll have to take up the slack. Can you do that, new blood?"

I enjoyed the hint of nerves in his voice. "I guess we'll find out."

In answer, Fade slung the brat over his shoulders and climbed out of the container. I sheathed one knife and clenched the other in my teeth to follow. Thankfully, I'd been watching our turns and counting; I passed him and set the pace at one he could keep, bearing the brat.

"We're likely to see trouble," he said softly, beneath the splash of our feet in the stagnant water.

"Freaks can smell weakness," I agreed.

And if Fade was right, and starvation drove them toward our enclave, then that made us meat on the move. In sufficient numbers, they could take a hunting pair. Hunters died—it was part of the job—but never without a fight.

At the four-way, they hit us from all sides.

Ambush

They lunged for Fade and the boy he was trying to protect with one arm and one knife. I whipped my club from out of its sling. This time, there were four, so that called for a bigger weapon. Winding up, I swung hard and cracked one's skull wide-open.

The other three spun, correctly judging me the greater threat. I braced for the lunge, and at the last moment, rolled away. Filth smeared the back of my shirt, and I came up behind them. I took one across the back of the knees at the same time I launched a sideways kick.

Close up, I could see these Freaks were starving to death; Fade had been right. In comparison, I was fast, strong, and well fed. There was no contest. They didn't fight as a unit. They lunged and snarled and lashed. I met each advance with a kick or a well-placed slam of the weighty end of my club. Blood spattered into the dirty water and bone crunched. In the end, we had a pile of corpses that the other Freaks would eat.

Best not to think about it.

The brat on Fade's shoulder wept. I guess if I was forced to listen to that while hanging upside down, I'd cry too. Fade patted the boy on the back until he quieted. I'm not sure it qualified as comfort so much as warning. *Shut up, shut up already.*

"Did you notice how they hit us?" he asked.

"Yeah. From all sides."

Judging by his troubled look, he shared my concern. If the Freaks were getting smarter, we were in real trouble. Right now, they lacked the ability to plan or strategize. If they evolved, became more like us in their thinking, well—we were barely hanging on as it was. Any shift in the delicate balance could wipe us out.

Still, we had to get back to the enclave before they missed us. If Silk heard from one of the other Hunters that we weren't investigating the back ways, as she'd asked, there would be hell to pay. The only way to handle this mess was to get there first.

Vaulting the bodies, I led the way back to the barricades without a single misstep. Pride swelled. I'd only seen the route once, and I remembered all the turns. I glanced over my shoulder at Fade, but he didn't recognize the accomplishment.

Instead he'd shifted the brat from his shoulder to the crook of his arms. The guard stopped us, not surprisingly, when we came back in. "You're not supposed to be off duty. And what've you got there?"

"I have to talk to your elders," the brat wheezed.

In the better light here, he didn't look good. His small face was sunken with hunger and dehydration. Dirt crusted his skin and he had sores at the corners of his mouth, where his lips had cracked. The white of his eyes gleamed even more unholy and disturbing. When the guards got a good look at him, they recoiled and blocked our path, weapons drawn.

I just knew this wasn't going to go well.

"What's going on here?" Silk demanded.

I glanced at Fade, who lifted a shoulder. I guessed that meant I should do the talking. "We found him in an emergency shelter, and he says he has important news." That was an exaggeration, but I didn't want to admit I hadn't been tough enough to leave him. The Hunter's number one tenet: "The strong survive." I'd proven myself soft today, when it came down to it, and who knew how Fade would tell the story.

"I do," the brat wheezed. "They sent me from Nassau." He named the closest settlement, three days in the tunnels if you were fast and strong. I couldn't imagine why they'd chosen him. "They sent me because they could afford to lose me," he went on.

That, I could believe. It sounded like a decision our elders would make.

"They had no Hunters to spare. We're surrounded by Freaks and they hoped if I got through, maybe you would send help."

Unlikely. Though College traded with Nassau, we had no terms of alliance, no policy of rendering aid. Each enclave governed itself and survived—or not—according to its own strength. But Silk had wanted information on whatever had the Freaks so stirred up; this counted. Maybe I could use this as my defense when I was accused of weakness and dereliction of duty.

"They're all over Nassau too?" Silk asked, her face somber. "Our elders do need to know this. Thanks for the news." She turned to Fade and me. "As for the two of you . . ." She smiled.

Yes, I could see we were going to be sorry.

"Since you thought it best not to follow your orders and we now have new information, you can check it out. You're going to Nassau."

I froze. "Just us?"

Silk *truly* didn't like Fade. I saw it in her eyes. "Do you have a problem with your orders, Huntress?"

"No, sir. What would you like us to do there?"

Her smile turned ugly. "If they are present in such numbers as the brat reported, I don't expect you to kill them. This will be recon. If you can, find out what's causing this behavior shift. In the old days, they attacked the enclaves nonstop and then they learned to fear us—our weapons and our traps. Discover *why* they don't fear us anymore. It may be important."

"What about him?" Fade lifted the boy in his arms.

Silk shrugged. "He's served his purpose. Even Nassau doesn't want him back."

Part of me wanted to suggest giving him food and water, having the medicine man look at him. I froze beneath the weight of her cool eyes. With a flicker of distaste, she handed the brat over to the guard, who handled him as if he were already dead. I bit my tongue until I tasted blood. I had to be tougher. *Had* to be. Or I'd never make it as a Huntress. Rarely, people lost their jobs. They couldn't take away my marks, but they could make me cover them with cloth armbands. They could still make me a Breeder.

A good portion of the enclave occupied that role. It kept our numbers up. Far fewer became Builders or Hunters, and the new blood *always* heard about our Breeder heritage from the older ones. *Maybe you should be a Breeder after all,* they'd say. It did no good to point out, *but nearly everyone comes from Breeder stock.* Defending the claim only threw fuel on the fire, and there were always those elite few whose sire and dam had been Hunters before age rendered them unfit.

So I said nothing. The brat was crying again, but this time Fade didn't comfort him. He stood beside me, silent for his own reasons, and I had the unmistakable feeling—it buzzed about me like an insect—that I'd disappointed him. I felt sad and sick and scared, because tomorrow we had to go to Nassau. I didn't think Silk expected us to survive. I might've been the best of the last group, but I wasn't irreplaceable. She wanted me to know that—and if I lived, to come back cowed and ready to follow orders, no matter what.

"Are we dismissed?" Fade asked.

"Yes. Be on time tomorrow," Silk said smiling.

He took my hand in a painful grip and dragged me through the warren of partitions. I didn't know where we were going, until we stopped at a random living space. By the way he stepped inside, it had to belong to him. One simply didn't treat anyone else's home with such disrespect.

For that reason, I stood outside the curtain until he said, "Get in here."

It wasn't the politest invitation I'd ever received. Frowning, I stepped in. His space looked more or less like mine. We all had the same amenities. "What?"

He dropped onto a crate, elbows on his knees. His face held an emotion I couldn't read and had never seen, but it hit me in a raw place. My skin prickled. I needed to go wash up and take care of my weapons; my club especially needed a good cleaning. I was in no mood to spend another minute with him. He'd been nothing but trouble since the first moment Silk stuck me with him.

"They're going to kill him," he said hoarsely.

And how I wished I didn't know that—or *care*. As a Huntress, I wasn't supposed to. I should care about the greater welfare of the enclave. My job existed to keep our citizens safe. Protection didn't extend to brats we found in the tunnels, unless they were like Fade, strong enough to survive on their own. We couldn't afford to feed and care for weaklings.

"I know."

"That could be me."

"It couldn't," I pointed out. "You're not defective."

He glared with black eyes that burned like coals, lunging to his feet. "That's disgusting."

When he stepped into my space, I didn't back away. "Then why do you stay? I'll tell you. Because it's better than being *out there*."

"Is it?" he asked. "How would you know?"

I flushed at the implication that I was ignorant and inexperienced, but I didn't back down. A Huntress wouldn't. "If you had anything better waiting, you'd be long gone. You hate it here, and you hate all of us too."

"Not *all* of you. At least, not until today."

"Because of the brat."

"Get out," he said, wheeling away from me. "I was stupid for thinking I could talk to you, for thinking you'd understand anything."

Grinding my teeth, I shoved through the curtain and out into the warren. A passing Builder leered at me. "You know you can get in trouble for visiting a boy's personal space. But if you do something for me, I won't tell anyone."

Oh, *not* today. Yes, I'd broken a minor rule by going in without a chaperone, but I was in no mood for this. "I wasn't in there long enough for anything to happen. If you shut up and walk away, *right* now, I won't shove your nose through your face."

When I reached for my club, the boy ran. Apparently he had some brains. Sure, he'd probably report me, but it was my word against his. And since I was heading off for Nassau tomorrow— and might not make it back—minor disciplinary action for uncivil behavior didn't bother me much.

After stopping in my space for clean clothes, I went to the female facilities, a part of the enclave curtained and off-limits to males. A constant trickle of more or less clean water came from the metal tubes arrayed in this area. We didn't know who had planned this place, but we were glad for the running water. Anything we drank, we boiled, but this was clean enough to wash in.

At this hour, nobody else was around, and I honestly preferred it that way. I didn't like the way some girls compared bodies. My body was a machine, plain and simple. I worked it to stay strong; I fed it to keep it running.

I got undressed. It was cool in here and the water was cold too, which made it worse. Taking a scoop of soap from a pot on the floor, I washed up quickly beneath the unsteady trickle. If I turned the wheel, I could get more at one time, but then I'd hear about it from Twist, who monitored our resources.

By the time I finished my shower and dressed in my spare outfit, my anger had cooled slightly. It wasn't fair to be angry at Fade; he couldn't help his crazy outlook. As we were told from the time we were brats, where you were raised made all the difference. The people in Nassau had some wild ideas for sure; they didn't have a breeding schedule like we did, so they looked . . . strange when their trading parties visited, and from their smell, they didn't care much about cleanliness either. We always offered to let them wash up in our facilities, but they'd smile with black teeth and say, "Why bother? We're just going to get dirty again on the way back."

But it had been a long time since we'd seen any of them, apart from the brat.

And Fade came from even farther away. At least, I assumed he did. It wasn't like he'd told me—or *anyone*, as far as I knew.

I just wished he hadn't involved me. If only I'd refused to

follow him, if only I'd stayed in the back ways, where we'd been assigned. We never would've found the brat, and we wouldn't be going to Nassau tomorrow. But the second Hunter tenet wouldn't let me do that, either. First, it was, "the strong survive." Second, it was, "trust your partner." My bad luck to be stuck with Fade.

No point dwelling on it—I had chores to do. First, I washed my filthy clothes and hung them up to dry. By the time I finished caring for my club, cleaning and polishing it, so the Freak blood wouldn't stain the wood, I felt almost resigned. We could've been punished worse for disobeying orders. At least we had a chance of surviving this run, so long as we were quiet and careful.

I went to try and relax a little before bed. Thimble and Stone found me in the common area, after their shifts ended. I sat watching random Breeders and Builders play some stupid guessing game. The Hunters socialized elsewhere, but I didn't feel like facing them. Fade might be there, for one thing, and I didn't want to see him at the moment. On another level, I wasn't sure what they thought of me. I was still new blood, and a troublemaking one at that.

"Is it true?" Stone whispered.

I didn't bother asking what they'd heard. "Probably."

"You *really* left your patrol route?" Thimble asked, incredulous.

It was worse than I'd thought. "We did."

Part of me wanted to lay the blame on Fade. I wanted to say, *It wasn't my idea. He ran off, and it's my job to follow him.* But I hadn't objected. I hadn't yelled, *Where are you going? Our route is this way.* My instinctive response had been to help whoever was making that noise. I could tell myself I'd been investigating a possible Freak presence, but Freaks didn't signal. They just attacked. So out there, I'd made a choice and now I had to live with the consequences. Stone and Thimble wore identical looks of shock and disbelief.

"Why?" Stone finally asked.

Because I'm weak. I'm not a Huntress. I have a Breeder's heart. But I'd never say it aloud. That left me with no answer at all. Thankfully, they didn't press.

Thimble patted me on the arm. "At least we got news from Nassau. The elder Builders had been wondering why we haven't seen any trading parties in a while."

They couldn't know about the brat. Or maybe they did—and didn't care. Like I wasn't supposed to. I shouldn't be thinking about his thin little face or his white eyes.

"Is it true you're being sent there?" Stone wanted to know.

"It is. Recon only." *Allegedly.* I guessed my misgivings showed on my face.

"Oh, Deuce," Thimble whispered.

When they hugged me from either side, I didn't fight at all.

Journey

In the morning, at the briefing, the other Hunters refused to meet my eyes. With Fade as a partner, I'd never earn their respect or share in the tight bonds I'd always admired. To make matters worse, I'd compounded the problem with my tardiness, leaving my patrol route and bringing the Nassau brat back instead of following orders. Jaw clenched, I let Silk's voice wash over me until I heard the customary words:

"Is everyone clear on their jobs today? Then good hunting."

The others headed off, but Silk stepped in front of Fade and me, blocking our path. "It's a hard three-day hike. I'll expect you back in seven days. If you're not here, I'll assume you've been eaten and promote two likely brats to take your places. Is that clear?"

"Yes, sir," I muttered in unison with Fade.

"Do you have provisions ready?" Silk asked.

Water, dried meat, a blanket, a map of the tunnels, my spare outfit, and my weapons—if those counted, then yes. I nodded. Satisfied with our responses—and that we were suitably cowed— Silk stepped aside. I'm sure she knew that if we survived, she'd have no more trouble with us deviating from our assignments. Next time, I'd keep Fade on task if I had to hit him from behind and drag him.

Heart heavy with dread, I led the way to the barricades. The guards didn't taunt us, but since they'd been on duty yesterday, one smirked at me. I wondered if he'd been ordered to kill the blind brat personally. Not wanting to think about it, I broke eye contact first and vaulted over the first barrier.

Rules exist for our protection, I told myself. But I couldn't kill the sick sourness in my stomach. Maybe Stone was the lucky one after all, even suffering through loss of the brats. He didn't have to deal with punishments like this.

Fade had his map in hand when he landed beside me. His silence burned like the hot knives Twist had used to make my marks. Still without speaking, he brushed by me and jogged toward the first turn. If I didn't keep up, he'd leave me alone in the dark; I didn't doubt that at all.

We ran all morning without a break. I sipped from my water bottle on the move. It was made of a light, strong substance, a relic of the old days. Someone had scavenged it from the tunnels, brought it back and cleaned it up. Even as a brat, I'd coveted it, knowing how valuable it would prove to a Hunter. As soon as I got my hands on something good, I bartered for it.

I got used to stepping where he did, running in the dark. Sometimes rays of light through broken stone illuminated the murk, but that only made it worse. Then I had to see the bleak tunnels, dirty water standing in the center, and the things that scurried away from our feet.

Like Fade, I'd memorized our route early on, so I tracked his leadership. I wouldn't put it past him to head away from College, away from Nassau, and lead me into the black to die. He'd seemed mad enough the day before to make sure I came to a bad end. Not for the first time, I wondered about the death of his first partner.

He wasn't as good as Silk claimed, he'd said. But maybe what Fade really meant was he'd disappointed him by not sharing his crazy, selfish ideals. Maybe the poor guy had only been guilty of serving the enclave first. Fear tightened my stomach. I would have to be on my guard at all times out here alone with him. At a few points along the way, I smelled Freaks, but we moved too fast for them to hit us. They cried and growled from adjacent passages.

I had no way to gauge how long we'd been running, but he called a halt, long after the stitch in my side became a brand. The tunnels even looked different here, splashed with red and black paint, more remnants of the old days. Our smoke hadn't penetrated this far. We were unquestionably in the wilds.

The stone ledge to the right permitted us to scramble off the ground, away from the metal and chunks of fallen rock. With a wall behind us, we rested without worrying about threats from all sides. I opened my bag and pulled out a chunk of dried meat. We didn't have a lot of variety even in the enclave: fresh meat, dried meat, and mushrooms. Occasionally, someone found a tin and once we pried it open, the contents smelled fine and enticing, but that was the exception, not the rule.

I ate and drank a little more water. We had to make it last until we reached Nassau. Worse, there was no guarantee we'd be able to access their supply. If the brat had spoken truly and the settlement was lost, the place might be overrun with Freaks.

"It's time to get moving," Fade said, after a while. Those were the first words he'd spoken to me all day. "We still have four more hours to go before we can make camp for the night."

"How do you know?" At the enclave, we had a few clocks that kept time for us, scavenged in long ago Topside runs. We had no idea whether they reflected the correct time, of course, but it didn't matter. We only needed to share a common schedule.

In answer he pushed up his sleeve and showed me his wrist. Unlike most, he preferred to keep his marks covered. He wore a small clock; I'd never seen anything quite like it.

"What is it?"

"A watch."

The glowing hands meant he could see it, even in the dark. That explained how he knew when our patrols were done, and that we still needed to run for four hours. Nodding, I stowed my gear and vaulted down from the stone ledge. We had been lucky to eat undisturbed. Time to get moving again, though my muscles felt weak and watery.

This time, I set the pace. I didn't like letting Fade run at my back, but I didn't want him to think he frightened me, either.

Along the way, four near misses with Freaks kept us sharp. They tried to hit us as we ran, but they were weak and slow. By tacit agreement we didn't stop to fight. Fights risked injury, making us even more attractive targets. We killed them near the enclave as part of defending our territory. Here, it was best simply to keep moving.

By the time we found a place to camp for the night, my whole body ached. Here, the tunnel widened. There were double metal lines and a raised area, littered with broken glass and covered in festive paint. Fade pulled himself up, and then offered me his hand.

Unlike the last time, it didn't hurt when his fingers curled around mine. His strength surprised me, because he tugged me up using his upper body only. I landed beside him and took stock of the area.

A metal gate blocked off one end. On the other, I saw a couple of doors. Fade was already moving toward them, trying the handles. Though the enclave didn't use doors, I'd seen them before. One of them pushed open, but the smell was so horrific I gagged.

"Did something die in there?"

"Probably," Fade said.

The white tile was stained black in spots, filth and dried blood. Doors blocked off tiny rooms, except for the last one, where the metal hung askew, revealing a squat chair with a hole in it. Curiosity got the best of me, then overwhelming disgust.

I took a step into the room, intending to check out the place, when side movement caught my eye. I whirled, knives slipping into my palms. The other girl did the same. When I froze, she did.

The mirrors I'd seen had all been tiny and, most of them, cracked. Though I knew I had brown hair and gray eyes, I'd never seen a full-sized reflection of myself before. Fade came to stand behind me, watching me as I did, and discomfort twined like razors around my spine. He made me feel small. Right then, I felt stupid too.

"I'd rather sleep out there." I jerked my head toward the open, raised area.

"Me too. You can use the facilities first."

"Facilities?"

"It's a bathroom."

I didn't see how anyone could bathe in here, but looking at the squat chair, I took his meaning. It held a black, foul water, and probably other stuff too. At home, we did our business above a grate, some distance from the rest of the enclave. The smell in that part of the settlement matched the stench in here, so I got it.

Fade stepped outside, leaving me to it. I was careful not to touch anything, and then I went out to give him a turn. Weird, seeing the echo of how people used to live.

The other door wouldn't budge, no matter how we pushed or pulled on it, so we took the corner in between the doors, as far back from the edge as we could get. I ate more dried meat and drank a few swallows of water. Thankfully it was cool enough that we wouldn't lose much fluid through sweat.

"I'll take the first watch."

He didn't argue. "You'll need this, then." After unfastening his watch, he passed it over to me.

The leather held warmth from his skin; I couldn't help but notice as I wound it around my wrist. It fastened easily enough. Now I could keep time too.

"Thanks."

"Wake me after four hours. That's four revolutions."

I spoke through clenched teeth. "I'm not an idiot. I can tell time."

Even if Twist kept time for the enclave and rang a bell at the important hours, when meals were served and shifts stopped and started, I knew how. That was part of brat schooling, what you learned in between chores. From three to eight, we learned basic things. From eight to fifteen, we took job training. But he might not know that; he'd come into the enclave late, and gotten his name not too long after. He probably hadn't spent too much time with our brats in their early years.

"I never said you were an idiot."

"You seem to think it." The words just slipped out. I didn't want to fight with him. Out here, just the two of us, it was the opposite of smart. Maybe I *was* an idiot.

"No," he said softly. "You've just been taught to think wrong."

And we were back to the blind brat again. I saw in his eyes

that he thought I should've done something when they took him. Well, he'd stood silent too. I swallowed my instinctive reply and substituted, "You're welcome to your opinions. Just don't let them get in the way of doing your job."

He sent me a hard look. "Are you implying something?"

"Am I?"

"You *know* you are. You actually believe I let my last partner die because I didn't agree with him. Yet here you are. Alone. With me." His black eyes gleamed wickedly.

No, I realized. I didn't think that. If the death of a worthless brat troubled him, Fade wouldn't let a Hunter die for any reason, if he could help it. It wasn't his fault; the odds must have been stacked against them, or maybe his partner made a mistake.

"I'm following orders," I said mildly. "But no. That wasn't what I meant. I'm sure you did all you could to save him."

That shut him up for a good minute. I knew because I had his watch and I found the movement of the skinny little line mesmerizing. Because we were still and quiet, I heard the soft ticking. It reminded me of a heartbeat.

"Nobody else thinks that. Not even Silk." For a moment, I recognized how alone he was, ostracized from the others. He came from nowhere. Nobody knew anything about him; he worked to keep the others distant and off balance.

And then I registered hurt. Until I turned up late for briefings and disobeyed orders, I'd thought Silk liked me. Certainly she encouraged my progress through the training circle and told me I'd make a great Huntress someday. So why had she stuck me with Fade, if she'd thought he had something to do with his partner's death?

He must've read the question in my face because he gave a wry smile. "She said if anybody could survive me, you could."

Ah. A nod at my skill, then. I took it as a compliment. But even if she'd liked me once, I had lost her regard. She thought I'd supported Fade, against her authority, and at base . . . I had. Becoming a Huntress was nothing like I'd dreamed, none of the belonging I'd wanted, none of the respect.

To counteract the bleak feeling, I made myself say, "We'll get through this."

Nodding, he rolled himself into his blanket and went to sleep. I admired that ability because I didn't have the knack. Hunters were supposed to be able to turn themselves off and on, but I found it hard to shut down my brain, my biggest weakness.

Through the quiet hours I kept watch. Movement would help me stay alert, but it might also attract attention. I ran practice matches in my head, pitting myself against more experienced Hunters. I had watched them spar and learned their styles when I could, when they didn't run me off for being a nosy, annoying brat. I didn't ever remember seeing Fade fight. But then, he chose not to socialize with his colleagues.

Though he'd gone to sleep facing away from me, he'd rolled, so now I could watch his face. At first I tried to avoid the temptation to study him, knowing he wouldn't like it, but there wasn't anything else to do. He had graceful black brows, darker in contrast to his pale skin. But then we were all pale.

I looked away and tried to think of something else. Our fish pools kept us from suffering like other settlements when hunted meat ran lean. From the elders, I knew it was important, and that other enclaves coveted our resources. It was why we limited our trade; we didn't want too many people coming and going. That invited invasion.

Eventually, my gaze found Fade again. His nose was sharp, like his chin and his jaw. Likewise, I could cut myself on his cheekbones. His mouth offered the only softness, and even then, only when he slept. I didn't like how I felt, strange and prickly.

Uncomfortable, I went back to staring into the dark. I felt I had invaded his privacy, and now I'd find it even harder to sleep, fearing he might do the same to me. The usual regulations didn't apply on a mission. In the enclave, we wouldn't be permitted to spend this much time together without a chaperone. It cut down on accidents occurring outside of sanctioned breeding. But the elders all knew that a dirty, Freak-infested tunnel was the last place any Hunter would be tempted to break the rules.

In the third hour of my shift, I heard the scrape of claws on metal.

Hidden

In the same movement, I bounced to my feet and found my weapons. I nudged Fade in the ribs. He snapped alert, started to ask, and I lifted my finger to my lips. *Listen.* He caught the telltale sound immediately and readied himself for a fight.

Club in hand, I stepped to the edge, braced, and waited. There was no point hiding; they knew we were here. They sniffed, searching for us. I could smell them too, worse than the filthy waste closet. They reeked of rotten meat and diseased flesh. In another instant, they burst into view, maddened with the scent of fresh meat.

They rushed the platform and I met the first one with a crushing blow from my club. The skull caved with a wet crunch, and blood bubbled from the wound. It fell and did not rise. Fade took down another, but two more scrambled up, and we fell back so we had plenty of room to fight. Based on my limited experience, I hated Freak eyes most of all; in them I could see a remnant of something human, something comprehensible, swimming in a sea of hunger and misery and madness. I tried not to look at its eyes as it rushed me.

After a day of running and without sleep, my reflexes had slowed. Instead of a clean dodge, claws raked across my arm. My recovery was off, but I drove it away with a kick solid enough to give me the crunch of bone. I followed with a hard swing. I didn't have the stamina for finesse. *End it fast.*

I did.

"I'm sorry you didn't get to sleep," Fade said. "But we have to move on."

He was right, of course. The corpses would draw more Freaks. I ripped the bottom of my shirt, used my daggers to cut strips and tied off the wound around my biceps to stop the bleeding. More precise treatment had to wait.

"It doesn't matter." I snagged my pack and leaped down from the platform. We had another two days of this to get through. And then it would get worse. "Have you been to Nassau before?"

"Once." He broke into an easy run.

"What's it like?" We probably shouldn't be talking, even in whispers. But my curiosity got the best of me, and words took my mind off the throbbing pain.

Fade shrugged. "Like any settlement. Like yours, but worse."

That damped my desire to ask further questions. We'd been running awhile when I realized I still wore his watch. Though I couldn't be sure, I thought we'd been moving for about an hour. My eyes felt grainy and dry; my head ached. It only made sense to run as far as I could before I had to rest. An hour later, I stumbled.

"This has to be far enough," I said. "I have to sleep."

We stood in a tunnel that showed little sign of use in recent years. There was no lingering smell from Freak occupation. I hitched myself onto the stone ledge, which was wide enough for me to lie down on, if I curled onto my side. Far from the comfort of the stuffed rag mattress I had at home; that was a cozy nest by comparison, but right then I thought I could sleep anywhere.

"My watch?" He held out a hand.

I took it off, head spinning with weariness. This time, exhaustion would keep my mind from working too hard. "Sorry."

After wrapping in my blanket, I propped my head on my arm, curled my knees toward my chest, and closed my eyes. I didn't care if Fade watched me. The dark tide of sleep took me.

I dreamed of the thin-faced brat with his blind white eyes. Unlike in life, his neck twisted at the wrong angle. He staggered toward me, arms outstretched. *I trusted you.* His pale fingers shone like bones twisting in the air.

They killed you.

You *killed me.* He was nearly on me now, and I was frozen by the white of his eyes. *And now, you can't kill me again. Can't kill the dead.*

Fade woke me. It felt like only an instant, but it must've been longer. He wouldn't have bothered me unless my time was up. A hard breath shuddered through me as I became aware how cold I was, even beneath the blanket. Fearful sweat made my shirt stick to my back, and when I tried to pack my gear, my hands shook.

"You were whimpering. Want to talk about it?"

I closed my eyes. How embarrassing. I felt like the baby he'd accused me of being, the first time we met. But I didn't want him to think it was something minor, like a Freak attack or being away from the enclave.

"I dreamed about the brat."

Fade nodded. "That would do it. You good now?"

"Almost." I had a little water to steady myself and then I got to my feet. "Another eight hours?"

"That would be best."

Though I'd believed I was tough, considered myself as strong as any veteran Hunter, I thought that day would kill me. We took only minimal breaks because the Freaks had the scent of my blood. They hunted us through the tunnels, their numbers growing. Movement became a test of will, putting one foot after the other, until I wasn't thinking about anything at all.

I ran in time to the pounding of my heart. With each step, my weight grew. More than once, I stumbled over broken ground. Fade never paused. I don't know if that meant he trusted in my strength or that he'd leave me if I dropped. Either way, I wouldn't test it. I could go as long as he could.

Eventually we stopped; we'd put in our eight hours and we needed rest. Fade found us an empty metal shelter, like the one where we'd found the brat. Unlike his, this one hadn't been over-turned. It simply sat abandoned on the metal lines.

We took turns using the facilities down the track a ways, and then combining our strength, we managed to pry the doors open and slip inside. They slammed shut at once, lending the illusion of safety. This would help, for sure. Freaks didn't tend to consider teamwork. If one of them couldn't open the door, they'd look for other ways in, and it would be noisy.

In addition to chairs, this box had benches bolted to the floor. I scanned the place for possible threats, but other than webs and dust, I saw nothing that could hurt us. My arm throbbed fiercely, the ache biting toward my shoulder, and I flinched as I dropped my bag.

"I need to look at that." Fade stood beside me, indicating my wound.

Sinking down, I gave a jerky nod. "Go ahead."

He unwound the makeshift bandages. I craned my neck so I could see too. Four parallel marks scored my shoulder, red, bloody, and puffy. I swore, recognizing the early signs of infection. Let go, this wound could cost my arm and then my life.

Back at the enclave, tending it would be no problem. Out here, well, fear shivered through me.

Like he didn't know the danger, he joked, "And here's your first battle scar. How about it, new blood?"

"Hurts."

"I know. I was lucky. I got blooded on my first patrol. Wasn't quite fast enough and the Freak hit me." He pulled his shirt up to show me the scar on his ribs.

"Was that with the guy who died?" Awkward way to ask, but I couldn't think of any other.

Fade shook his head. "I've had two partners. The first was venerable. I learned *so* much from her. Eventually, they had to pull her off duty. She died of old age."

"When?"

"A year ago."

"And then you got the new blood. Who wasn't as good as Silk said he was."

"Pretty much."

"So you've been hunting for two years." That made him roughly two years older than me, give or take. A lifetime in field experience.

"That sounds about right."

Well, while he's in an answering mood . . .

"How long were you on your own?"

"You mean outside a settlement, living like the wild boy?"

I didn't know what that meant exactly, but I did know we'd had to teach him civilized behavior. "Yeah."

"About four years, I guess." Like the rest, I had a hard time believing that, especially now I'd seen what it was like out here. I wanted to learn his secrets to augment my own survival chances.

But he turned away, letting me know the conversation was over. Fade dug into his bag and produced a little tin. Unlike the one that had nearly gotten us in trouble with the Wordkeeper, this one was silver and faded. He pulled the top off and a strong smell hit me; it wasn't unpleasant, but more . . . medicinal. After daubing some on his fingertips, he smeared it on my wound, and it stung, bad.

"What is it?" That seemed like a safe conversational choice.

"It's a salve one of the Builders made for me. Great for cleaning wounds. But I have no idea what's in it." He smiled at me. "Probably fungus."

That surprised me. Not that he had something good for cleaning wounds that might be made out of fungus, but that there was a Builder who liked him well enough to do special work. "Who?"

"Girl named Banner."

I knew who she was. Thimble had talked about her, before my naming. Back when I was still stuck in the brat dorm, while Stone and Thimble had moved on, I used to be jealous of how much she liked her. *Banner showed me how to make a leather bag,* she'd tell me in the common room. And I'd roll my eyes, because big deal, who wanted to make a stupid bag? I was going to be a *Huntress,* and I told myself that every night as I trudged back to the brat dorm while Stone and Thimble went to their private spaces.

"Maybe she'd make some for me?" Once the stinging stopped, it felt better. I felt it cleaning and tightening the skin. I'd take clean scars over seeping wounds any day.

"I don't see why not. I'll introduce you." The warmth in his tone said he liked Banner, unlike the rest of us.

I frowned. First Thimble, now Fade. I should meet the girl, if only to find out what was so great about her. And request some of that salve too. I didn't kid myself this was the last injury I would suffer. Assuming we lived.

I cut another strip from my shirt. His fingers brushed mine when I handed him the cloth, and his touch was gentle when he wrapped my shoulder. Part of my hair had come loose from its cord, and Fade brushed my hair away, keeping it out of the knots he tied. I felt strange, like I should move away *right now*, but he did it for me. I watched without meaning to, without wanting to, as he put the salve away.

By that point, I felt almost too tired to eat. I went to lie down, but he said, "No way, new blood. Eat. Drink. You have to stay strong, because I'm not carrying you."

"I didn't ask you to," I muttered.

Growling mentally over nearly making such a basic mistake, I got out my provisions. I went about it mechanically. He ate with a little more enthusiasm, but he'd been patrolling longer than I had. No amount of training could substitute for actual experience. I'd get stronger. I had to.

"We should both be able to sleep," I said. "If they find us, we'll hear them trying to get in."

"Agreed. And if we don't get a full night's rest, it will cost us down the line."

In reflex, speed, and stamina, certainly. I didn't want to think about other costs. "Will another day of running get us there?"

"It should."

"What will we do then?"

He shrugged. "Impossible to say until we scope things out."

A moment later, he delved into his bag a second time and produced a silver square. Fade flipped the top of it, rubbed his thumb along the side, and a thin flame shot up. I scrambled back. "What're you *doing?*"

"Remembering."

"What?"

"Before."

My patience ran thin; I didn't care to drag his past out of him. "What is it?"

"A lighter." For the first time, he volunteered information. "It used to be my dad's. Like the watch."

I paused amid dragging my blanket out of my bag. "You remember him?"

"Yeah."

That rocked me. In the enclave, we barely knew who our sires were. Most of them died before we got old enough to recognize their faces, and it wasn't like it mattered. All Breeders looked after us until we were old enough to take basic brat schooling.

"Fade," I began.

"That's not my name." He sounded angry, but not at me.

"It is now. Maybe somebody gave you a different name before, but you *earned* this one. That makes it true." With every fiber of my being I believed that.

A sigh escaped him. "Yeah. I guess. What did you want to ask me?"

"Where are you from, really?"

I figured he'd name one of the distant settlements. Most people thought he'd gotten lost and somehow managed to survive on his own in the tunnels until our patrols found him. I *didn't* expect him to say:

"Topside."

"Fine," I muttered. "Lie to me. I don't care."

Nobody lived up there. Nothing grew. Water fell from the sky and scored everything. We'd all heard the stories from the Wordkeeper. Disgusted, I rolled up in my blanket on a bench that ran parallel to the exterior wall. From this spot, the Freaks wouldn't be able to see me from the outside. They might smell us all around this car, but they wouldn't see us, and they weren't very bright as a general rule. I ignored Fade pointedly until I fell asleep.

This time, oblivion brought no bad dreams. I went where everything was dark and quiet, and I stayed there until I awoke naturally. Fade appeared to be asleep as I pushed the hair from my eyes. It had fallen out of the tail I wore to keep it neat.

His voice stilled me, no more than a thread of sound. "Don't move."

"Why?" I breathed.

And then I didn't need to hear an answer. Movement outside told me all I needed to know. Freaks prowled around outside the car; I couldn't tell how many from the motions, but they suspected our presence. They smelled us.

I jumped as one slammed against the glass, trying to see into the shadows within. I willed myself smaller. Another thud—a Freak climbed onto the roof. *How many?* I needed to know the odds if they started pounding until glass splintered everywhere.

Maybe if we're really still, they'll go away.

The moments felt endless while they snarled and growled and yelped outside. I resisted the impulse to cover my eyes like a baby brat in hopes the scary things would go away. Instead I listened and tried to gather information. Based on the noise and the movement, there had to be fifteen of them out there. Maybe more.

And we were trapped.

Nassau

"I've never seen so many of them together," I whispered.

I shouldn't have spoken. Though I'd thought my words were so quiet as to be barely audible, one of the Freaks heard me. It went wild, slamming repeatedly against the glass until it began to splinter.

"Up!" Fade shouted. "They know we're here. Get your weapons."

There was no room for the club, much to my dismay, so it would have to be daggers. Thanks to Thimble, they fit my palms perfectly. I rolled to my feet as the glass broke. The Freak pushed its torso into the car and I went for the jugular. Twin slashes opened its neck and its disgusting blood jetted out. Then it hung in the broken window like a grotesque blockade, until other Freaks began to tear at it. A few of them fed; others were obviously trying to remove it to get to us.

"How much trouble are we in?" The one on the roof started to jump, as if its weight could break through the metal.

"Depends on how smart they are."

"Have you been in a situation like this before?"

Incredibly, he smiled. "I doubt anyone has."

Why did Silk have to put me with a *crazy* partner? So many solid, experienced Hunters to choose from and I got Fade. Life wasn't fair at all.

The stench hit me like a club; the Freaks had torn the one in the window apart. At least half of them entered a feeding frenzy. They knelt and shoved the bloody gobbets of meat into their mouths, their razor-sharp teeth and claws shining red even in the dark.

"As long as they don't start breaking other windows, we should be fine," I said.

And then they attacked the other side of the car. Fade vaulted over two rows of seats to position himself, daggers in hands. I had to stay where I was and guard this opening. I didn't let my-self think what would happen if they spread out farther.

Another Freak threw itself at the opening. I missed the neck this time, but I caught it with a side shot, vital organ territory, as it struggled to clear its legs. Like the other, it hung, wretched and dying, while its kin ripped at it.

Fade was doing fine on his end, employing the same tactics. The dead bodies served as an excellent distraction. While Freaks wouldn't attack their own kind while they lived, if they were dying, it became a different story. Meat was meat.

Their screams and snarls made the hair of my arms stand on end. We held our ground, guarding the two breach points, until they went to work on another window. Two Freaks pounded repeatedly on the glass until it stressed. While killing another, I watched the growing web of cracks with dismay and then fear.

We were going to be overrun.

Before either of us could get there, one managed to climb inside. Without the barrier, another pushed in behind it. If we stepped away, we'd have them behind us on all sides. Grimly, I dispatched another one, and then whirled to take on the one running at me inside.

It dove at me, jaws snapping, and I drove my dagger in through its eye socket. In a smooth motion, I spun and took the fresh one scrambling in the window. Fade dispatched his with cool efficiency. He was better than any of the Hunters I'd watched with such admiration. Even his moves were unique, so graceful I had to work not to watch him when I should be fighting. I didn't need the distraction.

And then they broke pattern. Two ran at Fade while his back was turned, dealing with the one at his window. Though it meant abandoning my post, I launched myself over the seats, swinging around a pole for momentum, and planted my feet in a Freak's chest. I lashed out with a powerful kick, caving in its temple, and then I took its partner with twin slashes of my daggers. In saving him, I'd opened a path, though. More crawled through.

"You should run!" Fade shouted. "We'll kill you all if we have to."

The Freaks snarled back, wet, hideous sounds that sounded almost like words trapped behind predator's teeth. I fought on, back to back with Fade, conscious that my muscles were tiring. Humans had limits. But after we dropped ten of them, and the remainder fed on the fallen, they broke and ran. Apparently, we fought too hard to be worth the effort. That troubled me because it showed a certain mental capacity. They might even have taken his warning to heart.

Fade shared my unease. "They decided to cut their losses."

"That means they're not just creatures of impulse and appetite, like we thought." Panting, I wiped my knives on the rags worn by the dead Freak nearest to me.

"You think they'll believe us?"

I sighed. "If they don't, we're in real trouble."

"Well, Silk already knew their behavior has changed. We've been asked to find out why."

I raised a brow. "You think that's an attainable goal?"

"I think it's meant to break us."

Standing in this car, filthy and blood spattered, I realized it might. I collected my things. We needed to eat before moving on, but it wouldn't be here. The smell wouldn't let me keep anything down.

As if he shared my revulsion, Fade launched himself headfirst out of the window. I started to shout at him for being an idiot, but my breath caught when he flipped midair and landed on his feet. When he faced me, he was smiling.

"Showoff," I muttered.

My center of gravity wouldn't let me match the feat. I'd have to jump from higher up to stick the landing, so I kicked at some of the glass shards to level it out and then jumped feet first. I didn't *need* him to steady me, but I appreciated it.

His hands were surprisingly gentle. "You saved me."

"That's my job." Discomfort blazed through me.

Even in the shadows, I could see his black gaze as intent. "You're as good as Silk said you were."

Hearing that pleased me so much it hurt. No more scornful "new blood" from him. No more cracks about my skill. Maybe we could work together after all.

I ducked my head, unable to say more than a choky "Thanks."

"I think it's safe now."

Safe was such a relative word. The bodies mounded in dismembered chunks all around the car. Blood smeared the outside, trailing downward in a hideous memorial. Some of the limbs had been gnawed until they showed bone. Nothing in my training had prepared me for this. Nothing.

I wanted to sit down and shake in reaction. Fade shoved me around the carnage and got me moving. I wasn't sure I could've done it on my own. Once more, we ran with minimal breaks, but the sleep helped. Today I didn't feel like I might die from the trip, at least, even if every noise made my heart jump in my chest. So far from the enclave, I didn't think Freaks were just a minor annoyance, either. They counted as a legitimate danger to the settlement.

We made such good time that we started seeing signs for Nassau earlier than I expected. They were accompanied by the normal warnings about traps. ENTERING NASSAU TERRITORY. WATCH YOUR STEP. I avoided a couple of snares along the way, and as we got closer, I noticed with a sinking heart that they hadn't been checked in days. Some of them contained rotten meat.

My flesh crawled with the smell as we made the last turn. I'd long since gotten used to the darkness and the chill, but the stink was new. It was like the Freaks that had surrounded us in the car, only a hundred times worse. Fade stilled me with a hand on my arm. I read from his gestures that he wanted us to stay close to the wall and move very slowly on the approach. He got no argument from me.

We came up on the busted barricade first. There was no guard posted. Inside the settlement, Freaks shambled about their business. They were fat in comparison with the ones we'd encountered on the way. Horror surged through me. For a moment I couldn't take it all in; the silence of corpses drowned every thought.

There was no one here to save, and our elders had killed the sole surviving Nassau citizen. That meant our nearest trade outpost lay four days in the opposite direction. Fade put his hand on my arm and cocked his head the way we'd come. Yes, it was time to go. We could do nothing here but die.

Though I was tired, terror gave my muscles strength. As soon as we gained enough distance through stealth, I broke into a headlong run. My feet pounded over the ground. I'd run until I buried the horror. Nassau hadn't been prepared; they hadn't believed the Freaks could be a large-scale threat. I tried not to imagine the fear of their brats or the way their Breeders must have screamed. Their Hunters had failed.

We wouldn't. We couldn't. We had to get home and warn the elders.

Fade took us back a different way. These tunnels were narrower, and I saw no signs of Freak presence. I found hidden energy reserves and though our pace dropped down to a walk, I kept moving. By the time we broke for a rest, my arms and legs trembled.

He turned into a doorway and went up some steps. I slowed, gazing into the dark. Over the years it had been ingrained into me; steps were bad. They led Topside.

"Come on," he said impatiently.

Shaking, I swallowed my misgivings and began to climb. He stopped on a landing and followed a narrow hall around a couple of turns. It ended in a room swimming with dark shapes. To my amazement, Fade did something, and then we had light. We had scavenged lamps before, of course, but we didn't have the power to make them work. This one contained a flickering flame at its heart.

"How did you do that?"

"It's an old storm lantern. Runs on oil."

I wished we had some of those in the enclave. The torches

we used smoked a lot. Fade shut the door and turned something while I took stock. Full of relics from the old days, the room looked as though nobody had touched anything in years. A thick film of dust covered all the shelves, the desk, but it didn't conceal the nature of the artifacts. There were four tall, slim books here, all colorful and full of pictures. I started to reach for one and stopped, casting a guilty look at him.

"It's okay," he said. "I won't tell anyone if you look before taking them to the Wordkeeper."

It didn't count as hoarding, I reasoned, as long as I turned the stuff over as soon as we arrived. I picked one up and stared with disbelieving wonder. It showed a brightly lit tunnel and one of those cars, connected to a bunch more, zooming along the metal bars. And people sat inside it: cheerful, reading, talking.

"It used to be like that," I said, surprised.

"Yeah. People just came down here for transportation. Then they went back up."

I marveled at the weirdness of it. "You were born Topside?"

"It's not like you'll believe me if I say yes," he muttered.

Well, I had that coming. I ignored the impulse to apologize and instead buried myself in the thin books. They had slick, glossy pages and lots of pictures. The blue skies and greenery enthralled me. I'd never seen anything grow but a mushroom.

Finally, I stowed them in my bag and searched the rest of the room. Anything I carried back would help restore my reputation with Silk and the rest of the Hunters. Nobody had stumbled on a treasure trove like this in a long time. I ransacked all the shelves and furniture; my bag bulged by the time I finished taking everything I thought might interest them back at the enclave. The desk held tons of interesting paper, smooth and fine, even if it had started yellowing with age.

"Are there more places like this? Full of artifacts?"

Fade shrugged. "Probably."

For a moment I was tempted to look. But then Silk could claim we'd disobeyed our primary command. This room, I could state confidently we had found by chance. Regretfully, I ate a mouthful of dry meat and downed some water.

Now that the wonder had worn off, reaction set in. I remembered—and didn't want to—the horror of Nassau. To contain the shakes, I pulled my knees to my chest and wrapped my arms about them. I tried to control my breathing. A Huntress didn't crack under pressure. She might bend, but she could handle anything.

I felt Fade hovering beside me. "Is it your shoulder?"

"No. It's that everyone at Nassau is dead." I raised my head and looked at him.

"I don't want to go to sleep," he admitted.

He dropped down beside me, wrapped his blanket around my shoulders, and left his arm around my back. Hunched over, I felt the strength of him even more clearly.

I had enough resolve left to object. "That's against the rules."

"You're cold and scared. Relax. It's not like I'm trying to breed you." His tone said that was the last thing he'd do.

Good enough. I'd take his hand off at the wrist if he tried anything. Honestly, it felt good to sit next to him. He was the only living soul who could understand how I felt right now, my head crowded with images I didn't want and couldn't banish.

"Have you ever seen anything like that before?"

"Never. The balance has shifted."

"We have to be able to tell Silk why. Otherwise we haven't completed our mission."

"I know why," he said.

"Tell me."

"If they didn't take what Nassau had, those Freaks would've starved to death."

I recoiled. "You sound like you sympathize with them."

"I'm sorry for the people who died. But I understand why it happened."

"You think that'll be enough for Silk?"

"It'll have to be," Fade said. "It's the truth."

Darkness

The next day, I lacked the strength to run. We set our pace accordingly. Fear gnawed at me with relentless teeth, and the darkness made it worse. First my mind conjured monsters and then I imagined I heard them creeping along behind us, worse than the Freaks, smarter and scarier too.

The dark didn't seem to bother Fade. He led the way without faltering whereas I found myself living for those rare moments when we found a broken tunnel. Light fell in crossed threads, lightening the gloom for precious seconds before we passed through.

Gravel crunched underfoot, and I stumbled. My knees buckled. I almost went down, but Fade was there to steady me.

"Maybe we should take a break."

"We just started."

"It's been two hours."

That surprised me. In the dark, it became easy to lose track of time, along with sense of direction. With his hand on my arm, Fade guided me to the stone rim to the side of the tunnel. Maybe it was exhaustion, but things seemed darker this time around. I hadn't noticed it as much going to Nassau. Now it closed in on me, threatening to choke me. My breath came in ragged gasps as I boosted up and rested. I fumbled in my bag for the water bottle; to my dismay, I downed the last few swallows. Dry meat would only increase my thirst, so I opted not to eat.

"That's enough," I said. "I can go on."

Fade leaped down. "Would it make you feel better to lead?"

"Not really." I hesitated, not wanting to admit weakness, even to my partner. "I might get us lost."

"I have your back, Deuce."

"All right." Maybe I'd feel better in the lead. At least I wouldn't think monsters lurked inches away, waiting to grab and eat me.

We walked for hours more in silence. Up ahead, we faced the darkest part of the tunnels. There were no broken areas nearby, no ambient light. In this section, we used our ears to compensate. I thought I heard footsteps, but when I stopped to listen, the sounds stopped too. Maybe it was only an echo.

"You heard it too?" Fade whispered.

Then something did grab me. Hands snatched my arms and yanked me sideways. Fade lunged for me, but he missed. I heard him fumbling and felt the breeze from his movement. Kicking as I was dragged, my captors towed me toward the wall—or what *should* be a wall—instead I slid through a narrow chink in the tunnel. There was no room to fight here. Whatever had me, its hands were strong and it pulled me some distance. I tried to dig in my heels, but they slid in the loose stone covering the ground. They'd dug out secondary tunnels behind the ones left-over from the old days—or maybe these had already existed too. But they were older and more primitive, more natural rock, and less of the artificial stone.

A distant trickle of light illuminated my captor. He looked human, more or less, but his eyes were bigger, and he stood shorter than I did. His skin gleamed white; his people had adapted to the environment. Heart thumping, I wondered what his teeth looked like.

"Dem following you," he said.

So it hadn't been my imagination. I *had* heard something following us in the dark. A chill crawled along my skin, rousing fear bumps.

"Freaks?"

"We call dem Eaters. Come."

"What about my partner?"

A shrug. "We doan want him."

"I can't leave him out there. He'll *die*."

"Doan care. Come."

I could hear Fade's steps tracing away into the distance, running. He wasn't yet calling my name because that would be dangerous, but he'd start soon. He must be worried; I'd simply vanished on him. While screaming might catch his attention, it would also enrage my captor and might draw the Freaks down on us in numbers.

He led me into a room with low-sloped ceilings. I couldn't stand upright. Twenty others like him milled around me, fingering my hair and sniffing at me. I realized I didn't smell great after days in the tunnels, but if they tried anything else, they were meat—or I was. It couldn't end any other way. I had room enough to fight in here. Maybe not at the top of my game, but these creatures looked quiet and crafty rather than strong. They'd survived by sneaking and hiding, not fighting.

"What do you want?" I demanded.

They exchanged a look, and then the one that had yanked me out of the tunnel said, "New blood."

I just knew they were hiding mouthfuls of sharp teeth. "Not mine."

"Not like dat."

I didn't care if they wanted me for decoration, company, or to sing them to sleep. I shook my head, taking a step back toward the narrow tunnel. Even the wider room was too small to permit free-swinging my club, but I drew my daggers in a smooth motion.

"I can't stay. I have a job to do."

"You doan stay, Eaters gonna chew yer bones."

"How can you be so sure?"

"You got da smart ones stalking you now."

Smart, like the ones that slaughtered Nassau?

"There are different kinds of Freaks?" I asked.

"You din figger dat out on yer own?" He shook his head in disgust.

"The ones down near our enclave don't act like the ones we saw at Nassau."

"Dat's the dead place? Nah-saw?"

I nodded. "We were ordered to go check the place out."

"Your folk doan like you much, den. Why not stay?"

I looked around the room, caught the pale, avid faces and the huge eyes. They were creepy, but harmless. I didn't think they'd resist if I tried to leave. The idea of going back into the dark alone, however, paralyzed me.

Then I thought of Fade, out there on his own, and searching for me. He wouldn't just keep heading for the enclave. I felt sure of it. After the loss of his first partner, they'd kill him if he came back alone. I could no longer doubt it, after the way the elders had treated the stray brat.

"If you're willing, I'll accept your hospitality in offering a place to rest, but that's all. And *only* after I find my partner. We need a new place to trade." I didn't know much about supply and demand, but I knew one thing we had that others always coveted. "We have fish pools. Maybe your people would be willing to barter goods?"

They conferred briefly, and then the one that had snagged me nodded. "Deal. We share our fire til da Eaters pass. But *you* find da other one and bring him."

I could do that. Nodding, I turned and slid back out the way we'd come. I stepped into the inky darkness of the tunnel. For a moment I stood still and tried to orient myself. I listened for any breathing or hint of movement, but I could only hear the thundering of my own heart.

Which way would he have gone? Not back the way we'd come, surely. I turned left and crept along, listening every few feet for some sign of him. As I came to a fork in the tunnels, I paused again, sensing . . . something.

"Fade?" I whispered.

Movement. I didn't see him until he was almost on top of me. He curled his hands around my forearms, sounding considerably less panicked than I would have in the same situation. "Are you all right? Where were you?"

"Come on. No time to explain."

My skin prickled as I retraced my steps. Despite my concentration, I doubt I would've found the crack in the tunnel, if my benefactor hadn't grabbed me again. This time I kept ahold of Fade and dragged him in with me. He had to turn sideways to ease through the gap. The side shaft was just wide enough for his shoulders.

The small man began fitting loose stones into the gap, a smart measure, even if it made me feel trapped. But it should confuse Freaks—even the smart ones—if they happened to track us this far. I didn't speak until we were well away from the opening.

Fade gazed around in surprise. "What is this place?"

"Home," one of them said. That time, I caught a look in his mouth as he spoke, and was relieved to see normal teeth, teeth for chewing, not tearing flesh.

"We need a place to rest before the last leg of our journey," I told Fade. "They've volunteered. In return, we'll try to set up some trade." I paused, lowering my voice. "Freaks are following us."

He grasped the problem at once. "Instead of attacking, they're looking for the bigger prize."

"They want to see where we live." That definitely indicated a level of intelligence we'd never encountered in them before.

"We have to lose them before heading back to enclave."

I nodded. "Yeah."

He leaned in to whisper, "You're sure we're safe here?"

I pitched my voice low. "Relatively. We're bigger and stronger, and I *do* think they want to trade. They wanted me for breeding at first, but I convinced them it wasn't an option."

His teeth flashed white in the smoky torchlight. "And no bodies? Impressive."

Wearily, I sank down onto the stone floor. Around us, they went about their business. There were more of them than I'd first realized, though few in comparison with us. Considering their relative proximity, it was more impressive that we hadn't known of their existence before. Silk would probably want to kill them.

They brought us a thin gruel that appeared to have been made from mushrooms and stuff best not inquired about. I forced myself to eat it and thanked them for the meal. Fade sat close beside me, practically keeping a hand on me at all times in case I disappeared again. His subtle concern warmed me.

I was starting to be able to tell the Burrowers apart. Though they shared a certain resemblance, the one who'd rescued me first was a touch taller than the rest. He gave me a little bow and said, "Am Jengu."

"Deuce." I pointed at my partner and said, "Fade. You want to tell us what you have to trade?"

"Why doan I show you?"

I figured that was a good idea; I could tell the elders specifically what the Burrowers had to offer. With Fade close behind, I followed Jengu down another tunnel. We negotiated some twists and turns. The fatty torches made the air taste as bitter as burned meat. I tried to breathe only through my nose.

We emerged on a platform like the one where we'd rested. There appeared to be no other access, due to a collapse and heavy tons of rock. Despite the blockage, this area was brighter and better ventilated. But that wasn't even the most remarkable part—I'd *never* seen such a collection of old stuff. They had piles and piles of it, just sitting on the platforms. Most of it, I had no idea what it was or what it did, but this was the kind of treasure trove that would make the Wordkeeper run all the way here in person, just to examine the artifacts.

"Worth a few fish?" Jengu asked.

"And then some."

I didn't look through the stacks of stuff, although I longed to. But time was ticking away for Fade and me. We needed to rest and then get moving. Surely the Freaks would've lost our trail by the time we woke.

"Do you mind if we sleep here?" Fade asked. "You can search our bags now to see what we have, and then again before we go. We won't take anything."

"You wan sleep in storage?" Jengu seemed puzzled.

I understood Fade's request, at least. The ceilings were higher, and it smelled a little better in here. Good-hearted they might be, I didn't think our Burrower friends practiced much in the way of cleaning.

"If you don't mind." I held out my pack so he could rifle through it.

"Got dis where?" he asked, pulling out one of the slim books.

"On the way back from Nassau. There was a room up some stairs—"

"Ah," he said. "Up near Topside?"

I nodded. "I guess."

"Anything else?"

"Sure," Fade answered. "We didn't take it all. Couldn't carry it."

Jengu seemed pleased. It was more for them to collect when it came time to trade. Once he was satisfied as to what belonged to us, he shuffled off toward the smaller tunnels. I guessed he felt more at home in the darkness with the coziness of low ceilings. It made me feel trapped.

"You're all right?" Fade asked, once he'd gone. "They didn't hurt you?"

I shook my head. "They're harmless. It would do the enclave good to make friends of them, I think. Look at this place."

"It's amazing. They must've been scrounging for generations."

"Thanks for waiting for me. But it was a big risk. Anything could've happened to you."

He touched my cheek very lightly. "I have your back. I didn't mean only when it's easy. *All* the time."

Wow. Warmth blossomed within me. Even if nobody else liked him, even if the rest of them never accepted me, I couldn't have done better for a partner. I doubted the other Hunters would've acted the same. They would've followed orders to the letter and gone back to the enclave, leaving me to fend for myself. Silently, I thanked Silk.

"This should be our last stop. Tomorrow, we make it home." I got out my blanket and wrapped up in it.

A gap in the piles offered us the perfect place to curl up. We went to sleep a whisper apart and when I woke, he lay on his side, facing me. He always seemed different with his eyes shut. The contrast of his pale skin and sooty lashes made me want to brush my fingertips across the dark and light of it. My heart thumped inside my chest as his eyes opened and met mine.

Fade grinned. "Still tired?"

I groaned and rolled to my feet. Lying on rock had taken its toll. I felt like I could sleep for a week. Not like that would happen. As payment for our survival, Silk would probably assign us double shifts.

We got our things and went into the smaller tunnels. The Burrowers were already awake, and Jengu checked our bags to make sure we'd kept our word. I don't think he had any doubt, but it reassured the others.

After saying good-bye, we felt strong enough to handle the last leg of the journey. It would be a tough run, and there were Freaks to dodge, but we'd make it. We were Hunters, and the enclave needed the news we carried.

Homecoming

A day later, Fade and I staggered toward the barricades. We'd been forced to fight a group of Freaks when we could least afford to expend the energy, and we had very little left now. The guards broke from their posts to help us. I guessed they could see we were in a bad way. My lips burned with thirst.

Someone fetched Silk, who demanded, "Get them food and drink. They can barely move, let alone give a report."

She was kind enough to let us sit down in the kitchen area. I collapsed on a crate and thought I might never rise again. Gratefully I took the water and emptied the cup in careful sips. I remembered my lessons about how too much on an empty stomach could make me sick. Then I accepted a tiny bowl of stew and ate it with my fingers. It was lukewarm, which made it easier to rake it into my mouth.

As Fade and I ate, we gathered an audience. Not just Silk and the elders—Copper, Twist, and Whitewall—but Builders, Breeders, and brats too. I guessed they didn't think we were coming back. Everyone waited to hear what we had to say. As senior Hunter, it was only right Fade take the floor. I put down the remnants of my meal and a wee brat scurried off with it.

"Well?" Silk demanded.

"Nassau has fallen. It's Freak occupied now." Fade put the problem more bluntly than I would have.

Disbelief whispered through the crowd. Whitewall motioned them to silence. "No survivors?"

"Not one," he said. "They're living where the Nassau citizens used to and feeding on the bodies."

"And why is that?" Silk asked. "Were there signs of disease?"

I wasn't about to say we didn't get close enough to check things out in detail. Hopefully Fade wouldn't either. "No, they died fighting. Sickness didn't do this." He outlined the theory he'd given me in the little hidden room. "Therefore, we need to change our tactics. Lay more traps. We also need a battle plan in case they hit us in numbers, like they did Nassau."

Silk laughed. "You make it sound like Freaks are a force to be feared, a thinking enemy, rather than just vermin."

Oh, no. She doesn't believe him.

"It's true," I said. "We fought a number of them on the way to Nassau, and I think—" I almost couldn't speak the words because I knew what disagreeing with her in public, siding with Fade would mean. "He's right. They almost seemed to understand us at times."

Her jaw tightened. "We'll take your ideas into account at the next meeting."

"Thank you, sir." I ducked my head, exhausted.

We'd done everything we could, completed the mission, and delivered the requested information. If they chose to ignore us, we couldn't help it. Dread crawled up my spine nonetheless.

"Move along," Silk snapped at the gawkers. "There's work to be done."

There always was. I heard murmurs as people dispersed.

"What do you think?"

"Nassau never kept as clean as they should. They probably died of the dirty disease and then the Freaks ate them."

Someone laughed. "It'll serve them right when they die of it."

Great. They thought we were insane. That we'd cracked out there in the dark and were imagining threats where none existed. But they hadn't seen what we had. They didn't *know*. I sat miserably on my crate, head bowed, until I recognized Silk's boots.

"Because you completed your mission in the time allotted, I'm giving you tomorrow off patrol to rest and regain your strength. I don't want to hear you talking about your crazy ideas, do you understand? There's no reason to get people worked up, if they happen to believe you."

I understood the bribe/threat combo perfectly. "I won't talk to anyone about it."

"Good. Dismissed."

It took all my energy to drag my tired body to the bath area. I still had my clean clothes, at least. There had seemed no point in putting them on out there; I'd never smelled this bad in my life. I washed up longer than usual and then dried and dressed. A few other girls watched me, whispered and giggled, but they didn't address me directly.

Afterward, I started on my clothes. Though I hadn't noticed her arrival, Thimble came and took them from me. She went to work with silent efficiency. I leaned against the wall. My shoulder had scabbed over, and the salve Fade had used on me seemed to have warded off infection. But I'd always bear the scars as a reminder.

"How bad was it?" she asked softly.

"I promised not to talk about it."

Her eyes shone with hurt, as she held my wet clothes. Blood trickled from the fabric and down the drain. "I'm your best friend."

"I know. And you are. But I *promised*. I don't want to get in trouble. Silk already has it in for me."

"I wouldn't repeat anything you tell me."

Maybe not. But what if she yielded to the impulse to tell just one person, maybe Banner, who also told just one person? And pretty soon it got back to Silk. I couldn't take the chance.

"I can't. I'm sorry."

She slammed my half-washed clothes back into my arms. I worked on them until my fingers were raw. Back in my living space, I hung the clothing up to dry. I almost flopped down on my pallet before I remembered that would sentence me to exile. My bag bulged with important relics; before I could rest I had to see the Wordkeeper. Shouldering my pack, I picked a path through the warren.

To my surprise, I found him in the common area. He was twenty-two, but he looked older, older even than Whitewall. He had wispy hair, so fair it looked white, and a face folded into a perpetual frown, as if he knew the day would disappoint him.

"Sir," I said, and waited for him to acknowledge me.

"You have something to report, Huntress?"

Exhausted as I was, the title still thrilled me. "I do. On the way back from Nassau, we took shelter in a room filled with things that will interest you. I have them here."

"Permission granted to make your offering."

Before him, I laid out all the glossy, colorful books, the yellowed papers, every last trinket I'd collected, including some unknown items from the desk drawer. The Wordkeeper stared at it all with the sort of dawning wonder I'd felt. For the first time, I felt a glimmer of liking for him.

I checked my bag three times to make sure nothing got stuck in the crevices. "That's everything."

"Magnificent, the greatest find of our generation. It will enrich our culture in countless ways." The Wordkeeper was already reading, murmuring to himself. "Repair switch in blue line . . . I wonder what that means."

Well, "repair" spoke for itself. The rest I couldn't help with. I stood quiet until he remembered me. "Ah, yes. You've distinguished yourself among all citizens. For your contribution, I will see you rewarded. What would you like?"

For Silk to take me seriously. I almost said it. At the last moment, I bit my tongue to keep the words back. She would not take it well if a reprimand came from the Wordkeeper; she would see it as me going outside the chain of command for preferential treatment. Such behavior was weak and soft, and she'd be right to name it so.

"Any reward you think suitable will please me," I said.

He smiled. I didn't think I'd *ever* seen the Wordkeeper smile. "Very good."

"That's not all."

"Oh?"

"There's a small settlement only a day from here. They're not Freaks, but they don't look like us, either. I'd never seen anything like them." Strictly speaking, Whitewall should be here as well, but I was too tired to care about protocol.

"Friendly?"

"Yes. They gave us food and shelter, or I doubt Fade and I would've made it. Our water wasn't adequate for the journey, and it wasn't safe to get supplies at Nassau."

"Good news," he said neutrally.

"It gets better. They had the most artifacts I've ever seen in a storeroom there. It could take years to go through everything."

"Books?" he demanded.

"I think so. But there's old technology, relics, things I didn't even recognize. The Burrowers don't seem to value it. They want some fish in exchange."

"Fish?" The Wordkeeper laughed. "They can't be very smart."

That term was relative, I thought. You could *eat* a fish; you couldn't eat the stuff the Burrowers had stacked up. Wisely, I said nothing of the kind.

"That's all, sir. May I go?"

"Before you sleep, give Silk the location of these Burrowers. I'll make sure she sends a team. And then rest, Huntress. You've earned it."

I certainly had. My legs barely carried me to find Silk. She was watching a crop of likely brats when I stumbled up to her. I relayed the location as close as I could, per the Wordkeeper's instructions. Silk seemed scornful, but she agreed to talk to him. I was glad I was out of that business now.

Had anyone ever gone to Nassau and back so quickly before? I didn't think so. Generally, they stayed to visit, share news, and replenish supplies. Fade and I hadn't had that option, and without the Burrowers, we would've died. Maybe Jengu knew that too—and that was why he grabbed me.

So tired. It took everything I had to make it to my living space. The rag pallet seemed the height of comfort compared with what we had been sleeping on. It felt a little strange to be alone, after so many days with Fade. Like me, he'd probably showered and gone to bed. He had to be exhausted too.

Unlike other days when I lay there, unable to rest for the buzzing of my head, I winked out as soon as I closed my eyes.

When I woke, I had the unprecedented realization I had nowhere to be. No patrol. No training. If I wanted, I could stay here in my space and stare up at the ceiling. Ambient light from torches mounted on the walls stole in, brightening it enough that I could see my stuff.

My weapons.

In my stupor, I'd forgotten to care for them. The daggers wouldn't stay sharp and shiny if I didn't look after them. My club was much worse for the wear too. So that had to be the first thing I did today. After running my fingers through my hair, I bound it up in my usual tie and carried my things down to the Builder workshop, where I could find the proper supplies to clean and sharpen. I also had an ulterior motive—meeting Banner. Though I told myself I just needed some of the salve, I also wanted to learn about the girl who put warmth in Fade's smile.

As usual, the place bustled with activity. Anything we had came from this part of the enclave. Clothes, shoes, boots, weapons, soap, bags—it all began here. Work went at a furious pace. Things were mixed, poured, measured, hammered. I was sure there was some method to this madness, some organization, but my untrained eye couldn't pick it out. They recognized me as a Huntress from the marks on my arms. I answered their greetings with a nod.

On the other side of the workshop, I saw Fade, talking to a small dark-haired girl. She was pretty in a quiet way, and by the tilt of her head, she liked him. That had to be Banner. Without realizing it, I cut a path directly to them, forcing a couple of workers to detour around me.

"Were you looking for me?" he asked. "We're off today."

I shook my head. "No, I'm looking for her. I think. Banner?"

Her genuine, friendly smile said she didn't mind my intrusion. "That's me."

Fade nodded. "Right. I promised to introduce you." He did so quickly.

"I was hoping you wouldn't mind making me some of that ointment. It helped me out in the tunnels."

"I can make another batch, no problem. Other people don't like it because of the smell, but I'm glad somebody's getting some use out of it."

That taken care of, I had no reason to stay and listen to their conversation so I excused myself with a muttered "Great. I need to go work on my weapons. Nice meeting you, Banner. See you, Fade."

I had finished with my daggers and was working on oiling the stains out of my club when I felt him behind me. "You didn't do that yesterday?"

I sighed. "Bad Huntress, I know. My knives are my best friends."

"That's kind of sad. You mean *nobody* likes you?"

What's his problem today? I thought we were all right with each other. Scowling, I spun on him, ready to deliver some serious verbal hurt when I saw the smile in his dark eyes. *Oh. He's messing with me.*

"Funny."

"Have you eaten yet?"

I shook my head. "Came straight here."

"We could go to the kitchen and scrounge something up."

Hesitating, I said, "I still need to finish this and then I should have Bonesaw check my shoulder."

"You'll be better off if he doesn't. He got his name because he likes cutting parts off people."

I smiled, though I'd heard the joke before. Bonesaw had gotten his name like the rest of us, from the talisman his blood found in the pile of naming day gifts. But it only seemed right he apprentice to the medicine man; Whitewall was a big believer in signs. Now, three years later, the old medicine man was gone, and we had only Bonesaw to care for our sick and wounded. Most agreed he wasn't very good at it.

"Maybe you're right." I rotated my shoulder, and I didn't feel any of the tightness or heat that accompanied an infection.

"I am. Let me give you my tin of Banner's salve. Then she can give me what she makes for you." Kindness, I wondered, or an excuse for him to go see her sooner? As I was debating, he added, "I'll get it while you make that club shine. Then we can go eat. Sound good?"

It did, actually. Stone was busy with the brats, and Thimble was mad at me. I didn't look forward to eating alone. I agreed with a nod and Fade loped off.

Oiling a rag, I polished my weapon until it shone. I even dug all the dried blood out of the carvings Stone had made. He might not understand my job, but he cared. I had to give him that. Nobody else had anything so fine.

Someone stopped behind me.

"Back already?" I asked without turning.

"I never left," came Banner's puzzled voice.

Oops. I spun to face her. "Sorry, I thought you were someone else."

She grinned. "Someone like Fade?"

I couldn't help but smile; she had that kind of open, friendly face. "Kind of."

"He likes you," she said. "He was just telling me about you."

"Really?" I couldn't help but feel flattered by that.

"Yeah. He's a little hard to get to know, but worth it. He tells the most fascinating stories." By her indulgent expression, she thought he merely had a good imagination.

Based on my experiences with him so far, I suspected he'd seen and done more than anyone in the enclave would believe. I stifled a sigh. We weren't always inclined to credit the truth around here, if it ran counter to our experience.

"I like working with him." Any other response would be inappropriate, and could be repeated to my detriment. Hunters were supposed to trust and respect their partners, nothing more.

Thimble caught my eye then, radiating angry hurt. She saw me talking to Banner and her brows drew down. Oh, surely she didn't think I was telling her about the trip to Nassau. I'd just met the girl.

Before I could try to make amends, Fade jogged back into the workshop. He cut a straight line toward us. He greeted her with a smile and me with the words, "You ready?"

I nodded and waved to Banner. Thimble pointedly didn't look at me. Weapons in hand, I followed him out of the workshop.

"I just need to drop these off. Meet you in the kitchen?"

"Sounds good," he said. "I'll see what there is to eat."

"Let me guess. Meat and mushrooms."

"Might be fish."

Yeah, they did cook fish every now and then to keep us from getting sick. The elders put a lot of thought into what we ate and how much. Without their careful planning, our enclave would've died out long ago. It was a sobering thought. Just yesterday, I'd seen the consequences of careless behavior—and they didn't *believe* us.

Whitewall, Copper, and Silk seemed to think such things could never happen here. We were too smart or too lucky. I'd bet the Nassau citizens thought that too, up until everything went wrong.

Treasure

week later, the team they'd sent returned, weighed down with relics of the old world. I eyed the bags with dismay. I hadn't been on duty when the team went out, but I didn't think they'd taken enough supplies to trade with the Burrowers to merit such a big haul.

They wouldn't. Though my faith had been shaken, I didn't want to follow the thought to its natural conclusion. I took a deep breath and steadied myself.

Fade and I had just come off patrol. I'd cared for my weapons and cleaned up a bit, but I hadn't yet gone to see who was in the common room. Instead, I went looking for my partner.

He was in his room, so I swished the curtain to let him know he had a visitor. A few seconds later, he poked his head out. Surprise lit his features.

"Something up?"

"I'm not sure." I summarized what I'd seen, but no more. I wanted to know if he'd share my instincts without undue influence.

"They took everything by force."

I squeezed my eyes shut. Jengu had saved our lives. Whatever happened to them, it was *our* fault. I should've realized—the first Hunter tenet, "the strong survive," dictated their actions; they took everything because they could. But it wasn't right, and they'd made liars of us.

"What are we going to do?"

"What *can* we do?"

It was an unanswerable question. "Should we go see the Wordkeeper?"

"Isn't he the one who made Silk send a team?"

Right. I'd always thought once I became a Huntress, I'd have some power, influence over the way things were done. In truth, precious few had any. Even Silk followed orders; hers just came from Whitewall and the Wordkeeper. It would be years before I qualified as an elder, and even then, there was no guarantee.

"So we live with this, just like we live with what they did to the brat," I muttered.

"Maybe they traded," he said, but from his expression, he didn't believe it any more than I did.

"I might know how we can find out."

"I'm listening."

"Twist might tell me. Meet me in the common area later?"

"Sure."

We couldn't stand here any longer anyway; we'd already started to get some looks. With a wave, I went to look for Twist, and found him running an errand for Whitewall, deep in the warrens. I fell into step.

Twist cut me a suspicious look. "What's broken?"

"Nothing. As far as I know. I just wondered if I could do anything to help."

"Didn't you pull a shift early today?"

"Yes, but I'm fine. And bored without work to do. You always seem to be busy."

"The place doesn't run itself," he snapped. And then he ran a tired hand through his hair. "I'm sorry, I shouldn't take it out on you. I'm trying to put together a naming day ceremony, and the Builders haven't brought me their gifts yet."

"When is it?" I asked.

"Tomorrow."

I winced; I could see why he was impatient and angry. "Why don't I go talk to them for you?"

"Why would you do that?" He stopped walking, canting his head to study me.

In answering, I could be honest. "Look, you do so much, and nobody seems to notice. Whitewall tells you what to do, but he seldom says 'thanks.' He just takes the credit when it goes well and blames you when it doesn't. You've always been nice to me, even when I was a brat. I thought maybe I could help you."

Twist smiled and patted me on the shoulder. "You're a good one, Deuce. It would be great if you could round up the gifts."

"I don't mind at all. I know you have other things to do. Where should I have the presents taken?"

"Same place you were named."

I hadn't been sure since that was the only ceremony I'd ever attended. A prickle of excitement went through me. This unknown brat was to become a Builder, which meant only they had to supply presents from which a suitable name might be drawn. But the rest of us would bear witness.

From the warren, I made my way to the workshop. As ever, the noise nearly deafened me, a combination of clanging, banging, hammering that always had a good result, but I didn't know how they all stood it. I saw Thimble at once, but we hadn't talked since I came back. She might still be mad.

To my surprise, she waved me over. "I want you to know I understand. It was wrong of me to mind that you put your orders first." She paused in her work, surrounded by the various parts of some piece of furniture. "I had a chance to think about it, and Stone kind of yelled at me. I mean, if the senior craftsman told me I couldn't tell you how to make the torches, I wouldn't go up against him. No telling how miserable he could make my life in here, you know?"

I nodded. "And I'd never ask you to spill Builder secrets."

Until she hugged me, I didn't realize how much I'd missed her. Thimble smelled of smoke and tallow. Though we'd outgrown brat-hood and had other responsibilities now, our friendship would endure. Just because some things changed, it didn't mean everything had to. I wrapped my arm around her shoulders, feeling better already.

"So what are you doing here?"

"Besides coming to see you?" That was a side benefit, actually, but it was better if she thought I'd come specifically to make up. "I'm also doing a favor for Twist." I explained about the naming day presents. "Who should I talk to?"

"That would be Rod's territory. I think he's working on it." Thimble led me across the workshop, neatly sidestepping various projects.

We stopped before a tall, gangly boy a few years older than us. He was scowling when we approached, which made Thimble slide me an apologetic look and disappear. That left me standing alone when he noticed me. His gaze flicked to my bare forearms and he barely contained a sneer.

"What do you want, *Huntress*?"

I ignored the slur he gave the title by using that subtle stress. "Twist sent me to collect the naming day gifts. I'm sure you have them ready."

"As a matter of fact, I do. Four boxes, right there. I can't spare anyone to help you move them."

I turned in the direction he indicated and stifled a groan. They were sizable, so it would take me a while, and I'd have to make four trips. Instead of arguing, as he clearly expected, I just nodded and strode over the far wall. It took both arms to lift the first one, and as I staggered toward the door, I collided with someone. I peered over the edge of my burden and recognized Banner.

"You need a hand?"

Glancing at Rod, who was already busy elsewhere, I said, "Sure. But I don't want you to get in trouble."

"I'm off shift today. I came in to say hi to Thimble and see if she needed any help with the shelves she's building, but I can take time for you first."

"This way, then."

I headed for the great room we used for all ceremonies, which took us through the heart of the warren itself. Going past the kitchen, I smelled something good, better than usual, or maybe I was just hungry. With Banner's help, it only took two trips, but my arms were still burning when we finished.

"That wasn't so bad."

If I had to pick two words to describe her, they'd be "relentlessly cheerful." I wondered what she'd say if she knew about the brat, or what the elders had done with the Burrowers. But I still didn't have those answers, and I didn't want to add weight to her shoulders. Better if Fade and I kept silent.

"Thanks."

"Oh, I finished your salve. Fade said to give it to him, but if you want, we can get it now." Her blue gaze bored into mine, as if she were asking a silent question.

"Fine."

With a shrug, I went with her to her space. I wondered why she didn't store it in the workshop, but I didn't think anything of it until we stepped inside her quarters. At first glance, it looked just like mine. And then she lifted her crate to reveal a depression in the floor.

Hoarding. There was no doubt in my mind the elders would exile her if they got a look at what she'd hidden. Instinctively I took a step back.

"Fade said I could trust you. He said you're one of us. Was he wrong?"

"One of who?" I whispered. I averted my eyes from her stash, willing her to put the crate back. I wasn't sure I could lie to an elder—or even Twist—if confronted directly. The idea sent me into a cold, anxious sweat.

"Our leadership is flawed. It doesn't serve the people anymore, if it ever did."

That much, I agreed with, so I gave a cautious nod. The elders had lost my blind support, first through their treatment of the brat, and then Silk's response to our report about Nassau disappointed me. College citizens would pay the price for their determination to permit no change. I understood the rules existed to protect us, but if we didn't adapt to the new balance in the tunnels, we would die.

All that being true, I still didn't want to hear any of their plans. I was still a Huntress, not a traitor or a revolutionary. "Could you just give me the salve? Please?"

Her face fell in disappointment, but she did as I asked, and then I backed out of her space like she had a disease I could catch. I only wanted answers. I didn't want to join some secret rebellion. Obedience was ingrained too deeply in me.

Determined to put some distance between Banner and myself, I hurried toward the kitchen. I had yet to eat my evening meal. I wanted to search for Twist to see if I could parlay the favor into information, but he'd get suspicious if I did it tonight.

Copper ran from pot to pot, stirring and poking and slicing. I ate my meal standing up, much later than the other Hunters, and I had been right; it was good. She'd done something different with the fish and mushrooms, maybe augmented by something the Burrowers had sent. The place was full of brats, in fact, a testament to how long I'd waited. They all snickered to see me sharing their mealtime.

A girl grinned up at me. "Remember how you said on naming day you'd never eat with us again?"

I smiled. "Joke's on me."

I didn't feel like being social tonight so I went to my pallet and just lay down. Unfortunately, I wasn't destined to be left alone. Before I'd been there long, my curtain rustled, indicating I had a visitor. Throat clearing followed.

With a faint sigh, I climbed to my feet and stepped out. *Fade.* I'd forgotten I'd told him to meet me in the common area.

"What did you say to Banner?" he demanded. Rage pulled his mouth into a taut line, and he spoke through clenched teeth. "She's been crying and she's scared to death."

"Nothing!"

"She wouldn't be this upset over nothing. Did you go to Whitewall? Or the Wordkeeper?" His hands fisted at his sides as if to keep him from reaching for me.

"No!" I leaned in because I didn't want to chance anyone overhearing. "Look, I'm not going to tell on her. I just . . . I don't think it's a good idea, that's all." Her willful hoarding was risky and dangerous.

"Why should I believe you? You ran to them on your naming day. You didn't even sleep when we got back from Nassau because you were so scared of exile. Is that the way you want to live? Do you think it's *right*?"

It hurt that he didn't trust me, more than I'd expect, especially after all we'd gone through together. I had saved his life, and he'd saved mine. We'd protected each other every step of the way. I would never do anything to hurt someone he cared about, even if his friend's behavior was reckless and unwise.

"The rules exist to protect us." But I didn't speak the words with conviction anymore. I'd seen too much.

Some of the anger drained out of his face. "She's really upset. Would you mind coming with me to talk to her? I promise we won't involve you in anything." He shrugged. "I just thought, after everything, you might—"

"No. I can't. But I'll go with you to reassure her."

But we didn't find Banner in her personal space. Nor was she in the kitchen, the common room, or the workshop. Thimble stared at me strangely when I popped my head in for the second time, but I just waved and went on. Fade's scowl grew in proportion to the mystery.

"Builders never leave the enclave," he said flatly.

"I know. Maybe she's bathing?"

"Let's find out."

It was the only place we hadn't looked. He walked with me, but he couldn't go in. I slipped into the room, finding it darker and colder than usual. The steady *plink plink* of water added to the hiss of the torches. I found Banner in the corner. Fully dressed, she sat hunched over, paying no mind to the trickle dropping on her head.

"Don't worry. Please. You were right. You can trust me."

When I knelt down to touch her shoulder, she fell forward in a pool of blood. Banner wasn't just upset; she was dead.

Recompense

Nobody cared. The elders sent her body out into the tunnels as a gift for the Freaks. That was all. People talked about the shock, but everyone agreed she must've killed herself. A girl in the baths with two slit wrists? What else could it be? They speculated that perhaps she'd snuck around and gotten herself in trouble. Bred without permission, maybe. That kind of offense got you exiled.

Almost *anything* could get you exiled. As a brat, I hadn't realized the magnitude; I didn't dare articulate my thoughts or my fears. The safety of the enclave was starting to feel like a prison. Life went on for all us, and only Fade wore his grief nakedly. He didn't talk to me anymore outside of patrols, as if I might've had something to do with it. And that hurt, more than I wanted to admit.

After the naming ceremony, Twist came looking for me. "Thanks for taking care of the gifts."

So much had happened I'd almost forgotten I had an ulterior motive for doing that. I'd wanted to find out what they'd done to the Burrowers. I wasn't sure I did anymore. The knowledge might only prove a burden.

But since I had him here, I figured I'd try. "I'm glad I could help."

I fell into step with him as he talked, venting about the strain of working for Whitewall. Twist didn't have any friends that I knew of, so maybe he didn't have anyone else to talk to. Listening cost me nothing.

When he wound down, I said, "I saw the team come back with a lot of stuff. I guess you have to sort and organize it for the Wordkeeper."

He sighed. "Of course I do. They don't trust anyone else."

"How much did we pay for it all?" I tensed.

"A few bags of fish. The way I heard it, those Burrowers are smart and wouldn't let the Hunters in until they passed the trade goods through a narrow gap in the wall."

Relief spilled through me. I'd nearly let suspicion poison *everything*. Just because the elders had made some tough decisions, it didn't make them brutal or merciless. A weight lifted from my shoulders.

I talked with Twist a bit longer, so he didn't suspect I'd been after that information all along. Since I liked him—and few people did—I didn't want him to think I'd only been using him. In the kitchen, we went our separate ways: him to other work and me to patrol.

Fade waited for me beyond the barricades this time, one foot tapping with ill-concealed impatience. As soon as I scrambled over, he spun and led the way into the dark. I thought we needed to talk, but plainly he disagreed. The hours passed with excruciating speed, between the silence and the tension.

At last as we turned back toward the enclave, he spoke. "Do you believe them?"

"Who?"

"The elders. The gossip."

"About what?" I thought I knew but I wanted him to spell it out.

"Banner. They're saying she killed herself because . . ." He trailed off, unable to say it aloud.

He'd been close to her. That made him a likely candidate for the sire of her unborn brat, if the story was true. I didn't like how that made me feel. I cast back to the day we'd found her, remembering the cuts on her wrists, how the skin looked—

Sickness overwhelmed me.

"No," I said quietly. "I don't."

He froze for a long moment and then spun to face me. "Why?"

I could see in his eyes he'd noticed right away. I just hadn't wanted to think about it until he forced me to remember. "The cuts were wrong."

If I wanted to die, I'd use one long motion, no stop and start of the blade. The ones we'd found on Banner showed where the knife dragged and paused. Someone had killed her; I didn't know why. If they'd found her hoard, she should've been exiled.

But maybe it ran deeper. Maybe the elders knew something about the silent rebellion. In that case, Banner would've been killed as an equally quiet warning. *Associate with them and you'll wind up like this.* It was nothing they would want to confront openly because that would mean admitting some citizens mistrusted their leadership. Acknowledging discontent would only breed more. I understood the way they thought.

"They added all of her things to the archives," he said softly. "And fed her to the Freaks."

I flinched. "I'm sorry."

"What are we going to do about it?"

"What *can* we do?"

In answer he turned and headed for the barricades. I feared he might do something stupid, and I couldn't think how to help him. If I pushed, I'd end up like Banner. And so would he.

A few weeks later, as promised, they rewarded me for my contribution to culture. With Banner's death hanging over me, I didn't want the credit, but there was no refusing. They held a feast, and the Wordkeeper sat me beside him in a place of honor.

Once everyone had assembled, he rose. "We're here to honor Deuce, a Huntress who, despite considerable risk, brought back a bag of artifacts. She did not attempt to keep anything she found for her own personal pleasure. As one should always do, she thought first of the enclave." The Wordkeeper droned on about the importance of putting the group before self. He also mentioned how I'd been principal in a trade that gave us access to more artifacts than we'd ever seen before.

I felt strange, being lauded for something that had been coincidence. I ducked my head, hoping the enclave wouldn't hate me for making them listen to the Wordkeeper, but everyone seemed happy to take the day off. When he finished, he threw his hands skyward in a dramatic gesture. "Let the celebration start!"

An answering roar went through the crowd. Pipes and drums echoed through the enclave. The torches smoked; people whirled and stomped while brats ran around underfoot. Roasting meat and mushrooms smelled unbelievably good, and there was fish too. For once, they didn't limit us and I took seconds of each dish. Brats immediately snatched my plate, running off to lick it and then wash it up so someone else, someone less honored, could use it.

From the sidelines, I watched the party until a Hunter came

to get me. Gazing up at him, I realized he'd been patrolling longer than Fade. As a brat, I'd watched this one train and he was smiling at me. What was his name? Silk had introduced me, but that first day, I'd been so nervous, I couldn't remember more than half of them.

Crane, I remembered belatedly.

"Come on," he said. "You're going to miss it."

"Miss what?"

"We're doing a demonstration."

A thrill went through me, despite my dark mood. How could I have forgotten? At any feast, the Hunters assembled and sparred as part of the entertainment. Citizens often bet on the outcomes. Rising, I tried to look serious when excitement bubbled inside me.

I glanced at the Wordkeeper, who had been sitting with me, watching the others dance. "May I be excused, sir?"

"Certainly. Fight well, Huntress."

I didn't think I'd ever get tired of hearing people call me that. Hurrying, I kept pace with Crane. He led me to the training room, where everyone else stood already waiting. As we slipped in, Silk was handing out the assignments, telling people who they'd face first in the tournament.

The elder Hunter beside me whispered, "It's by elimination. The winner of each round progresses to the next until only two remain."

That much I remembered. When Silk paused before me, she said, "Deuce, your first opponent will be Pinwheel." It was a terrible name, and the girl who owned it scowled at me. She was tall, which meant she had a good reach—better than mine. I could see her assessing me in turn.

"Pin," the other Huntress muttered, not that Silk cared. She had already moved down the line.

Once she finished, she went and got a box. "The senior Hunter will choose a number that determines the order in which you'll fight."

I stood by while Pin picked for us. No question I was low in seniority, even if I'd completed a dangerous mission and brought back some artifacts. She held up the wood chip so I could see it read "5." Good, other people had to go before us, but not so many I'd have too much time to get nervous.

Pin slipped over beside me. "Don't worry. It'll all be over soon." But her tone was friendly. I wasn't used to that.

"Make sure you give them a good show," Silk ordered. "Now move!"

I followed the throng of Hunters into an orderly formation to the side of the training area. The rest of the enclave filtered in, forming a circle around the fighting ring. As a brat, I had pushed my way to the front, kneeling down so nobody complained about me being in the way. I'd watched so many of these tournaments, and now I was finally going to compete. For safety's sake, we didn't use weapons.

Random pairings meant no consideration had been given to skill level. I watched as a slim Huntress faced an older Hunter. She fought hard, but his experience dominated. In the next match, two Hunters circled each other, but the elder had the greater reach and better timing. Speed would help the smaller one in time, but at the moment he lacked the experience to parlay it into a win.

So the first two went quickly. The opponents were too unevenly matched for it to be otherwise. Anything else would've amounted to fakery, and the Hunters had too much integrity for that. The next two pitted veteran Huntresses and Hunters, and they were so fierce and graceful, they had me bouncing on my toes, cheering and oohing along with everyone else.

Then it was my turn.

Heart pounding, I took my place in the circle, where I faced Pin. She wore a fierce, focused look. At Silk's signal, we faced each other and bowed.

"Begin!"

We circled. She was wary enough of me to want me to go on the offensive first; I took it as a compliment. Seeing I wouldn't, Pin spun at me with her big move first. I leaped away from her lashing leg. I faked an off-balance landing, hoping that would bring her rushing in. It didn't. She grinned at me and shook her head.

Pin blocked both my attempts to punch and countered with a kick aimed at my knee. I wheeled her arm into a lock and flipped her. *Ha. Didn't see that coming, did you?* She landed hard on her back, but she pulled until I fell with her, flipping over the top. I turned the fall into a roll and came to my feet with a bruised shoulder. The sounds of the audience hooting and cheering faded as I narrowed my eyes on her movements.

We exchanged a flurry of hits and blocks. My speed came into play then, but when she connected, it rocked me. Her fist felt like ten pounds of solid rock slamming into my stomach. I doubled over, but when she went to finish me, I snagged her ankle and pulled. Immediately, I dropped all my weight on her chest and sank an elbow into her throat. Not enough to hurt her, but enough to prove my dominance. I held her there until she slapped the floor three times.

I staggered to my feet and Silk threw my hand in the air.

I don't believe it. I won. Proud and happy, I beamed at the audience, despite my new bruises. Afterward, Pin shook my hand and slapped me on the back. I went to stand with the other victors.

The other fights were good, but I was too pleased with myself to pay close attention. I should have. I might've learned something.

In the second round, I got my butt handed to me by the Hunter who had come to get me. Crane rushed me, ignoring my attempts at finesse. Up in the air, I tried to overbalance him, but he was holding me too tightly. I could feel the bruises forming. He slammed me to the ground and shoved my face in the floor before I had time to get my balance. I felt like he'd break my spine before I tapped.

Afterward, I shook his hand and limped to join the other losers, but even that didn't dim my glow. I hadn't lost in the first match, at least. As far as I could tell, no other new blood had made it out of the first round besides me.

Bets flew fast and furious while the fights went on. In disbelief, I watched Fade claw his way up the ranks. He was grace personified, compared to most of the Hunters. He fought with lethal beauty and an escalating sense of urgency. Sometimes, after a fight, he stared with such ferocity the spectators backed away. Even the other winners gave him a significant amount of space.

Eventually, it came down to Crane . . . and Fade. Final match. This would decide who held the title until the next feast. Fade was taller, leaner, but Crane had more muscle mass. He had brute strength in contrast to my partner's agility. After watching them both, I didn't know which way this would go.

The big Hunter charged but Fade dodged. He was so fast he made Crane seem lumbering in comparison. I knew how strong Crane was, but he had to get ahold of Fade first.

Three times, Crane lunged, Fade evaded, and the crowd got restless. Fade was losing them. They wanted a final match, not to see him refuse to take a hit. *Come on,* I said silently. *You can do this.*

He attempted his first strike, and he was just fast enough to clip the big guy's jaw. But that brought him close enough for Crane to grapple. He crushed Fade in a rib-breaking hug and lifted him up off the ground. I realized the mistake as soon as he did it. Fade slammed his brow into the other Hunter's temple.

Yes, that's the way. Fight to win. While the big Hunter staggered, dizzied, Fade went for the kneecap. He gave no quarter, becoming more ferocious with every passing minute. It was almost as if he'd forgotten this was a match, as if he thought he'd die if he lost. On his last hit, he dropped Crane to the ground and he went with him, fist upraised to pummel his face.

The big guy tapped.

The crowd stilled, breath caught. They expected Fade to hit him anyway. So did I. I shook my head slowly, hoping he wouldn't, hoping he wasn't crazy. Slowly, he lowered his arm, and let Silk pull him to his feet. When she threw his arm in the air, he stumbled. He'd fought a lot of matches today. His black eyes flashed as he glanced around. His fists were still clenched, despite Silk's grip. I wasn't sure he knew the fights were over, or that he was safe.

"Our winner!" she shouted, and the citizens surrounded him to thump his back.

He was the best the Hunters had to offer, and he was about to attack the congratulatory crowd. Before I could think better of it, I pushed my way through the throng toward him. When necessary, I connected with a discreet shoulder or elbow to clear a path. I snagged his hand and towed him out of the mix.

The pipers and drummers started up again, distracting every-one with a festive tune. All the better for us to make our escape. The dancers stomped and clapped, and I pushed clear, leading him away into a quiet section of the warren. He leaned against the wall, seeming grateful for my intervention, even though he blamed me for my inaction after Banner's death. His breath churned his chest as if he'd been running, and sweat trickled down his face.

"I'll get you some water."

"Stay. I just need a minute."

"It's hard for you," I said. "Because you fight to live, not for show."

Eyes closed, he nodded. "I participate because Silk won't let me sit out. But once I get going, I . . . forget it's not real."

What must those years have been like for him outside the enclave? This wasn't the time to ask, but I wondered. I noticed he had a host of new bruises from all the matches he'd fought today, but they didn't seem to trouble him. He pushed away from the wall, skin gleaming pale in the torchlight. For a mo-ment I wanted to put my hand over his heart so I could feel it beating, and the impulse frightened me. I took a step back.

"You sure I can't get you anything to eat or drink?" Ordinarily I wouldn't offer; that was brat work, but he'd earned it. Tonight he stood as the Hunters' champion, and he could have whatever he wanted, including a Huntress for a serving girl.

"You did enough getting me out of there." The flat, un-friendly tone cut me, and my smile died. For a minute, I'd felt like we were back on the old ground.

I didn't know why I was still trying to help him. If he still thought I had something to do with Banner's death, then we shouldn't work together. Hurt curled through me.

"If we don't hammer this out," I said, "I'm going to ask Silk for a new partner."

"I would have already if I thought it would do any good."

I exhaled. "I'll go talk to Silk."

As I turned, he grabbed my arm and wheeled me around. "You want to tell me why you did it? This is on me. I told her she could trust you."

I'd thought he *trusted* me—and that he was angry because I wouldn't do anything after I admitted I knew she hadn't killed herself. It was much worse than I'd imagined.

With fierce resolve, I broke his hold on me. "You want to fight this out? I didn't *do* anything. If someone found out her secret, it wasn't through me."

His black eyes studied me. "You willing to take a blood oath on that?"

"Get your knife."

For obvious reasons, we couldn't do this in the hallway, so he dragged me off toward the hall we used for ceremonies. That was fitting enough, and nobody would bother us. Once we arrived, he produced his dagger and offered it to me.

I cut a line on my palm and spoke the words. "On my blood, I swear I had nothing to do with Banner's death. May it boil in my veins if I speak untruth."

Fade watched me as if he expected it to happen, no matter what I said. He didn't relax until I handed back the blade. I curled my fingers in as if I could trap the blood. Instead it trickled out between my fingers.

"I'm sorry," he said. "She was my only friend, and I needed someone to blame."

After our trip to Nassau, I'd thought *we* were friends. But I didn't let on that his words bit deep. I kept my face blank. "Maybe I'd feel the same if it had been Thimble or Stone."

"He's that big Breeder I sometimes see you with."

"Probably."

He hesitated. "I never had a partner pay this much attention to me before."

That made me feel I'd overstepped. He'd had two before me, so he knew better than I did what constituted normal behavior. Maybe I watched him *too* closely. It was unsuitable, and Silk would demote me to Breeder if she ever found out.

"I should get back," I muttered.

"Not yet." In an unspeakable liberty, he snatched the tie from my hair, so it spilled around my face.

"Why did you do that?" My breath caught when he brushed the strands around my face just so. Touching me. We were on shaky ground here. If someone saw us—

"I wanted to see what you'd look like."

Back off, I told myself. *Walk away now.* Instead I froze, gazing up into his impossibly dark eyes.

He bent his head and brushed my lips with his. His hair spilled against my forehead, sleek and startling. Shock held me immobile, shock—and something else. Part of me wanted to lean into him. I shouldn't want that. A Huntress wouldn't. Shame, confusion, and longing warred for dominance. Against my better judgment, I let my brow graze his jaw, just a whisper of heat, wrapped around me like a pair of arms. And then I drew back.

"What are you *doing*?" I demanded.

"Apologizing. I missed you, Deuce. I'm sorry I doubted you."

Maybe the kiss didn't mean anything. Maybe it was just an

apology, like he said. "Accepted. But if you ever misjudge me like that again—"

"Got it." He smiled. "Now come on. We're missing all the fun."

To my surprise, he took my hand and led me back to the dancing. As a brat, this wasn't something I'd ever done, but I learned the rhythm easily enough. They circled in a long progression, and the two of us joined at the end. Fade let go of me after the second circuit, carried away by well-wishers.

I danced until I had no breath left. A brat tapped me on the arm. When I turned, I recognized one of the younger ones. She'd joked with me in the kitchen a while back, and I'd shared dorm space with her until my naming day. Her small, dirty face reflected the same kind of admiration I'd felt. I remembered her number too.

Her eyes lit when I said, "What's up, Twenty-six?"

"Do you think I could ever learn to fight like you?"

"If you work hard and don't skip lessons, I think you could."

She confided, "I don't want to be a yucky old Breeder."

"I don't blame you. You can do it, if you want it enough." Once, those words would've meant the world to me. The new bloods were busy trying to impress the older ones, and experienced Hunters had no time for brats.

After 26 ran off, I followed the other Hunters back to the section of the warren they'd appropriated as their own. Nobody else dared come in here. *I'd* never even been in here, as a matter of fact, although I could have. Torches lit the darkness and the Builders, understanding our importance, had filled the space with proper chairs and cushions. This was the nicest section of the enclave by far, even better than what I'd seen of the elders' area—unless they had hidden comforts.

Making sure not to look at Fade, I sat down beside Crane, who flashed me a grin. "No hard feelings, new blood?"

"No," I said, smiling back.

They dealt me into a game they were playing, and I basked in the simple pleasure of being one of them. *Deuce. Huntress.* This was the best day of my life.

Countless hours later, Silk tugged me aside, wearing a smile. "You're welcome."

"Thank you," I said. I didn't ask what I was thanking her for. It only mattered that I spoke the words.

"I run them." She gestured all the assembled Hunters, who had surrounded Fade to congratulate him. "I told them the two of you are forgiven and part of the team again—that you've done your penance, and I don't expect any more trouble out of you." She paused. "I won't get any, will I?"

Ah. I got it now. She wanted me to know Fade had been accepted, because she ordered it, and if I enjoyed the pleasure of being a Hunter, it was only because of her. Which meant I wasn't to spout off about Nassau or the Freaks or the Burrowers, if I wanted to enjoy such simple things. My job wasn't to think or to plan. I was a Huntress—and new blood at that. Leave the important stuff to the elders. The more I got to know Silk, outside of the hero worship that lasted through my brat-hood, the less I liked her. But maybe she had to be this way to keep everyone in line.

I shook my head. "We'll follow orders, sir."

Sacrifice

For several weeks, morale stayed high. Patrols passed with relative ease, we met the meat quota, and I enjoyed being a Huntress. Apart from the occasional clash with Freaks, things stayed quiet. I had the awful feeling that once they stopped gorging on Nassau, they would head for the next nearest enclave. Us. Still, I kept my misgivings to myself.

When I least expected it, disaster struck. But not in the way I thought.

Fade and I were among the last to return from patrol that day. We had to range wider than usual to fill our bags. Half the snares sat empty, worrisome enough, but we managed to take enough prey to justify calling ourselves Hunters. We also dropped a couple of Freaks, but I hardly called that a deed worth mentioning. These had been near death, nothing but skin and bone and bloody teeth.

When we clambered across the barricades, I knew instantly something was wrong. The guards stood facing away from their posts, for one thing. They barely glanced back at us to make sure we were human before returning to the common area just beyond.

I glanced at Fade, who hefted his bag in a shrug. We put the meat in a pile with the rest—Twist would tend to it later—and inched closer to hear what was going on. The Wordkeeper held court with Whitewall and Copper standing to either side. They had a big sandy-haired guy trapped at the center of the circle. Everyone had stopped work to watch events unfold. My movement drew the Wordkeeper's eye and he *smiled* at me, as if we shared a secret.

"You stand accused of theft and hoarding," Whitewall said, his voice hard.

"How do you plead?" Copper asked.

"I didn't. I would never!"

Oh, no. Even before I cut around enough to recognize his face in profile, I knew Stone's voice. He cradled a brat in one arm, his face drawn with terror.

"Silk found this hidden beneath your pallet." The Wordkeeper held up one of the slim, colorful books I'd brought. "You were seen lurking around the archives. Can you offer any explanation before we sentence you?"

Tears streamed down my friend's face. The brat in his arms caught his mood and started to cry in little gulping sniffs. "It's not mine. I don't know how it got there."

Watching them, *I* knew. With a terrible growing sickness, I knew. Skittle probably hadn't done anything, either. Every so often, they picked a citizen at random. They put artifacts in his private space and then they accused him of hoarding. They needed the consequences to be fresh in everyone else's mind. This was how they kept us from questioning their decisions. I'd once believed the elders to be benevolent and wise.

But no more.

Stone had no chance Topside *and* he had a brat. He'd sired one; it could be the boy tucked into the curve of his arm. I couldn't watch this happen. If the tunnel brat haunted me, there was no way I could live with watching my friend's exile.

"That's no defense against the evidence," Whitewall said.

"It's mine." I spoke before I knew I meant to.

Unfriendly hands shoved me toward the center. I stumbled and then restored my balance, approaching with my heart thumping like mad. I didn't want to do this; I *couldn't* be doing this. I didn't want to leave the only home I'd ever known.

The Wordkeeper narrowed his eyes on me. "You claim you stole it? After presenting yourself as a model citizen?" His tight expression said he knew I'd done nothing of the kind.

"Then how did it wind up in Stone's private space?" Silk demanded.

I don't know what I would've said, but Fade pushed forward then. *No, don't do this. Stay and be safe.* In that moment, I tried to will him not to speak. I even shook my head, but he didn't look at me.

He focused on the elders. "I put it there. I was jealous of their friendship, and I wanted him to be blamed for what she'd done."

After the initial gasp, silence.

I could see them weighing the benefit of seeing two former heroes brought low, two sacrifices for the price of one. Fade had proven the best Hunter among us, so he would make an excellent example. *See,* they would say. *Anyone can stray. That is why constant vigilance and obedience is so important.* They conferred far too short a time, unlike after my naming day. This was serious, and someone had to pay.

Whitewall said, "I accept your confession. From this moment forth, you are banished, stripped of your titles, and will be offered no aid or shelter by any College citizen, on penalty of exile. Go Topside, lawbreakers."

Though I had expected it, the weight of the pronouncement crushed me. I tried to catch Thimble's eye but she turned away. One by one, everyone else did the same. As a brat, I'd taken part in a shunning; I just hadn't realized how it felt. I'd been secure in my status. *Every year,* I realized. *We sent people Topside every single year.*

With some part of me, I recognized they'd targeted Stone as a warning. Because I cared about him, because we'd been brat-mates. It was a reminder to keep silent about anything I might've learned from Banner or Fade. They couldn't have expected me to react like this. Even *I* couldn't believe it.

Stone wore a bewildered look, as if he couldn't understand what was happening. He patted the brat on the back and dried his tears while staring at me with mute hurt. We'd been through so much together. Did he *truly* think I—

"Thief," he spat and turned his back, like the others.

He didn't know I'd saved him. There would be no acknowledgment of the sacrifice. The knowledge rendered me numb.

"You have five minutes," Silk said. "You will not be permitted to take our food or water. We will allow you your personal effects, but you will be searched before leaving the enclave for the last time."

Her eyes reflected a sad, quiet awareness of what I'd done. Of what Fade had done. Though I didn't like her, I didn't believe this was her policy; she merely enforced it. I knew why I'd spoken up for Stone; I was less sure of Fade's reasons for getting involved. Whatever they were, he now had no choice but to follow me into the exile.

With shaking hands, I put my few belongings in the bag I took on patrols: spare clothing, my blanket, the tin of salve Banner had made, and a few of my shiny baubles. All told, there wasn't much. That left only my weapons, and I strapped them on feeling hopeless and heartsick.

Twist stopped me on the way and tugged me into his private space. I'd never seen it before. "We don't have much time." He rummaged in his crate and came up with an item that looked like a leather harness. He filled the packets with dry meat and the pouches with water. "Here, put it on under your shirt."

"They'll kill you if they find out you're helping me."

His mouth curled. "Like they did Banner?"

"How do you know?"

"Who do you think deals with the dead?" Twist closed his eyes for a moment, but not before I saw his grief. Banner had been important to him. His hands curled into fists, and he slammed one against his palm. "Someone betrayed us."

"Us?" This couldn't be a trap, not at this point. But I still didn't feel comfortable admitting what I knew.

"I'm one of the rebels."

I froze, wondering if he, like Fade, suspected me of playing some part in Banner's death. But he wouldn't be helping me if he did. "I'm sorry. I wish I'd helped her, like you're doing now."

He shrugged then. "It's not that big a risk. They're going to kill me for what I do after you're gone."

For the first time, I looked at Twist and saw him as he was— not the cowed, scurrying figure who went to do Whitewall's bidding. His eyes carried an angry fire; his shoulders might be narrow, but they were straight and sure. I almost asked what he was planning, but we didn't have any time to waste.

"Don't throw your life away," I said softly. "Whatever you do, make it count."

He nodded. "You were always nice to me, and Stone is a good person. I know he didn't do this. Neither did you."

"Nobody did," I said softly.

Twist gave a jerky nod, stuck his head through the curtain to make sure there were no witnesses, and pushed me out. The harness made little shape against my shirt. With luck, the guards would only search my bag, not my person.

They spat on me as I passed through the warren toward the barricades. I lifted my chin and pretended not to see them. Fade met me there. We stood mute while they rifled through our things. Pin flung my bag at my head, and I caught it. I hardly dared breathe when she stepped close.

"You disgust me," she said, low.

I said nothing. Like so many times before, Fade and I climbed across and left the enclave behind. But this time, we weren't heading on patrol. No safety awaited us. Without thinking, without seeking a direction, I broke into a run.

I ran until the pain in my side matched the one in my heart. At length he grabbed me from behind and gave me a shake. "We're not going to make it if you keep this up."

A choked laugh escaped me. "Are you stupid? We're not going to make it anyway. If Nassau died, what chance do we have? Why did you come with me? Now I have to feel bad about *you* too."

"You're my partner," he said, as if the words meant something different.

"But you lied. I know you didn't put the book in Stone's space."

"And I know you didn't steal it."

"He didn't either," I whispered. "And it wasn't fair. It was *them*."

"I know."

"How long have you known?" Heartbreak and disillusionment cut me like shards of glass.

"Always," he said simply.

"That explains why you hated them so much."

He wrapped his arms around me and my first impulse was to push him away. But there were no rules anymore. I wasn't a Huntress. Now I was just a girl with six scars on my arms. So I laid my head on his chest and listened to his heart.

"You can't look on this as a death sentence," he said, after a moment.

"You really think we can survive?"

"Down here? Not for long. But Topside isn't like they said, Deuce. It's dangerous, true, but going up doesn't mean instant death."

My teeth chattered at the idea. I'd prepared my whole life for the dangers one faced in the tunnels. I knew nothing else. I tipped my head back as if I could gaze through the tons of metal and stone to the wonders he'd seen and the horrors he'd survived. The surface world sounded like a tale told to a brat during a quiet moment. I couldn't imagine what it might be like up there.

"If you say so."

"Come on. Let's keep moving. We need to be out of their territory before the next patrol or we'll have to fight any Hunters we see."

I didn't want that. By his expression, neither did he. "Did you kill Skittle?"

His silence served as its own answer.

"We're not going to be down here long," he said eventually. "Remember the platform where we slept that first night?"

The place with the horrible waste closet—yes, I remembered. I nodded.

"Well, the metal gate on the other end blocks off the stairs. Those lead Topside."

"You think we can get it open."

"If not, the Burrowers might know a way out. They have all kinds of subtunnels."

I nodded. "We also need to warn them about trading with the enclave, assuming Twist told me the truth. We owe them that much."

"Agreed."

I fell in behind him. Fade set a bruising pace; I knew what he wanted—out of these tunnels. He could've left at anytime, but maybe he didn't want to go alone. I could understand that.

With each stride, I left the known world behind.

two

topside

From the cellar she got into a long passage, into which the moon was shining, and came to a door. She managed to open it, and to her great joy found herself in *the other place,* not on the top of the wall, however, but in the garden she had longed to enter.

—George MacDonald, *The Day Boy and the Night Girl*

Unknown

The platform looked the same—with one notable exception. There were no Freak bodies, not even bones, just the smear of blood where they'd been dragged off. Ears sharp, we took a break for food and water, and then Fade strode over to the metal gate.

It had a lock on it, but the gate itself was old and rusted. He kicked it repeatedly until it finally bent and gave enough for us to slip through the gap between the gate and the wall. The fit required us to turn sideways and it scraped a little, but we made it.

Then we stood on the other side. Steps led upward with a metal divider separating the two sides. Fade led the way, and we climbed toward the surface. It took far less time than I expected. If everyone in the enclave knew just how close we were, figuratively speaking, people would've suffered some sleepless nights.

The air felt different, the higher we went. It moved against my skin, carrying new scents. But the stairs ended in a mound of rocks. The wind could slip through, not people. We stood there for a moment, stymied in our attempt to escape before we ran into the first hunting party.

"It will have to be the Burrowers," I said.

"If not, I think the steps near where you found the relics go all the way up."

That was halfway to Nassau. With the scant provisions Twist had supplied, it would be a terrible run. The closer we came to the dead settlement, the greater the risk we'd run afoul of the Freaks too. But there was nothing else for it. I retraced my steps with Fade on my heels and we scraped back past the metal gate.

"You know the way from here?" I asked.

"It's not that far."

Relatively speaking. We ran at a strong clip for several hours. Noises echoed in distant tunnels, but we didn't see any Freaks. Our patrols had done a good job of clearing the area in the past days.

When we came to the split where I'd lost Fade, I started counting, and the correct number of steps brought me to where I thought we'd found the Burrowers. I ran my fingers over the stones until I found the loose ones. I pushed one until it plunked out. A pair of huge eyes stared out at me.

"Deuce." I recognized Jengu's voice at once.

He made a wide-enough space for us to slip through. As we continued down the narrow shaft toward the wider common area, I heard him rebuilding quickly; they gave the Freaks no sign of their presence. This couldn't be the only entrance or exit, just the only one we knew about. The other Burrowers stared at Fade and me, but they didn't speak. None of them looked wounded, and a weight lifted.

"Doan spect to see ya so soon," he said with a friendly smile.

"Did you have any problems with the first trading party?" Fade asked.

Jengu grinned. "Not once we make clear we don't open up til dem give us fish, and maybe Eaters find dem before den."

Relief sparkled through me. In its own way, cleverness counted as strength. The Burrowers could trade with the enclave on equal terms. "How much did they take?"

The Burrower shrugged. "Lots. We doan need it. Can't eat it."

That was more or less what I thought. Fade was smiling. "We wanted to warn you not to trust them completely, but it looks like you were one step ahead."

"Doan trust nobody completely," Jengu said, philosophical. "But fish is fish."

I declined an offer of a steaming cup of something. It smelled none too good. I'd rather eat the last of my dried meat and drink the tepid water Twist had given me. But right now, I had business to discuss.

"We need to leave the underground," I said.

Jengu tilted his head, wearing an expression I interpreted as concern.

I went on, "We're not asking you to reveal any of your hidden tunnels. But if you could point the way out, we'd appreciate it."

The Burrower considered. "I can. But dem"—he jerked his head toward the other Burrowers—"gonna wan know how you paying."

I hadn't factored that. "What do you want?"

"What you got?" he countered.

With a shrug, I dumped the contents of my bag onto the floor. We were close enough to the torches that he could see everything I owned. The few baubles I'd held on to over the years caught the light and sparkled. Jengu bent down, entranced with a small blue object that shimmered. I showed him how to open it. Inside, it had a tiny mirror. Unlike most it wasn't broken or anything. The item carried a nice scent too. I had no idea what it might've been used for, but I liked to open it up and look at my eyes. It was the one thing my dam had passed along to me, a family treasure. I'd had it for as long as I could remember.

His hand curled around it in a possessive gesture. "Dis. I show ya for dis."

Of course. I suffered a little pang but acknowledged the price must be paid. "Deal. Is it a long way?"

"Two sleeps."

"Can we rest in storage again before we go?"

"Plenty room now."

He didn't bother guiding us. I'd counted the way before, and that was one of my chief skills, besides fighting. This time, the platform stood half empty. Hunters had taken a lot of relics for the Wordkeeper to catalog; the work would keep him busy for a long time.

If I portioned it away, one step at a time, the fear of the unknown wouldn't overwhelm me. Maybe Fade knew how I was feeling. We went to sleep on the platform without talking about what the future held.

After we woke up, we ate the last of our food. Then Jengu came to get us. The path took us back into the common area and down another tunnel. I counted the steps, but the twists and turns soon had me lost. Even counting, I doubted I could find my way again.

These tunnels were dank and damp, and they smelled terrible. Jengu carried a small torch with him, which told me there were no Freaks in here. Dark water trickled down the center, so we stayed to the edges and tried to dodge the floating, furry corpses.

It was a miserable journey. By the end, we were reduced to eating what Jengu gave us and hoping it wouldn't make us sick.

The air tasted disgusting, so I tried to breathe through my nose. Our Burrower guide didn't seem to mind and Fade never showed his discomfort.

At last we came to slimy wall that had metal bars fastened to it. Jengu tilted his head. "Climb up. Push. And ya out."

"You're not coming?"

"Dem doan need nothing from Topside now. But we go sometimes. Get things."

They did occasional supply runs to the surface? *Interesting.* Maybe Fade knew what he was talking about. Maybe we could make it.

"Thanks for everything," Fade said.

"Yes, thank you."

"Welcome."

The Burrower didn't wait to see how we fared. He turned with the torch and trudged back the way we'd come. Soon the shadows devoured us and I could only see the vague Fade-shape nearby.

"I'll go up first."

I didn't argue, but I didn't let him get far ahead of me either. As soon as he started to climb, I did too. The metal was slick beneath my palms; several times I nearly lost my balance and fell. Grimly, I continued up.

"Anything?"

"Almost there." I heard him feeling around, and then the scrape of metal on stone. He pulled himself out of what looked like a small hole. Diffuse light spilled down, a different tint than I'd ever seen. It was sweetly silver and cool, like a drink of water. With Fade's help, I scrambled up the rest of the way and saw the world above for the first time.

It stole my breath. I spun in a slow circle, trembling at the size of it. I tilted my head back and saw overhead a vast field of black, spattered with brightness. I wanted to crouch down and cover my head. It was too much space, and horror overwhelmed me.

"Easy," Fade said. "Look down. Trust me."

He was right. When I looked at the ground, the terror dialed back. From that point, I didn't look up more than I had to. Tall things surrounded us, mostly blocking my view. Shards of glass and broken stones littered the ground. The air was full of sounds I couldn't identify, after having known only enclave noises. Wind rustled through rock, creating a mournful kind of song. Chitters and scrapes alarmed me. We weren't alone, and I didn't like not knowing what waited in the dark.

Down below, I always knew.

I refused to show my fear. *Lock it down, Huntress.*

"What are those?" I asked, pointing.

"Buildings, mostly abandoned."

Some towered, spearing up to unimaginable heights. I couldn't even imagine how such a thing had come to be built. Others had buckled and toppled, leaving rubble strewn all over the ground. That, I was used to.

The air didn't burn the inside of my chest, at least, and it smelled fresher than I'd expected, based on the stories. No rot, no fetid wind like that down below. And I didn't feel sick from standing here. I shouldn't have been surprised that the elders had lied. Or maybe things had changed Topside since we first took shelter down below.

While I tried to get my bearings, he fitted the metal circle back in place and stomped it down. We stood in the center of an endless stretch of old rock. It didn't look natural. Despite its age and poor condition, I thought it looked like something poured down and left to harden.

"I think you better tell me everything you know about this place," I said shakily.

"I will," Fade promised. "But first we should find shelter. There are no Freaks up here—at least there didn't used to be—but from what I remember, there are other dangers."

"There are places to hide all around us."

He nodded. "But they're marked. See?" As we walked, he pointed out bits of white or red paint marking the buildings. "The Topside gangs take their territory seriously. We don't want to cross anyone."

"What's a gang?"

"Kind of like the enclave," he said. "But meaner."

"Is that why you left? To get away from the gangs?"

"Partly."

I saw I'd get no answers while he was distracted and scanning the buildings, so I tried to help. I might not know what the symbols meant, but I could tell if they were present. We'd been walking for a while over the rough stone path—it buckled in spots as if the world had lifted up and given it a sound shake—when Fade spotted a crumbling red building that bore no marks at all.

"Here?" I asked.

"Let's check it out." He ran up three stairs to the door; it swung open when he tried it. But he stumbled away, one hand pressed to his face. "Stay back. There's a reason nobody has claimed this place."

The distance we covered seemed incredible to me. All the while, I fought my urge to panic. I couldn't *be* up here. To combat the feeling, I focused on the new sights. Something flapped above us in the dark and I ducked down, curling myself into a ball.

"What *was* that?"

Fade was smiling. "It's a bird. They can't eat you. You're too big."

It sailed upward, riding the wind. The wings showed in silhouette, tapered and graceful. I marveled at the existence of such a marvelous creature, and wondered how it must feel to move like that, all elegance and velocity.

"All the old stories are true," I breathed.

"Most of them."

We walked until my feet hurt. I saw more birds, perched on poles and buildings. Rusted metal wrecks sat here and there along the street. Fade told me they were called cars and they'd once owned the surface we walked on. I found that hard to believe. Plants had forced their way through the cracks, giving the rock a mossy, uneven look.

The sky had begun to lighten by the time we found a building that didn't smell terrible and didn't bear any gang markings. Fade tried the door, but it was locked.

"Maybe there's another way in?"

We circled and found in the back something Fade called a window—low enough for me to slide through. Fade wanted to, but it was too small. I waved off his concern.

"I'm a Huntress," I said, out of habit. "I'll be fine."

And then it hit me all over again. I had no right to call myself that. I squashed the sadness and let him boost me up. The window slid open and I wormed my way through it. I hung upside down and managed to twist to my feet as I dropped. On the way down, I banged my shoulder on the wall.

When I got my bearings, I saw I stood in a dark room, but I could make out the shape of the door. Even the dark didn't seem as black as it had down below. Maybe there were benefits to being Topside. I avoided the junk: dusty piles of broken glass and items that had rotted away or crumbled into dust. Still there were a few things I recognized like eating utensils, bottles, plates, and cups in different colors and patterns. The Wordkeeper would die of excitement if he could see this place.

After some fiddling, I managed to unfasten all the bolts, and then I opened the door to let Fade in. He joined me, redid all the latches, and then took a look around.

"It's a storeroom. I think this was a shop of some kind."

"A shop?"

"Where people traded."

It sounded like a good idea. At the enclave, we'd held a shop on a regular basis in the common room, where we could examine what everyone else had and then barter for it with our best items. But if you lived in different buildings, people needed a place to gather and trade.

"Let's take a look around."

I led the way out, down a dark hall and into a bigger room. Metal shelves—we'd scavenged a few like that over the years— stood mostly empty. There were only a few tins left, nothing familiar, though, nothing I'd ever seen before. Broken glass crunched underfoot. Another door led to a waste closet, but this one didn't smell like the other. Nearby, Fade twisted a handle but nothing happened.

"There used to be water, sometimes," he said. "We used to drink it, my dad and me, but then he got sick."

"From drinking that?"

"Maybe. I was a brat. There was a lot of stuff he didn't tell me."

"I have a little water to tide us over. Turn around." Without asking why, he did. I struggled out of the leather harness. "Twist gave it to me. It has water pouches. The meat is gone, but I still have these."

"Why? He risked everything by doing that."

"I know."

"I wish I could thank him."

"I did for both of us. Let's see what else there is here."

We found another doorway off the hallway leading from the back room. I hadn't seen it the first time because I wasn't used to tunnels leading anywhere else. Fade noticed it and opened the door. Stairs led up.

"I thought this building had another level," he murmured, and went jogging upward.

I didn't know if going higher sounded like a great idea, but I wanted to stay by myself even less. Out of habit, I counted as I climbed, even though I could see perfectly well up here.

The steps opened into what I'd call a private living space. By my standards, it was unbelievably luxurious. Only the elders would've had something so nice in the enclave, but even they wouldn't have gotten this much space. The room must've been sixteen feet long and almost that wide. I recognized the objects as furniture, but I had to ask Fade their names.

I burned with embarrassment when he grinned and pointed. "Sofa. Chair. Table."

The sofa felt amazing when I sank onto it, despite its musty smell. Not even my rag pallet had been so soft. Leaning my head back, I closed my eyes. I could hear Fade moving around, checking the place out.

"There's another room," he said. "We can each have our own space."

"I'll take the sofa."

He sat down beside me. "So you had questions before."

That sounded like an invitation to ask whatever I wanted. "You were born Topside . . . how long did you live here?"

"Eight or nine years? And then after my dad died, it got too dangerous. They chased me down into the tunnels, where I just . . . lost myself." His eyes went dark and distant, as if the memories required careful handling.

I remembered how he'd been when the Hunters found him, barely human. Living alone in the dark for years would do that. I marveled once again that he'd survived.

"Why did you stay with us when you didn't want to join the gangs?"

"The elders didn't give me a choice," he said. "Well, they did, technically. Once the Hunters caught me, they said I could fight for them or die."

"Oh." No wonder he'd hated us. We'd held him prisoner.

"I'm bigger now, and I've learned to protect myself. It'll be different when we run across the gangs again."

"What's so bad about them? I mean, how do they compare with the enclave?" I still ached with disillusionment.

He half turned to face me, his arm resting behind my head. "You know all the rules you believed in? They exist to keep you safe, and the elders only want what's best for everyone?"

I nodded, barely managing to restrain a flinch. "What about them?"

"The gangs have *none*. It's . . . ugly, Deuce. My dad had weapons and they left us alone. Once he was gone, they were determined to recruit me. They don't always take care of their brats. Sometimes . . ." His eyes bored into mine, as if willing me not to make him say it.

A shudder rolled through me. "Oh."

At the enclave, there had been rare instances where the

elders discovered the Breeders were twisted in that way. Those Breeders weren't just exiled; they were also cut so the Freaks found them faster.

"You can see why I didn't want to be initiated."

I would've fought against it pretty fiercely myself. "Tell me what you know about the gangs. What we'll be up against."

"They'll want to breed you," he said without looking at me. "The only way to advance is to kill and keep killing until there's nobody tougher than you left alive."

"So it's not like the enclave, where age is a sign of wisdom."

He laughed. "No. We'd be considered elders. People don't live very long."

"But not because of sickness or age."

"No. In the gangs, they kill you because you have something they want or you're just standing in their way."

"They must breed a lot to make up for it."

Fade brushed my hair back, grazing the curve of my jaw. The heat of his fingertips sent a tingle through me. I tipped my head to one side so that his palm landed on the nape of my neck. His thumb skimmed along the tender skin, making me shiver. By the time he drew back slowly, I'd almost forgotten what we were talking about.

"That's all they think girls are good for. There are no rules about it up here, either. You have no power."

Pure cold seized me. So that was what he'd meant about it being dangerous in a different way. Up here being female meant something else entirely. The marks on my arms wouldn't give anyone pause, but maybe my skill with a weapon would.

"I don't think I can take any more answers tonight," I admitted without looking up.

"You know the important stuff now."

"Wait. Maybe one more."

"Go ahead."

"How did you get your name?" I'd always wondered.

For a moment I thought he wouldn't answer, because according to enclave rules, it was an intrusive question. If I hadn't been present, hadn't contributed to the stack of gifts, then it should wait until he volunteered the information. But we didn't live by their regulations anymore.

He delved into his bag and came with a tattered strip of paper. I took it, held it to the faint light, which was just strong enough to make out the shape of letters. They were so old that many of them had worn away:

C l rs w l n t fade.

His blood speckled lightly on the final word. I fingered the silky slickness of the paper, nothing like what we made in the enclave. It shone in the dark. He had attended my naming or I would produce my card. But he'd seen. He knew. Feeling honored, I handed the talisman back to him.

"It came off an old bottle," he said. "But that was too big to carry around, so I peeled off the paper."

"Do you know what it says?"

He stroked the edges with his thumbs; I could actually see the darker imprint where he'd done that often since his naming. "I think it says, 'Colors will not fade.'"

To me, it sounded like a wonderful message, a promise of loyalty and fidelity. His colors would not fade or change, no matter what. The name fit someone who wouldn't leave his partner, even when she disappeared in the dark, and who wouldn't let her go Topside alone.

"It suits you." I paused, wondering if I should ask. Maybe he didn't remember. Maybe he wouldn't tell me. "What did your sire call you?"

"Like you said, I'm Fade now. I'd rather not go back."

I understood. A dead man had given the old name to him. It didn't seem like a good idea to speak it. When he put his arm around me, I didn't resist. He waited a beat, as if gauging my reaction, and then he eased his head against mine. Sorrow cloaked him, losses I could neither see or know.

Such closeness felt new . . . and intimate. It had been different with Thimble and Stone, none of the awareness that prickled through me with restless sweetness. Because he seemed to need me, even if it went unspoken, I let myself answer by turning my cheek to his and I remembered the kiss.

Long after he pulled away, the phantom heat lingered and haunted my sleep.

Sunshine

When I awoke, I first thought the room was on fire. I scrambled off the sofa and started to bolt when my senses caught up to my instinctive fear. No smoke meant no fire; it was a simple relationship.

So why was the room so bright?

I crept to the window and gazed out, eyes slitted in pain. Everything glowed. If anyone had tried to explain this to me, I wouldn't have believed it. The light hurt.

Fade came up behind me. He wore something that wrapped around his eyes, and he offered the other to me. I slid it onto my face.

"Sunglasses. There were a few left on the floor downstairs." He smiled. "Good thing. I'm not used to the sun anymore either."

So the light had a name. I still wasn't sure I liked it, but with my eyes covered, I could bear it. "Will it hurt us?"

"It might. Remember how long it's been since I was here."

Through the smoky filter, I gazed out over the city for the first time. I had seen pictures before, of course, old and faded. The elders had told us they reflected a lost world, now poisoned beyond hope. There was nothing Topside except terror and death. Like most of their stories, they contained a grain of truth buried beneath the lies.

Tall shapes filled my view; some had collapsed and lay in ruins. Shorter buildings squatted at the base, holding their shapes better. They were built of old stone—some natural, others looked as if man's hands had shaped them. The colors had faded beneath the burning sun, much like the artifacts we'd found down below. Built side to side, not much space existed between them, and occasionally, time had pushed one to the side, so it leaned tiredly against its neighbors.

One building rose above the others, its sharp tower gleaming green. It was a different from the buildings that surrounded it, more beautiful and with rounded points atop the windows. Most of them hung in jagged shards, and it had been marked with white painted that identified it as claimed territory. For no reason I could name, the damage saddened me. Resolute, I turned.

"What's our plan?" I portioned out what was left of our enclave provisions. In my opinion, the first priority should be finding food and water.

"My dad used to talk about getting out of the city." Fade gestured. "That's what he called this place. He told stories about where it was green and clean, where you could plant food and watch it grow, where there were plenty of animals for hunting, and you could drink the water without getting sick."

That sounded unlikely, but . . . "Did he tell you where that was?"

"North. That was all he ever said."

"Then let's go."

I hoped he had some sense of direction. I wasn't altogether sure I could find my way around the corner Topside.

"We should wait until nightfall. We're more likely to run into the gangs during the day, and I suspect we might get burned out there."

"Burned?" I had visions of being roasted on a spit.

"By the sun." Fade smiled slightly. "The gangs won't cook and eat us."

"Then what can we do for water? We may be able to find food along the way, but—"

"I've been thinking about that. There's water downstairs. If we can figure out some way to boil it, maybe it would be all right."

"We could build a fire out back." There was plenty of stuff to burn.

I got up and rummaged through the cabinets. I turned up a pot, but we needed some way to suspend it over the flames. We occupied the day building a contraption out of scrap junk.

"Will this work?"

I shook my head. It took most of the day to put it together, and he stood watch while I started the fire. His vigilance made me nervous even as it reassured me. If there were any gangers around, he'd spot them. The noises were still too strange for me to tell what was threatening—I started at things he said were harmless, like the chittering of small animals and the flutter of wings. And my eyesight wasn't what it should be. Even with the sunglasses on, I could barely tolerate the sunshine. Though the warmth felt strange and beautiful on my skin, Fade shooed me back indoors.

"Small doses, Deuce. You have to get used to it, or it's going to sting."

Right. He'd said the sun could burn me. It certainly looked angry enough, all orange and glowing mad. I peered up at it through the dark filter, through the glass, and wondered how we could've lost all memory of something so huge. Down in the enclave, there had been no talk of day or night, no mention of anything but burning air and water that scalded like fire. Somehow we'd mixed everything up. Sorrow rose in me, as I realized the Wordkeeper dedicated his whole life to lies. What a waste.

I sat in the storeroom while Fade handled the actual work, and I kept busy examining the items piled in dusty, papery boxes. I found a metal object that appeared to be nothing much at first glance, but the more I played with it, the more parts I found. I recognized the knife, but not the other tools. Two looked like they might be good for stabbing, but I could only guess at the rest. Since it was light and it folded nicely, I stowed it in my bag.

Through the open door, I watched Fade work. He used the lighter his father had left him to kindle the smaller objects and then the sparks spread. Eventually the fire burned bright and clean, curls of smoke floating off toward the sky. In the enclave, we'd never have allowed it to get so big. Here, it didn't seem to matter. I had the fleeting thought that someone might see the blaze and come to investigate, but if so, we'd handle them.

He turned and saw me staring. "Find anything good?"

"Maybe."

I prowled some more, frustrated by his refusal to let me help outside. I wondered if I'd always be so useless Topside. On a tall shelf, I found a dusty metal box. I lifted it down and looked for a way to open it. Something important must be inside. An opening looked as though an item would fit, possibly opening it.

Eventually, I located the right object. I slid it in and heard a click. When I lifted the lid, I found the most marvelous thing. A book. Not *part* of one, not loose pages. *A whole book.* And it wasn't flimsy like the ones I'd found down in the tunnel. Still, I was almost afraid to touch it.

The beige front had raised letters and green paint, outlining a fanciful design with a girl in strange clothes, a winged brat, and a bird. With some effort, I read the letters: *"The Day Boy and the Night Girl*. Fairy tales by George MacDonald." Though I understood most of the words, others escaped me. Enthralled and breathless, I opened it. The book made a little popping sound, as if nobody had touched it in a long time. That was probably true. Using my finger to mark my place, I put more letters together slowly, and other words leaped out at me. "London: Arthur C. Fifield, 1904. Ed. by Greville MacDonald; printed by S. Clarke, Manchester."

With great care, I turned the page, and my breath caught. Someone had *written* in the book. The Wordkeeper would be livid. In faded ink, it read: "with love to Gracie from Mary." Those were names, I thought, and it implied this book had been a gift. Other hands had touched this, people who lived in the lost world. They'd known dreams like mine, and I'd never know how those stories ended. A marvelous sense of connection thrummed through me.

I forgot my worries. I forgot the danger. Using only my fingertips, I flipped to the next page, lightheaded with wonder.

There was once a witch who desired to know everything. But the wiser a witch is, the harder she knocks her head against the wall when she comes to it. Her name was Watho, and she had a wolf in her mind. She cared for nothing in itself—only for knowing it. She was not naturally cruel, but the wolf had made her cruel.

She was tall and graceful, with a white skin, red hair, and

black eyes, which had a red fire in them. She was straight and
strong, but now and then would fall bent together, shudder,
and sit for a moment with her head turned over her shoulder,
as if the wolf had got out of her mind onto her back.

"What do you have there?" Fade asked.

I almost hid it from him, and then with a burst of shocking relief, I remembered I didn't have to. Wordless, I held the book out to him. He looked at it, and his hands were as reverent as mine had been. He read faster than me, and when he finished that first page, his gaze met mine, glazed with awe.

"We'll take it," I said. "It doesn't weigh much."

He slipped the book into my bag and went back to work. By dark, we had enough clean water to last us a few days. Secretly, I feared leaving this place because I'd gotten used to these two rooms. Inside didn't scare me. Outside, that enormous, monstrous sky hung over everything, and the size of it made me want to hide.

But there was something different about the dark this time. I took off my glasses and stared up. A curve of silver hung amid the brighter specks; it looked to me like a curved dagger, pretty but deadly, as if it might slice the sky in two.

I didn't let him see how terrified I was. Instead I geared up as if this were nothing more than a routine patrol. I checked my weapons and our supplies; I shouldered my bag with the resolve of a Huntress. I could handle night.

But you're not a Huntress. You're just a girl with six scars.

At least Fade had them too. Maybe I'd been cast out of my tribe, but I wasn't alone. That made all the difference. If I'd been sent Topside on my own, I'd have already given up. It was simply too different from what I knew. But his calm resolve made me believe we might someday see the green land promised in his father's stories. If we didn't, it would be because it didn't exist, not because we hadn't tried.

As I stepped outside, a boom sounded, practically shaking the ground itself. I flattened myself against the building. While I cowered, water spilled down, like the pipes in the enclave, but a hundred times more powerful. It soaked me to the bone in no time, and I stood frozen in it, face upturned.

"Don't worry. It's rain." Fade stood close enough for me to feel his heated breath against my ear. A shiver rolled through me, echoed in distant crashes that shook the ground beneath my feet. He lifted his face as well, drinking it in, and I gazed at him through that silver curtain, watching as it glazed his features, all pallor and prettiness. Droplets spiked his lashes, so that I wanted to—

I shouldn't want that. *Rain*. Instead I focused on the other part of what I felt.

"It doesn't burn," I whispered.

In fact, it felt amazing. I hadn't bathed recently, and this was the next best thing. I started to smile. I turned slowly, admiring the flashes of light. Rain pounded against the ground until it sounded like a chorus of running feet combined with shushing whispers. I'd never heard anything so lovely. I didn't even mind we had to walk in it; I only hoped the book was safe and dry. At the first chance, I wanted to read more of it.

"No. They had that wrong too."

Along with so many things. For the first time, I felt sorry for the people trapped by the enclave rules, who would never break free, who would never see any of this. Who would live and die in the dark.

"I want to go back," I said. "The elders need to know the truth."

Fade put his hands on my shoulders. "They won't listen, Deuce. They'll kill us on sight. Besides . . . don't you think I told them?"

Sickness boiled up inside me. They didn't share the knowledge with us. Not even a whisper got out, after Fade's arrival. None of us ever knew where he came from, nothing he'd seen or done. I'd thought his silence meant he didn't *want* to talk, but now I realized the truth.

"They threatened you."

"Not a threat, so much. I could fight for them or I could die." He repeated what he'd said before, and only then, the enormity sank in for me.

All along, they'd known, and they'd chosen to keep us all in the dark. Literally, figuratively. I felt lost, as if I had nothing left to believe in.

"That's why you never tried to fit in. Why you didn't talk to anyone much."

Besides Banner, the girl he'd said was his only friend—and maybe only because she shared his belief that things needed to change. If I'd helped instead of running away, maybe she wouldn't have died. For the first time I accepted that the elders' spies might've overheard our conversation. If they'd suspected her, my exchange with her had caused her death.

"I was afraid they'd hurt anyone I cared about. As an object lesson."

"So you didn't feel safe, the whole time you were there."

He shrugged. "I had a place to sleep and food to eat. The work wasn't that bad once I was trained, and people left me alone, mostly. It would've been worse up here."

"I'm sorry. I had no idea."

His silence said he didn't want to talk about it anymore. I

understood. There was no point in discussing things that couldn't be changed.

We set off in the direction Fade said was north. Gradually hope sprang up within me, replacing the sick disillusionment. I hated walking off and leaving Thimble, Stone, and the brats, but I had to accept there was nothing I could do.

If a better place existed, we'd find it.

As we walked, I lost myself in the cool air and lashing water. It silvered the buildings, blurring them as if through a veil of tears. Fade watched the dark street and eyed the markings on the doors. The red and white paint hinted at hidden dangers.

"You're in our territory," a hard voice said.

The rush of the rain must have masked their footsteps because I hadn't heard them. They came from behind and were just suddenly there, surrounding us in a full circle—all male, most younger than us, and they all carried weapons. But I couldn't mistake their youth for weakness. In their eyes I saw a feral anger I'd never noticed in the enclave. I knew then Fade had spoken the truth. I understood why he'd chosen the more obvious risk of the Freaks and the darkness below.

Fade stepped forward, putting himself in front of me. It was pointless, as they'd come at us from all sides. So I turned, facing the gangers behind him. We'd fight back-to-back. He had made it clear what would happen if they took me. I'd die first.

Falling back on my training, I counted them. *Eight*. They all handled their weapons like they knew what to do with them, and they looked stronger than the average Freak, rested and well fed. This would be the toughest fight we'd ever faced. The prospect made me smile.

"We don't want trouble," Fade said. "We're just passing through."

The big one shook his head. "No, you're not."

Clearly he was in charge; the others looked to him for leadership, and they might scatter if he fell. I'd go after him first. In a smooth motion, I drew my daggers.

I grinned over my shoulder at Fade. "Let's see how many we can kill."

Resistance

I brought my knives up into a fighting stance. The weight of my club comforted me; even if I couldn't use it and stay close enough to Fade to guard his back, I liked knowing I had it. The gangers eyed us as if wondering whether we could be as good as we claimed. I guessed we were about to find out.

The headman rushed me and I met his swing with a dagger in the wrist. Quick in and out, I didn't want to lose my weapon. He danced back with a cry of pain, his eyes wide with disbelief. Soon I had three on me, but I hadn't been running in the tunnels all day. I had meat in my belly and a night's sleep behind me.

I blocked their movements with graceful speed; I never felt beautiful unless I was fighting, and even then it was something that went beyond skin and bone into the kinetic joy of successive movements. Kick, thrust, slash. I never doubted Fade at my back. I never faltered.

The big ganger went down first. I took another one before they broke and ran. Their footsteps pounded away through the rain, leaving me staring at a couple of bodies, and blood thinning away to pink trickles. I turned to Fade and found him smiling down at me, his lashes tangled and damp.

"I don't think we need to worry about them," I said.

"Not unless they bring more. And they will, next time."

"Then what're we standing here for?"

He answered by setting the pace. We walked through the night. Fade guided us. He used the compass on his watch. I'd noticed it underground, but I didn't know what it meant until I saw him using it. I'd always navigated by counting steps; that was how small my world was before.

"It tells me which way is north," he explained.

"Did your sire ever say how far north you'd have to go?" The distance and space aboveground still bothered me. If I watched my feet as I walked and didn't think about it, I could manage to function. But it was all so vast, and I felt tinier than ever.

"No. He didn't say a lot of things."

"At least you remember him. Sires and dams never played much part in the enclave. I mean, some Breeder looked after us, but we never knew . . ." I trailed off, wondering why I was telling him. It didn't matter.

According to Fade's watch, we had been walking for two hours when the rain stopped. It left everything clean, though I was wet and cold. The buildings climbed to insane, unimaginable heights—and yet they were obviously dead, relics of the old days. I had the impression of immense solitude laden with expectation, like when we dragged our dead out into the tunnels and left them for the Freaks. We were alone . . . but not wholly. Eyes weighed on me from unseen hiding places and left me uneasy.

Birds swooped after the small, furry creatures that scampered in the shadows. A fat, brave one paused some distance away, gnawing on a seed. This thing, I recognized; relief surged through me. I knew how to snare one, if we needed to eat. It made me feel more settled—not *everything* had changed.

Fade followed my gaze and nodded. "Rats live up here too."

Other animals prowled the dark along with us, different than any I'd seen before. Herds of something with horns clattered down the streets. *Deer*, Fade said. The word meant nothing to me, except he promised they made good eating. They were fast, though, and too big for a simple snare. More cries split the silence: growls and rumbles and yowls. I couldn't imagine what made those noises.

"Where is everyone?" I whispered.

The Wordkeeper had taught us enough that I knew these cities used to be filled with people, teeming crowds of them. Of course, he'd also taught us that the sky blazed fire and the rain would burn our skin from our meat and leave nothing but bones. So I couldn't count on anything I'd learned before.

Fade hesitated, looking young and unsure. "My dad said they left the city a long time ago. That people went north and west to get away."

"From what?"

"I don't know."

"Maybe we can find out," I said. "We found one book and we weren't even looking for it. There might be more."

He stopped and looked through me as if remembering. "He told me about a place filled with them. A library."

"A place for books? Do you know where it is?"

Fade shook his head. "We'd have to ask. It's too dangerous to stay in the city, roaming around searching. The gangers would take us sooner or later."

"Is there anyone we could ask?" I gazed into the darkness, and suppressed a shiver when it seemed to stare back. "And do you think it's worth it, trying to find out?"

"We can do what we want, now. So I guess the better question is, how much do you want to know?"

"A lot," I realized aloud.

I was no longer content to swallow the half-truths and out-right lies I'd been fed as a brat. I wanted to understand everything as nobody from down below had in generations. I needed to know the truth.

"Then there might be someone. My dad had a friend. . . . I'm sure he's gone now, but he had a daughter. Pearl could tell us—if she's alive. Her dad had maps."

I felt dumb, but I had to ask, "Of what?"

"Where everything is in the ruins. Or used to be."

If we had complete maps of the tunnels, I wouldn't need to count everywhere I went. How many steps, how many turns. I could memorize the paths and hold them in my mind before going into the dark. We had maps of trips we made often, like the route to Nassau, but we'd had no idea where the back ways led, or about hidden rooms full of relics, like the one Fade found.

My awe and elation faded as I recalled that wasn't my job anymore. I had no purpose. I wore a Huntress's scars but I had nobody to protect.

"Can you find her?"

"If she hasn't moved. It's a lot of ifs." He started walking.

"Why didn't you go to her, after your sire—"

"Because it was too far. I barely made it to the underground."

"But you think we can do it now."

"You're tough," he said. "And we're not stupid brats."

For the remainder of the night, we walked in silence. Fade watched for landmarks and familiar streets. I wondered what it was like for him, if he remembered passing this way with his sire and if those memories felt like another life. I tried to imagine living Topside, and even now, I found it more of a dream than a real thing, as if I would one day wake from this wild, unlikely world with Twist's foot in my ribs and hear him demand I get up and get to work.

In the dark, I could see as well as anyone, and I noticed the shadows almost at once. I tracked them in my peripheral vision. They seemed to be stalking us, more than readying to attack. But maybe that was worse. Maybe they were, as Fade had predicted, gathering numbers for their next attempt.

"Do you see them?" I whispered.

"Gangers. I told you they'd bring more."

"How many are there? Can you tell?"

He shook his head. "But there will be twice as many as last time. They won't underestimate us again."

Even as he spoke, they rushed. There had to be at least twenty, this time. Some were young enough that I'd call them brats. Their size made me hesitate; I'd been raised to protect brats, not fight them, so I didn't react fast enough. I fought, but they didn't fight like Hunters. They kicked and bit and scratched and leaped like wild animals. Sheer numbers overwhelmed me and one clubbed me across the back of the head.

I heard Fade calling to me as the world went away.

When I awoke, it was dark. Not nighttime, as I'd come to know it up here, or the blackness of the tunnels, but a soft, textured darkness. They'd tied something around my eyes. I tried to sit up, found my hands bound behind my back, and slammed my face against a hard floor. I could tell they'd taken my weapons. Another shift told me my ankles had been tied too.

Laughter erupted around me. I didn't give them the pleasure of seeing me struggle further. Worry ate at me. Where was Fade? A strip of cloth in my mouth prevented me from speaking, or I'd call out, even if it meant a boot in the face.

As the ringing in my ears subsided, I distinguished voices and then words. "Who gets her?" someone demanded.

A high, thin voice answered, "I do. I brought her down. I own her."

A different male spoke, low and mocking. "Good work, cub. But you wouldn't know what to do with her."

Instinctively, I knew I should fear the owner of that voice, even as he knelt beside me. He pulled my blindfold off and left me to recoil at the sight of him. His whole face had been carved up, not from battle like Fade's scars, but in a purposeful mutilation. The lines bit deep, and he'd painted them red as blood; they striped his skin in savagery. The marks shocked me, maybe because I didn't understand their purpose.

His eyes reflected the firelight; they were pale as rainwater and flames danced in their depths. "So you're awake. Where do you come from that you fight like a Wolf?"

He snatched the tie from my hair, but unlike when Fade did it, it wasn't a pleasant shock. It was invasive, and when he twisted his hand in my hair, it hurt. He turned my face side to side, inspecting me, and pure fear slithered through me at that gesture. Those light eyes examined me as if I were a strange creature.

I tried to tell him with my eyes that he didn't want to do this, that he would be sorry before we finished this story, but I didn't think it worked. In response to my look, he laughed. As I lay there, bound and helpless, I knew only one thing: I'd die first. I hadn't fought my way out of the tunnels to wind up like this. He pulled the cloth from my mouth, just enough to let me answer.

"Underground," I bit out.

Interest kindled in his savage features. He whispered, "Then you're worth something, more than just a Breeder. Later, I want you to remember how I saved you." He straightened and spoke loud enough for his Wolves to hear the order, this time. "Take her and clean her up. I'll break her in personally later."

Hands grabbed me and towed me away. I felt each seam and divot in the floor; they would leave bruises. The place flowed over me in glimpses. I had the impression of immense space and a tall ceiling as I jolted along. Then movement stopped. My head hit the ground again.

Someone pulled me to my feet and then knelt to untie my ankles. That person was smart enough to do it from behind, or I'd have certainly broken his or her neck with a kick. Twisting round to peer over my shoulder sent pain shooting through my skull, but I managed to see it was a girl. She was small and thin, liberally covered in bruises. Some were days old; others looked fresh. She didn't wear any marks, so I guessed gangers only gave such status to the males.

She left my hands tied. *Smart girl. Well, relatively.* She couldn't be *too* smart if she took those bruises without complaining, but as I knew, you got used to anything. If she had been born here, among the gangers, she probably didn't question that this was how things ought to be. I was having a hard time adjusting my worldview too.

With complete indifference, she left the cloth in my mouth and went to work on me with a knife. My clothes fell away in ragged strips and then she washed me like I was a piece of junk she was trying to make ready for use. Twisting didn't do any good; she only moved closer and completed the job.

Then she dressed me in a long, ragged shirt like she wore. It showed way more of my legs than I liked, and she didn't give me anything to wear underneath. I supposed that was the point. Fear tried to dilute my anger, but I didn't let it. Instinctively I understood the purpose of this ritual. They took away my things; they reduced me in rank to one of their cowering, subservient females. But they could never take away the marks on my arms. I'd *earned* them.

The strong survive, I told myself. Though it was a Hunter tenet, if anything could get me out of this, it was the resolve I'd learned in training. No matter how many times a bigger brat knocked me down in class, I got back up. I fought harder. I learned a new trick, or a new throw. Except in that match against Crane, I'd never been defeated.

Now I regretted not laying into those brats with everything I had, but it was too late to change my circumstances. I couldn't let panic paralyze me. This might be a new world, but I could survive it. I *would.*

Finally, she untied the strip of fabric from around my face. I spat on the ground to remove the stale, fuzzy taste. I studied her face. She might've been pretty if she wasn't so beaten down. The poor thing wouldn't even meet *my* eyes.

"I'm Deuce," I said. "And you are?"

She glanced up in surprise, as if she hadn't known I could talk. "Tegan."

"What did they do with my friend?"

"You have your own problems."

That made me smile. She stared at me like I was crazy. "I'm aware. But where is he? Is he alive?"

"For now. They're going to hunt him later."

My blood chilled. "What does that mean?"

"They'll cut him and give him a short head start. Then the Wolves will give chase, following his blood trail. When they find him, they'll kill him."

The word "Wolves" was unfamiliar to me, but I guessed it was the name these gangers used for themselves. I didn't doubt

Tegan was telling the truth. Somehow I managed to conceal my desperation.

"And what's going to happen to me?"

"Stalker's claimed you," she said with a shrug. "So I guess you belong to him until he gets tired of you. Usually, you'd end up with the Wolf who brought you in. Stalker doesn't often exercise his rights."

So it meant something when he'd said, *Later I want you to remember how I saved you.* Was I supposed to be grateful for his favor? Not likely.

"And then?"

"When Stalker's finished, they'll probably fight for you. You're new."

"But nobody wants to fight Stalker?"

I did. One on one, I had my doubts he could beat me, even with this lump on my head. If he didn't hide behind greater numbers, they never would've taken us in the first place. If only I hadn't paused over the idea of fighting brats. If only we'd run. But there was no use in treading over lost ground.

"They stopped trying," Tegan said. "You can't win."

Clash

My shoulders burned.

Since Stalker hadn't given her any instructions, beyond cleaning me up, Tegan didn't know what to do with me. So we waited. Right now the Wolves were occupied with the deathsport part of the evening, and if I didn't find some way to prevent it, Fade would die, bloody and alone. Because he'd lied for me.

I didn't want him to die for me.

We sat by the fire. The enormous building was mostly empty, and rain drummed on the roof. I craned my neck looking for anything I could use to untie my wrists. Nothing behind me that I could see. Ahead I focused on a sliver of glass. It would cut my fingertips, but it would slice through the cords as well.

I inched forward. Tegan didn't seem to be paying me any attention. The licking flames held her eyes; I hoped they would continue to until I finished my work.

My heart thudded in my ears. It took ages but I eventually set my fingertip on the shard. I shifted to cover the small scrape it made as I raked it behind me. Time pressed on me, weighty and inescapable, while I sawed.

Blood trickled over my fingertips, so I knew I'd cut myself, but I couldn't tell how bad it was. It slicked my hands and let me slip free at last of the loosened bonds.

When Tegan spoke, it surprised me. "Have you gotten free yet?"

I froze. "If you knew what I was doing, why didn't you stop me?"

"That's not my job," she said with a glimmer of spirit. "He told me to clean you up. That's all. They should've left some guards, but they're stupid and they only saw a weak female."

That wasn't entirely true. Stalker knew I was different. He'd asked *why*. So maybe this was some kind of test. But I wouldn't wait around to learn his agenda. I didn't care what he wanted with me; it wasn't happening.

"But they're wrong about you," she went on. "You're not helpless."

I acknowledged that with a nod. "Then you won't yell if I slip away?"

Her eyes locked on to mine. "I will if you don't take me with you."

I made my decision in a split second. "Where did they put my gear?"

The building was long and squat with windows set up high that let in very little light. Grime obscured the glass, and some panes were broken. It must be daytime, but the interior didn't reflect it. Then again, the rain pattering overhead might have something to do with the gloom.

"Over here." She led the way to a corner where my things— and Fade's—had been carelessly piled.

"Do you all live here or is this just where they bring their victims?" I hadn't seen any females other than Tegan, so I leaned toward no.

"We live wherever Stalker tells us to sleep," she said. "But no. Not here."

"Are there more girls?"

"Yes, but I'm the one they don't trust. That's why they keep me close." Her mouth tightened in the firelight, anger burning beneath her bruised skin.

"Why?"

"Because I wasn't born a Wolf. I lived with my mom until a couple of years ago. We hid a lot and we moved around."

Like Fade, I thought in wonder.

"They took you, after she died?" I didn't ask what it had been like. I could see the pain written on her skin.

Tegan nodded, her eyes flat and hard. "I've lost two cubs in the last year. The last time, I almost died. That was when I decided, if I ever got a chance to run, I'd take it. So I bided my time."

I listened, not having any idea what to say. In the enclave, if anyone had treated a girl this way, he would've been fed to the Freaks, piece by piece. Maybe the elders weren't as good as I thought, but they weren't nearly as bad as they could be.

While she spoke, I dug into my bag. My dirty clothes had been sliced up, but I still had the spares. Everything was still here, even my weapons. I closed my eyes on a surge of relief and then pulled the shirt over my head. I scrambled to dress before the Wolves realized Tegan was aiding in my escape.

She finished, "And so I fooled them. I made them think they'd beaten all the hope out of me."

I picked up my daggers and strapped them on. My club went across my back in a reassuring weight. This time, I wouldn't check myself. Until meeting Stalker and his Wolves, I don't think I fully understood when Fade talked about how it was Topside, how different the dangers. Now I did. The gangers were like Freaks in their way; they could not be reasoned with.

Tegan watched me with hunger in her eyes, but not for food. She sought strength, surety, and revenge for what they'd done to her. Without thinking overlong, I slipped the club free of the loop and handed it to her.

"This is simpler than the knives. It requires less finesse. Just swing it as hard as you can until they stop moving."

She gave a jerky nod. "This way. I'll show you where they always start the hunt."

Though she didn't move silently compared with a Hunter, the noise as we drew nearer drowned out any sound we might've made. A high, curling wail filled the air, raising the hair on my forearms.

I glanced back at Tegan, who whispered, "That's normal."

We crept closer, through the gaping maw at the back of the building, and into a strange yard mounded with relics from the old world: rusted metal, tilted gates, and hunks of dead machines. Overhead, the sky loomed like a rock about to fall; it was no color I had ever seen in my short time aboveground. Swirls of green and blue made it look angry and bruised.

At Tegan's word, I stayed behind piles of relics, moving carefully. The Wolves had Fade on his knees; he was completely surrounded. There were more than there had been earlier too. They tilted their heads back, all stomping and making that horrible noise. I couldn't tell how badly he was injured, but when Stalker curled his hand around his neck and went in with the knife, my whole body tensed.

Tegan pinched my arm fiercely. "Not now. Our best chance is after they blood him and then send him off."

The tactical part of my brain asserted itself. "Better not to face them all at once. If we can get to Fade first, we can take them out a few at a time."

The strategy was not unlike hunting Freaks down in the tunnels. We'd always done our best to stay away from huge packs, so we weren't overwhelmed. This would be the same principle, more or less.

So I stood silent while they cut him, and I counted their number, calculating how long it would take to dispatch them all. I didn't know how Fade had faced his naming day or the white-hot marks Twist laid atop his wounds, but he hung silent while the Wolves worked on him. Hate seethed in my gut. Stalker watched it all with an amused air, as if it were all intended for his entertainment.

"Done," Stalker said when the Wolf finished. "Run, meat. We'll take you soon."

Tegan and I broke from the shadows, slipping off as soon as Fade sprinted away. We made sure not to draw attention from the Wolves by rounding the building on the other side. It was a calculated risk. We might lose sight of Fade if—

He slammed into me coming around the corner of the building. His hands came to my arms to steady me automatically, and his battered face broke into a wide smile. The blood smearing his arms didn't detract from his Hunter scars. I'd never seen anything so welcome—or so puzzling.

"What are you doing?" I demanded. "You're not even trying to get away!"

"I circled back to cut you loose," he said. "I thought we had a better shot together. Who's this?"

"Tegan." Nervous energy had her bouncing with my club in her hand.

I didn't know whether to hug or hit him. "Let's get out of here."

"We're not going to get far before the Wolves catch up," she said. "You might surprise them at first—most meat just cries and dies—but they'll rally."

Fade and I shared a smile, and then I fingered my daggers. "That's all right. We don't want to run."

A nearby building proved ideal for ambush; it was like the one where they'd taken me initially, but this one smelled even more unused: of wild animals and feces and weird, damp growth. While we explored, we planned. The relics here would prove helpful and dangerous, if we could use them as we wanted to.

Several factors played in our favor. First of all, the Wolves thought Tegan and I were still sitting by the fire, waiting for their triumphant return. They also didn't realize Fade could turn almost anything into a weapon—and he fought even better bare-handed. They thought they'd laid hold of a couple cowards, a girl who would do as she was told and a boy who wasn't brave enough to become a ganger.

This was going to be fun.

In setting the trap, we didn't try to stem the bleeding. Fade's wounds were light and shallow, and we wanted them to follow the trail. Before long I heard rustling that indicated one of the Wolves had taken the bait.

"Fresh," a voice said. "He's in here."

"He didn't get far," another muttered in disgust. "I hoped he'd make this interesting."

Fade stepped out from behind a stack of crates. "You mean like this?"

Predictably, they rushed him, making that horrible wailing

noise. I guessed it was to tell the others they'd found us. I dropped one from above. My knees slammed into the boy's back and I heard bones snapping. Fade took the other down with a kick in the crotch, and Tegan finished them.

"Two down," she said, smiling.

I slid away from the unconscious ones, as footfalls sounded outside. They weren't even trying to be quiet, which showed a profound disrespect for our skills. I shook my head silently at Fade, who shrugged. *They're crazy,* he said with his black eyes. *Who understands what they do?*

Rows of crates offered hiding places, making it difficult for them to track us. Fade smeared his blood all over everything as we moved in and out of the shadows, avoiding detection. I had been born in the dark. Once, torchlight was the brightest light I'd ever seen, so this felt like coming home.

I listened for them, eyes closed. They came after us in twos and threes. It was almost unfair. Because they searched for Fade, we made sure they found him, time and again. When I joined the fight, their expressions shocked me. You'd think they had never seen a girl who knew how to use a weapon before. *Stupidity kills.*

"How many was that?" Tegan asked, breathless.

Fade looked at me. "I counted ten. You."

"Twelve. You forgot the two that tried to run."

Tegan wiped off the club. I'd have to explain to her how the blood would damage the wood if we didn't keep it clean. Later, if we could find supplies, I'd oil it.

"Then we're more than halfway there," she said.

My mouth tightened. "It's not over. We have to teach Stalker a lesson."

"Agreed." Fade led us deeper into a knot of old machinery and rusted metal.

More Wolves came hunting for easy prey. Too bad they didn't find it. I put a blade in one and then ran to retrieve it. Fade guarded me from a distance, as I pretended to be unaware of the boy sneaking up from behind. He got a knife for his trouble.

"My turn," Tegan said. "I've been dreaming of this."

We let her take the next two. She had good reason to be angry. It twisted me up when I thought of what she'd suffered—and just because she was born a girl. Wolves—and maybe all gangers—had a sickness in their brains that didn't let them grasp the truth: People's value came from their actions. In the enclave, the strong and the physically perfect survived, but *if* you were strong, you protected the weak until they had an opportunity to grow into their own power. At least, that was the ideal. In practice, it hadn't always worked that way in our settlement, and maybe in other enclaves, like Nassau, it had been even worse.

But I saw none of that balance Topside, and it sickened me.

At last, by my count, we had only two left: Stalker and whomever he hunted with. Footsteps warned us of their approach. I motioned Tegan to stillness because she had the least skill in stealth. Though she frowned at me, she complied, pressing herself against the crate.

"He dropped Mickey and Howe," a new voice said. "And there's blood all over. I've lost count of the bodies. Maybe we should let this one go." He sounded scared. And young. That bothered me until I remembered the gleeful way the brats had attacked me. It might even have been him that clocked me, and that possibility steeled my resolve. "Stalker, I don't think there's anyone else left. We still have the girl. That could be fun, huh?"

"The meat has teeth," Stalker replied. He sounded serene and certain. "But we'll take him."

"That's what you think," I whispered.

Rush

Stalker was every bit as fierce as I'd first thought. But he was smarter too. When the three of us stepped out into his path, he stilled. He didn't seem surprised to see *me* somehow. I'd guessed right about the test, but I couldn't believe he had been willing to see so many of his own injured in order to assess my skills. It was certainly an honest challenge, but it carried such a high price that it told me a lot about his character.

Silk would've approved.

His pale gaze touched on Tegan and he shook his head. "You're going to regret this."

So he hadn't foreseen her help. He'd thought I would best her and escape on my own. Good to know.

He winged a dagger at me and I dove wide. Instead of pressing the attack, as Fade charged toward him, he tapped his cub and they both took off running. I started to give chase, but Tegan snagged my arm.

"Don't. He isn't stupid."

Deferring to her greater experience, I called to Fade, "Wait!"

After he returned, she added, "He won't return until he has enough Wolves to deal with us. The hunt is over, and it's a matter of pride now."

My heart sank. "You mean there are *more* of them?"

"Those were just the cubs, who needed their first blood. The more experienced Wolves are guarding the den."

Kind of like the naming day ritual, I guessed, except we didn't hunt down some poor person to get our names. It came down to personal bravery instead. I didn't like much of what I'd seen from the surface so far.

"Sounds like you have some experience with this," he said.

She nodded. "We have one chance to get away. This is it."

I glanced at Fade. "Can you find Pearl's place from here?"

"I think so."

Before we took off, I wrapped his arms; we didn't want to leave a trail this time. It was a quick patch job, nothing more. Once we found a safe place to hide, he needed better care and some of Banner's salve. But as usual, he didn't show any pain.

It was dark again, thankfully, as we trekked through the city. I found the silence disconcerting. In the enclave, you could always hear human noises. Here, the buildings stood like dying sentinels, and I had the unnerving fear they could topple over at any second, crushing us in dust and rubble. Down below, I'd possessed the sense of being a valuable part of the community. Up here, I felt like nothing. The space filled me with disquiet, and I found it nearly impossible to believe this place had once been filled with people. I couldn't imagine it.

At dawn, Fade found us shelter. The building bore no paint, and the front windows were shattered. That made it easy for us to enter, but I held myself ready in case we ran into trouble. Though the place smelled of animal musk, I saw no signs of human habitation. Whoever had broken in first, they were long gone.

"We're far enough from the Wolves to risk a rest," Tegan

said. "With any luck, they've lost our trail in the time Stalker took getting the rest of them."

"How much do we need to look over our shoulders?" I asked.

"He's a good tracker, but we covered a lot of ground."

My aching feet could attest to that. Walking Topside was nothing like traveling in the tunnels. Our cured-skin slippers worked down below, but here, we needed something heavier.

Fade said, "I hope it will be enough."

After crawling carefully past the broken glass, we found a shop, similar to the one where we'd sheltered before, but bigger, with row after row of metal shelves. A huge blue and red sign hung sideways from the ceiling. Tilting my head, I read some of the letters: CAL'S MEGAMART. Wonderingly, I walked up and down between the shelves. Most had been picked clean, but I found a few tins. Those I slipped into my bag.

We split up by mutual consent to explore the place thoroughly. A few minutes later, when Tegan started yelling, I drew my daggers and sprinted in her direction. I stopped short when I realized she was excited, not scared. Clothing surrounded her. The styles and colors were bright and unfamiliar; the fabrics felt cool and slick. A few items tore when I picked them up, but others seemed to be in perfect condition.

"I haven't had anything that was mine since the Wolves took me," Tegan said, and her voice broke in a way that tugged at my heart.

"Find some that fit," I suggested. "If these traders had food and clothes, then they probably have a bag around here for you too."

Thanks to her work with the knife, I needed a spare outfit as well. Life in the enclave had taught me one didn't need more than could be easily carried, but I didn't like not owning anything to change into when what I wore got too dirty to bear. And I was getting there.

I prowled through the garments until I spotted a green combination of shirt and pants. The shirt had a metal strip running down the center; I yanked it up and down before deciding it was meant to make it easier to get dressed. The pants were as simple as I was used to with a simple string to tighten the waist. This would do; it was light, smooth and should be comfortable. The material was a little dusty, so I beat it against the wall; the slick, shiny stuff shook clean unlike any cloth I'd ever seen. That would come in handy.

I left Tegan searching for a bag to carry her stuff. In the next set of shelves, I saw a bunch of bottles, and they looked like they held water. Marveling at the luck, I took a couple with me. *There might be a waste closet here,* I thought. At the back of the shop, I found it, tucked into a dark hall. The shadows didn't bother me. My ears were good and I'd hear movement.

Inside, it was dingy, but not disgusting at it had been on the platform. The mirror didn't take me by surprise this time. I ignored the girl going about her business—even though with my brain, I knew she was me, I felt no connection to her, and every now and then, I looked up just to see if she would continue what she was doing, or stop and stare, as I did. Each time, her movements matched, but my sense of unease remained. *It was like a doorway,* I thought.

I cracked open a bottle. It didn't smell like the water we boiled, but I didn't intend to drink it. Instead I used it to wash off before putting on my clean clothes; they were warmer and lighter than I'd expected. When I'd done what I could to remove the bloodstains, I felt a little better.

"Deuce!" Fade called. "Come here."

I expected more clothing, but he'd found another room,

hidden behind a heavy metal door that read EMPLOYEES ONLY. This one was full of boxes and crates and beyond that, another space, this one smaller still, that held tables, chairs, tall storage units, and two dusty sofas. We pounded them until they looked clean enough to use.

"We can lock that door," I said. "And hole up in here while it's so bright out."

"That wasn't what I wanted you to see."

I sat down beside him while he pulled the top off a tin. It contained a red substance that made me recoil. Surely that couldn't be—then he lifted it to my nose so I could sniff it. It was the best thing I'd ever smelled, and my mouth watered.

"What is it?"

"Taste it." Fade dipped his finger into the tin and offered it to me.

I couldn't resist, though I knew better than to let him feed me like a brat. Sweetness exploded on my tongue, contrasting with the warmth of his skin. Shocked and pleased, I pulled back and dipped two of my fingers into the tin in a little scoop. This time I caught more than the sauce. A round little red thing sat in the curve of my fingertips. I ate it without hesitation, two, three more scoops until I was sure I had red all around my mouth, and I didn't care. He watched me with amusement.

"How did you know it would be so good?" I asked

His smile slipped. "I had some with my dad, once."

I turned the tin, which was covered in red things, and had a blue banner with white letters on it. They read, "Comstock," and below that, it said, "More Fruit Cherry." More new words. We were eating *cherries*, something I'd never had before, and they made my mouth water for more. I stopped because I wanted Tegan to taste them too.

"Do you miss him?"

Fade nodded and set the tin down. Hesitantly, I put my hand on his shoulder. I wasn't a Breeder, so touching didn't come naturally to me. If I was, I guessed I'd know how to comfort him. I might even have the right words instead of a throat full of silence. It was the first time I'd ever thought being a Breeder might come in handy.

For the first time, I looked at him and I didn't see reflexes or muscles or fighting potential. I saw only a boy who had followed me from the tunnels, who had been a friend no matter what obstacles we faced. Even while the Wolves had been hunting him, he thought of saving me. My heart shifted a little in my chest; it seemed to swell and beat against my bones until I couldn't hear.

"You were right, you know," he said finally.

"About what?"

"Why I stayed. I didn't have anything better waiting. The enclave was better than being alone."

"You're not alone," I said. "And you never will be. We're partners now."

Fade smiled then. I didn't know why. Until he said, "My dad had a partner. I don't remember her."

"Oh?" I wondered if his dad had been a Hunter too, some Topside variety I didn't know about. The whole world couldn't be populated with people like Stalker.

"She was my mother."

The words struck me like a question, but I didn't have an answer. "Come on. I found some water on the shelves. We need to clean your arms up."

"The cuts aren't that deep," he protested.

"And if they get infected—"

"I know." He followed me back into the shop, where I walked along the shelves finding things I might be able to use. Some of them even looked like they might be suitable for tending wounds.

Fade winced when I unwrapped the cloth strips. I tried to be careful, but the dried blood made it stick. With perfect gravity, I stared at the way they'd made the cuts run parallel to his Hunter marks. Now he bore twelve. Part of me wished I could seal them properly, so his arms would say to anyone, *I'm twice the Hunter you are.* But Topside such symbols were meaningless. They were just scars. Nobody would admire him for having more. I hated that loss too.

Head bent, I washed his wounds and applied the salve Banner had given me. The primitive part of me didn't think I should use it—whatever power she had given to its making would fail because of her death. But it was all we had, and I wanted him to heal.

He didn't show further signs of discomfort. I sliced up one of the shirts for bandages, and turned the soft white side to his cuts. The outside was slick like the clothing I wore, and should keep the rain out. It seemed like a very useful fabric. Too bad the making of it had been lost. But then, everything I knew was lost too. I felt like I must learn everything again, like a brat, or face painful consequences.

When I finished tying the cloth, I looked up to tell him he could go, only to find a steely, fixed expression on his face. He didn't look away. His hands came up to frame my face, warm against my cheeks. Before he bent his head, I knew what he was going to do. Touch his lips to mine. Oh, and I wanted him to. He left me the chance to back away and break his hold. I stilled, hardly daring to breathe. The old refrain of *can't* and *shouldn't* sank beneath the weight of new words like, *please* and *yes.*

This time I did wrap my arms around his neck. I met him on raised toes and melted into him. I breathed his breath and tasted the essence of him. He was the heat of a fire and the sweetness of the moon I'd only just met. *No wonder Breeders were so cheerful,* I thought, breathless.

"I never belonged anywhere until I met you," he said, resting his cheek against my hair.

"I thought I did."

Remembering the enclave gave me a pang. I would always miss Stone and Thimble. I would worry about Twist and hope the brats were doing well, especially Girl26. But it wasn't my place. I knew that now. There was a reason besides pity I had sacrificed myself for Stone.

"And now?"

I couldn't lie to him. "I was born there. I expected to die there. If I'd never left, I think I would've been content. I believed what they told me about the surface. When we started climbing that day, I thought I'd die of fear."

"Not you," he said. "I've never seen you defeated. You were so determined to prove to everyone you deserved to be a Huntress, when nobody questioned it but you."

That astonished me. "What do you mean?"

"You were among the best. If not for Crane's physical strength, you would've been facing me in the finals. But I think you doubted it because from the beginning you didn't have the same hardness as the rest of the Hunters. It's not *easy* for you."

"No," I said softly, thinking of the blind brat we'd failed to save.

"And that's why I—"

Before he could finish his thought, Tegan found us. "So this is where you two are hiding."

The moment was broken, so I led the way back to the room with the sofas, where we'd left the can of cherries. I handed her the open tin. "Try it."

"It looks—*oh*." After one wary taste, like me, she dug in with hooked fingers.

I saw why Fade had enjoyed watching me eat. Her pleasure was contagious and it found its way to my face in a quiet smile. We let her finish the rest; I figured she deserved something sweet.

"I have a couple more in here. Why don't you bolt us in for the night?" While Fade locked the door, I rummaged in my bag. "Let's see what else is for dinner."

The first can we popped open smelled fishy, but not rancid. Over the years, I'd grown fairly expert at detecting whether such food could be safely eaten. Judging by the color and texture, this actually was fish. The three of us divided it up. I knew we would need the energy, no telling how long before we'd eat so well again. I also had a tin that read, "Mixed Vegetables." The multicolored stuff in there tasted none too good, and it was mushy, but it filled our bellies.

"Thanks for taking me with you," Tegan said.

Fade sighed. "Don't thank us yet. We're heading north. By the time the journey's done, you might wish you'd stayed with the Wolves. We don't know what's out there."

"I'd like to find out." Her look held a sweet kind of hunger, a longing that didn't devour, only the need for truth.

I understood that look. Since I had let go of the possibility I could change everything for the brats, I had begun to throb with the desire to understand why things happened, why some people lived under the ground, like our enclave, the Freaks, and the Burrowers, and why some stayed Topside and turned into the greatest monsters of all.

"Do you still have that book?" Fade asked me.

Wordless, I laid hands on it in my bag and gave it to him. The light shining through the distant window was sufficient to see the pages. Without asking if we were interested, he opened it and began to read. I listened until my eyes grew heavy, and I slumped over onto his legs. I dreamed of boys who gleamed red-gold, and girls with shadows in their skin.

Pearl

I t took us two days to find the part of the ruins where Fade thought his father's friend had lived. We traveled in the dark and avoided the gangers as best we could. The markings helped with that, and we stayed away from the areas that bore the most paint. Still, it was slow going.

The air smelled different here, sharper, stronger. Each open-mouth breath tasted of that salty, tinned fish. Tegan noticed it too; she lifted her face and then took off. Fade called to her, but she ignored him. I ran after her because I wanted to know what was causing the change too. We drew up short when the world ended. Below, a sharp drop, down to loose earth, and beyond that, water. I had never seen anything like it or even imagined; it met the sky for vastness. In the distance, they kissed in whisper-ing shades of blue, deepening as the stars twinkled in reflected light. I drew in my breath, overcome.

"Have you seen this before?" I whispered to Fade.

"Once. But I wasn't sure I remembered right. I thought I might have dreamed it."

In my mind's eye, I saw him half his height, clinging to his sire's hand and watching the water tear high against the rocks. I saw no ending to it, just this beginning, or perhaps I had it wrong, and *this* was the ending of all things. Certainly it felt that way to me, as I gazed in aching silence, and refused to weep for the wonders the enclave brats would never see.

And so I saw the sun come up completely for the first time, rising over the water until it shone with a reflected light that arrowed toward me. I didn't know how long we stood there, rapt, but eventually Fade tugged on my hand. I hadn't even realized he was holding it. His fingers were strong and sure. Tegan looked dazed; perhaps it was only weariness.

"I hope we didn't get you lost," she said.

Fade shook his head. "No, I recognize that, actually."

"That" was a building, oddly shaped with a walkway that wrapped around it. Unlike most, it looked like rotten wood, long since given way and hanging in chunks. He continued north from there, following the water until we came to a short red structure. It had a few letters painted on it, but most had peeled away, leaving only the cryptic message OLEA L U GE. I didn't know what it meant, but Fade seemed sure of himself. He went to the side of the building, where steps led down to a door. The windows here had all been barred with heavy black metal.

He rapped urgently as the day grew brighter. I still didn't like being out in the sun, so I got out the glasses that shaded my eyes. It grew progressively warmer until I could feel it prickling on my skin. Fade banged on the door forever and then pulled a string that dangled from the top. We stood outside for a long while.

"Go away!" A female voice shouted eventually.

"Pearl?"

At last part of the door slid open, just enough for the person inside to see us. "Who are you?"

"My father knew yours. You're Oslo's daughter? We came to see you."

She spoke a word that I didn't catch as the sliding metal clanged shut. I heard the sound of her unfastening many bolts and chains, and then the door swung open. "Get inside, quickly."

We did as she asked.

She led us down endless flights of stairs to a solid metal door. She unlocked it and as we went in, I took in the place with wide eyes. Everything was clean. New looking. She had relics that looked as if they had just been made the day before. I recognized some of the items: sofa, chair, table, but the rest puzzled me. She also had a whole room devoted to supplies.

"It's been a long time," Fade said. "You've changed."

His smile held layers that I didn't like. Of course Pearl had changed. It had been at least six years since he'd seen her. She was his age, or a little older, and she was *pretty*. Clean. Her pale hair shone like stars, and her eyes were green as the water we'd marveled at only moments before. And her skin, her skin lacked the sickly pallor that was my legacy from a life underground. Instead it glowed with delicate warmth.

Pearl took in his scars. "So have you. Where did you go?"

"Down below."

"Ugh," she said. "I've heard they're little better than animals."

Funny. I thought the same thing about most Topsiders I encountered. Tegan touched my hand in silent sympathy, and I set my jaw.

"They're not so bad," he said. "At least, not all of them."

I stepped forward and pasted on a false smile. We were in her home, after all. The least I could do was be polite. "I'm Deuce, animal from the underground."

She had the courtesy to display chagrin. "I'm sorry. I don't get many visitors."

"Do you never go out?" Tegan asked. She had to be wondering why gangers hadn't snatched Pearl yet.

"Not often. I have just about everything I need here."

Fade nodded. "Your father left you well supplied."

Apparently his hadn't, or I would never have met him. All of a sudden, I wanted to know more about him, more than Pearl or anyone else would ever know. But this wasn't the time or place. I'd had my chance to ask questions, and somehow I still didn't know as much as I wanted to about him.

"Yes," Pearl said. "I'm lucky. His great-grandfather built a bunker down here, a long time ago. They were scared of the world blowing up, or something."

The word "bunker" was unfamiliar to me, but I didn't ask for a definition, as I might have done from Fade, if we'd been alone. I had the inexplicable impression that I shouldn't show weakness in front of Pearl, as if it might incite her to a feeding frenzy like a Freak. Tegan watched her with wary eyes, I think for different reasons. She simply didn't trust people; I wasn't sure she would've trusted us, except that we'd fought together, and that tended to create faster bonds.

"I was hoping you could help us," he said.

She smiled. "For Stepan's son . . . anything."

Encouraged and plainly pleased, he went on, "We need to sleep and then we'd like to look at his old maps, if it's all right."

"I have them boxed up. I don't have much room, I'm afraid, but you're welcome to my bed. They can bed down on the floor here." To us, she added, "You have blankets?" Her courtesy was false; it tasted like bad meat.

She didn't want Tegan or me sleeping on her floor or under her roof. Fade didn't seem to notice. He followed her into the other room, where they spoke in low voices. She told him how lonely she'd been. In the silence that followed, I knew he was hugging her and they were sharing childhood memories.

Since Tegan didn't have her own blanket, she had to share mine. That meant lying close and wrapping up together. I didn't mind. It reminded me of sharing space in the brat dorm. It cured some of my homesickness.

"I don't like her," Tegan whispered. "Why are we here?"

I explained what the library was and why we wanted to go there. She listened with a frown building between her brows. When I finished, she asked, "Does it matter why anything happened? I thought you were leaving and going north. That's what I want—out of this place."

"We are," I said. "But we want to find answers first. I thought if we knew what happened, we might be able to prepare better for what's out there."

"That makes sense," she acknowledged.

I lay back and gazed at the gray ceiling. "I don't know anything about this world. Well, nothing but what Fade tells me. And sometimes he doesn't seem sure either because he's spent years underground."

"I might be able to answer some questions," she said.

After thinking a bit, I settled on, "Your mom wasn't a ganger?"

"No. She and my dad were part of a small group that managed to stay hidden. It wasn't just us, at first. But people got sick.

My dad died first. My mom was the last to go. And then it was only me."

Fade said his dad got sick too. A common thread?

"There was a disease in the enclave, a long time ago. The elders told us about a time when nearly everybody died of it. Do you think it was the same thing?"

Tegan shrugged. "Maybe."

"Do you know why you didn't get it?"

"I wish I did. When the Wolves had me, I asked myself why I didn't die too."

Her mind surprised me. In the enclave, I'd never questioned why some brats lived and some died. There seemed no pattern to it. Sometimes brats I thought were small or frail, like Twist, would wind up thriving. Sometimes a strong, hardy one died in his sleep. The world made no sense at all.

"Maybe it was to make you stronger," I suggested.

"It did." She rolled on her side to face me, her eyes angry. "That's why I'll be watching that girl. I won't give anyone a chance to hurt me again."

I was glad she'd said it. Now I didn't have to wrestle with the uncomfortable suspicion that I didn't like Pearl simply because she knew more about Fade than I did. We listened to them talking until Tegan fell asleep. Rest wouldn't come for me, though. I kept waiting for something—a bad something—and expectancy coiled me tight.

Eventually, I slept. I dreamed of Stone and Thimble. When I woke, I wondered what they were doing, whether they missed me at all or if they still nursed righteous indignation about my exile. I missed them, regardless. They had been my best friends from the first.

That morning, I also discovered we'd been right to dislike

Pearl. Her voice carried from the other room; I'm sure she didn't know I was awake.

"You can stay as long as you like, of course, for old time's sake. But I don't have enough food to provide for your friends. I'm sorry."

Fade said, "Don't worry, we won't be long. I just need to finish looking over these maps."

So he was already working on finding the library. *Good.* I started to sit up, and then froze at her next words.

"I wish you wouldn't go," Pearl said softly. "I've thought of you often. I know your father wouldn't want you to leave me alone."

There was something off about her, something *wrong*, and not just because she was trying to talk him into abandoning me. I thought being by herself might've driven her crazy. I didn't like the way she looked at Fade.

His tone was gentle, almost conciliatory. "You've been fine all these years. Deuce can't make it without me."

I set my jaw. I didn't want him sticking with me out of pity. With Tegan's knowledge of the surface, and my ability to fight, we'd probably be fine. I almost said so, but then I'd have to admit I was pretending to be asleep so I could listen to them.

"Safe doesn't mean fine. I'm *lonely*, Semyon."

"Don't call me that," he said. "He died in the dark. And maybe what I meant when I said that about Deuce is I don't *want* to do without her."

Oh. My heart made that funny little turn again, as if I were frightened, but it was better and warmer than that.

"I see." Her voice went sharp and hard, covering hurt or some darker emotion. "Then whenever you're ready to go."

"I'm set. Thanks for your hospitality and the use of your father's maps."

I sat up then and nudged Tegan. Her hair tumbled into her face, making her look younger than she had before, too young to have suffered what she had with the gangers. Maybe she'd never be Stone or Thimble, but I already knew we would be close friends.

"I think we've outstayed our welcome," I muttered.

She assessed me and then whispered, "Did you hear him?"

Mutely I nodded, and her smile made me feel both pleased and ridiculous. It shouldn't matter that he'd picked me, but . . . it did. From her expression, she knew it. I wondered that she could trust us, even a little bit. Maybe, like Jengu, she didn't trust anyone completely, but we were better than anything she'd known since her family died.

By the time he came out of the back room, Tegan and I were ready to go. We both mouthed the right words to Pearl, but she just wanted us gone. I'm sure she felt rejected by Fade, but she hadn't spent long nights in the tunnels with him, or guarded his back when Freaks were determined to eat him. All she had to offer were maps, and he didn't need those forever. Apparently, he *did* need me. I quietly savored the feeling.

Outside, the night was chilly. My breath puffed from between my lips and I blew it out several times to make sure it wasn't a coincidence. The shirt I wore had an extra bit of fabric at the back so I tugged it up and was pleased to find it covered my head. Tegan did the same, as we wore matching clothes, just in different colors.

Fade guided the way back toward the water. I heard it and smelled it before I saw it. Instead of going down toward the wider body, he turned toward a narrow channel that angled into the land itself.

He read the puzzlement in my face and explained, "If we follow the river, it'll take us nearly all the way there."

Another new word. River. I stored it away. "You memorized where the library should be?"

"If you're ready, we'll go find it."

"And maybe some answers," Tegan added.

Together, we set out on the next leg of our journey.

Enlightenment

The trip took half the night. Where the river twisted and turned, so did we. This part of the ruins was quiet, a place where the spirits of the dead ghosted on the wind and whispered across my skin. So much had been lost. I marveled at the size of it all and tried to work out the purpose of the buildings we passed.

I liked the gentle light of what Fade called the moon. Tonight it had swelled from when we first came Topside.

"Will it get bigger?" I asked.

He followed my gaze upward with a faint smile. "Yes. It turns into a perfect circle. Sometimes it's silver and sometimes it can glow almost orange. Other times it's golden, but never as bright as the sun."

I didn't like the sun. Neither Tegan nor Fade seemed bothered by it as I was, but I hated the thing. I thought it might well burn me up, if given the chance. When it set fire to the sky, I wanted to hide, or I might end up like a chunk of meat on Copper's spit, all the juices crackling out of me. I tried to hide the worst of my fear because I didn't want them to think I was weak.

Tall, abandoned buildings surrounded us. Green covered the sides, growing in along the stone and rock. Parts had crumbled away from lack of care, showing the insides. I had the wild idea we could climb up, as if over the bones of a great beast. I had to pick my way carefully, avoiding enormous holes and sunken bits of rock. The plants had grown wild here for so long, they had reclaimed the whole area: Tall ones Fade called trees and long ones he named grass that flowed in the wind as if brushed by invisible hands.

Eventually we came upon an enormous structure built from gray rocks. It too had been claimed by the green; a web of leaves wound up the sides. A vast number of broken steps led up to the gaping doors, and two giant stone monsters guarded the entrance. I eyed them warily. We all stopped and stared. Unlike the others, this place had an air of majesty, even in its disrepair. I could tell great things had happened here.

"And this whole place is full of books?" Tegan asked.

"It's supposed to be. That's what my dad said."

She studied her feet. "My mom didn't talk to me much, unless she was saying, 'Be quiet, they're coming' or 'We have to run now.'"

"What was she like?"

"My mom?" At my nod, she grew thoughtful. "She looked like me, but she was always scared. I don't think I ever saw her when she wasn't."

If I had a brat to protect, I'd be scared too. Fade mounted the stairs at a run, as if trying to flee the memories Tegan's words evoked. Or maybe now that we were here, he was just eager to find out what secrets the building contained. So was I.

The doors had been broken at some point. No paint marred the exterior, so this wasn't ganger territory—a lucky break for us. But someone had been desperate to get inside. We stepped from the chill into a dark stillness. I could tell there were books all over the place, a few still on the enormous wall of shelves, but mostly they had been torn, broken and flung around, as if by wild animals. A certain smell made me think some might be nesting here.

"We'll have to wait for daylight before we can read anything," Fade said.

I agreed with a nod. "But should we check the place out while we do?"

Tegan shivered. "I hate the idea there's something in here with us."

"Something might be better than *someone*," I muttered, thinking of Stalker.

"True. Let's explore a little." Fade was already wending his way into the shadows, going at a near run. This place probably seemed wonderful to him, as much as he'd loved finding that old book. Here, was the prospect of countless books.

There was no point in sitting by the front doors until the sun rose. Now that my eyes had gotten used to the shift, I realized there was more light here than in the tunnels. It trickled in through the windows, painting cross-paths of silver on the dusty floor. My feet left visible tracks, and that made me uneasy. Topside, it was too easy to track us.

I told myself I was worried for nothing and I let myself be awed by the grandeur of this place. It must have been quite a world, where books lived in a house finer than anything I'd ever seen built for a person. The plants had gotten in here too, breaking through the floor in wild profusion.

"It will take hours to go through this whole place," Tegan said.

Fade grinned. "The sun will be up by then."

We explored each level, going up winding stairs. My nerves

coiled a little tighter with each one we climbed. I'd never been so high up. I could hear my heart thumping in my ears until I would have proven no help at all, if we'd encountered anything but small animals and nesting birds.

The high ceilings and endless rows of shelves created interesting shadows. We passed through vast open rooms filled with tables. A few locked doors barred our way. Whoever broke the front doors hadn't carried the attack all the way to the heart of the library. Here, I only heard the flutter of wings and scrabble of tiny claws skittering on the floor. If I were so inclined, this would be a decent place to lay snares for meat.

I was tired by the time Fade pronounced the place safe. Sunlight struggled through the dirty glass. Most of the windows were broken, though this part of the ruins had avoided the worst of the damage. Time had certainly taken its toll.

"What happened here?" I asked aloud.

Tegan put her hand on my shoulder. "That's what we're going to find out."

We made our way back down to the ground. I felt safer, but that wasn't the reason I thought we should begin there. It made sense to me that we should start looking at the doors and fan outward. Otherwise, we'd cross paths and might wind up covering the same area more than once.

The stuff nearest the entrance had been exposed to weather, and it was useless. It had gotten wet and shriveled up and dried, leaving the words illegible. Many of the books we touched crumbled in our hands. My hopes sank.

Farther on, we found sealed doors, and past them, an enormous room full of tables. Some of them held books; others yellowing papers. In here, the sunlight was sufficient for us to start reading.

I picked up a faded yellow bundle of papers. There were images, right on the paper, beside the words, but none of them were of happy things. I saw a lady crying, and a fire rising up from a car. I'd only seen them rusted and motionless. This one seemed to have been drawn at the exact moment it hit another one, and they both had flames all over them.

"'CDC reports vaccine failure,'" I read slowly. Most of the words were unfamiliar to me, and I sounded them out as best I could.

"Did you find something?" Fade asked, coming to my shoulder.

He rested his hand there as he leaned in, an easy touch like Stone would've bestowed, but coming from Fade, it meant something else. Not comfort or connection or a quiet way of saying he was there. I sensed the difference in every part of me.

"I'm not sure." I handed him the paper.

There was no shame in admitting his reading skills exceeded mine. I knew my letters and I would never be hurt because I'd failed to understand a warning sign. What else did I need? He skimmed the words, using only his eyes and not his fingers, as I did to mark my place.

"I don't understand all of it," he said at last. "But it seems like the disease my dad had—and Tegan's mom—it killed a lot of people. So they tried to make medicine for it, but it didn't work, and things got worse."

Worse. Like now? Or had life improved for people since then? That was hard to imagine.

"Are we the only ones left then?" Tegan whispered. "The underground tribes, the gangers, and a few survivors like my mom and me?"

Fade shook his head angrily. "No. My dad said people went north. That it was better there."

With a little twinge of pain, I wondered if those had just been stories, like the one he was reading to us—full of promise that could never be realized. Because I knew the question would hurt him, I didn't ask it. Maybe he saw it in my eyes because his sharp features drew in on a frown.

Presently Tegan came over with a different paper. "What's 'evacuation' mean?"

I shrugged as Fade took it and scanned the words. Maybe he could figure it out from reading the rest. Not for the first time, I admired his mind as much as I admired the way he fought.

"I'm not sure," he finally admitted. "But I think it has to do with people leaving. The person who wrote this seems angry. 'Evacuation plans are slanted toward the rich and powerful. This is going to be Katrina all over again,'" he read aloud.

"Powerful, like the elders," I muttered. "So whatever happened, the important people left first."

"There were people left behind," Tegan said. "That's why we're here."

It was a sobering thought. We came from those who hadn't been important enough to get evacuated. Though I might not be sure what the word meant precisely, I was positive its opposite was "left behind."

"We could spend forever here and not learn more than this," I said.

I was a little disappointed not to find all the answers in a single book, waiting for us turned to the right pages, but I now realized my expectations had been too high. A place like this couldn't tell us where to go, or what lay beyond the ruins. If we were brave enough, we'd have to find out for ourselves.

"I'd like to look a little longer," Fade said.

"Fine with me." But I sat down. I was done poking around

the dusty pages, looking to dead words for my answers. On the table beside me, I found what must be a child's book because it was mostly pictures.

On a whim I opened it. "A is for Apple. B is for Bear. C is for Cat." Intrigued, I went through, learning new words, things, and creatures with each flip. This book was sturdier than the others, so the pages had held up better. They still felt stiff. At *W*, I paused, wide-eyed.

"Tegan!" I called. "Come look!"

She got up with a sigh. I think she was ready to leave too, but we were indulging Fade, as neither of us really wanted to set out before nightfall anyway. We both preferred walking after dark.

" 'W is for Wolf,' " I read and tapped my finger on the picture. "Have you ever seen one of those?"

"Not for real. Just the human kind."

"But you knew what they were?" I was disappointed and cha-grined. Apparently I was the only ignorant one. Our schooling hadn't included much Topside lore, and most of what I'd been taught was wrong. I comforted myself with the fact that Tegan didn't know about Freaks or Burrowers. She didn't know what my scars meant. Unfortunately, my knowledge was useless up here.

"My mom had this exact book. She taught me to read with it." She sounded odd and choky.

There was no way it had survived her captivity, so I held out the book to her. "You want it?"

Her eyes got bright and teary. "Thank you."

Tegan took it and hugged it before stashing it in her bag. I fiddled with a few more books before losing patience and going to look for Fade. I found him sitting on the floor, surrounded by books. They were huge and old with tiny words. My head ached just thinking about trying to puzzle all of them out.

"Learning much?"

"Yes," he said. "But not about the things I wanted."

"Like what?"

"The old days."

I sighed. "Are you almost ready? It will be dark soon. I think we should get out of here as soon as we can."

Before he could answer, a long keening noise echoed through the halls. I recognized it, and it chilled my blood. Fade's black eyes met mine. "Where's Tegan?"

Library

"Come out, come out, wherever you are!" Stalker shouted. "Come on, *Semyon*. There's someone here who's dying to see you."

Fade closed his eyes. "He has Pearl."

I didn't care that much about Pearl, but I could see he did. "He'll have brought the rest of his Wolves."

Now I had a mental picture of them too: fierce and fanged with silvery gray fur and shining eyes. Stalker's human versions couldn't look like that, but if they came close, we'd have an awful fight on our hands, further complicated by Tegan and Pearl. Fade wanted to save his old friend for his father's sake. I'd concede her loss if there was no other choice. But not Tegan. We'd saved her. He couldn't have her back.

The darkness helped. I slipped along the edges of the wall until I could see what we were dealing with. Fade stayed close, his presence reassuring at my back. To my surprise, Stalker hadn't brought an army, just a few Wolves who looked every bit as frightening as he did. They wore the same scars on their faces, but they'd painted them different colors. I guessed his meant he was in charge and nobody better forget it.

They stood just before the broken doors. As I'd feared, he

held Tegan casually, a knife to her throat. One of his Wolves had ahold of Pearl. They were strong, well armed, and rested. To make matters worse, we lacked the element of surprise. They expected us to attack.

"What do we do?" I whispered.

Hiding was an option. If we slipped away, it was unlikely they'd ever find us. In fact, I was impressed he'd tracked us this far. I wondered if Stalker had only pretended to run and sent his cub for more Wolves while he tracked us, leaving quiet signs for them to follow. It was the only explanation that made sense.

"There are four of them."

But they wouldn't be like the cubs we'd faced in the warehouse. We'd tried not to kill them because they were brats, but these opponents would be like fighting four trained Hunters, I had no doubt. Were we good enough?

Stalker lost patience. "You have one minute before I start making new holes in these two Breeders."

I made the decision before I realized I had and stepped into view. "So you found us. What's the complaint? We're not in your territory now."

"You injured eighteen of my cubs. Two of them died."

"They had it coming," Fade said. "And they're lucky it wasn't worse."

I murmured, "Why don't you let them go? We'll talk."

Stalker smiled. "I don't want to talk."

Before he could give the order to attack, a horrible smell drifted to me on the wind. I'd only smelled anything like it once before, near Nassau. *Oh, no.* Before I heard the scrabbling movements, I knew we had Freaks incoming.

I didn't realize they ever came Topside, but as soon as they burst through the doorway, I saw we were dealing with the smart ones. Their eyes looked different, not swimming with hunger and madness. No, these were worse because I recognized cunning and craft. In daylight, these creatures looked more horrible with their yellow skin, bloody claws, and fierce, sharp teeth. Sparse hair sprouted from their misshapen skulls, stained dark with their kills.

"We're not your biggest problem now!" I shouted.

To his credit, Stalker whirled. His Wolves shoved Tegan and Pearl away and fell into a fighting stance. Unlike their brats, the Wolves fought well—and as a unit. Not up to the standards set by Hunters, but they had a surprising amount of discipline. But they weren't used to Freaks. I could see fear in the way they tried to block snapping fangs and raking claws.

My daggers in hand, I joined the battle with Fade close behind. As I whirled into the attack, I counted—part of my Huntress nature. Twenty Freaks. We'd once faced almost as many underground, but they had been weak and stupid, plus the shelter offered a certain amount of protection.

We stood back-to-back, blocking and striking in harmony; sometimes it felt like his arms and legs were an extension of me. I could count on him to keep them off me from behind. My daggers became a blur as I cut and thrust, driving the Freaks back. I couldn't spare any focus to see how Tegan and Pearl fared. I didn't use any of my flashier moves—no kicks or spins. My goal was to protect Fade's back. I heard Silk telling me relentlessly, *Take them down. Simple and clean is best. Don't waste energy.*

Now that he wasn't trying to kill me, I admired Stalker's style. He was incredibly fast, using two small blades strapped to the backs of his hands. *Slash, slash, slash.* Fighting him, you wouldn't die of one great wound, but instead bleed out slowly, surprised to find yourself weak and dying after a thousand cuts.

The Freaks dropped back after the first wave fell. They studied us with their red eyes, as if assessing for weakness. Beneath my feet, the floor flowed with blood. We'd lost three of Stalker's Wolves, and I didn't see Pearl anywhere. Tegan was hiding—smart girl. This wasn't like knocking cubs unconscious.

"What *are* those things?" Stalker asked.

That answered my question as to whether they'd seen them before. "We called them Freaks underground. I've also heard them called Eaters. I don't know what they are. I do know they're hungry."

His pale eyes widened as the Freaks decided to make another run at us. But he had no chance to ask further questions as the fight began anew. We'd taken ten of their number at a cost of three. The Freaks seemed to think math favored them—those who survived would feast on the dead—and I wasn't sure they were wrong about the odds.

But Stalker and his sole remaining Wolf went back-to-back like Fade and me. They didn't have our rapport or our rhythm, but they made up for it in desperation and ferocity. I slashed open a Freak's jugular and blocked with my left hand. But I was slow. It sank its teeth into my arm. I screamed and slammed a dagger into its eye. The pop and squelch turned my stomach every bit as much as the smell.

And Fade went feral. He broke formation, fighting as he'd done in the tournament; it seemed so long ago now. His hands and feet were a blur as he demolished the one trying to eat me. When all enemies stilled, red spattered him from head to toe and he was shaking.

The last Wolf had taken grievous wounds. He bled from four different bites and had a painful claw wound across his chest. I couldn't tell if Stalker was hurt. Like Fade, he had too much blood on him for me to be sure if any belonged to him. He stared at me with his odd, light eyes, wearing an unreadable expression.

So help me, I thought, *if he tries to fight us now . . .*

"Are there more of those?"

"A lot more," I said. "Underground. I guess they found a way out."

Part of me feared they'd broken through to the Burrowers and discovered those subtunnels with the holes that led up the surface. Jengu might be dead, and there was nothing I could do about it. The whole *enclave* might be dead by now. I feared for Stone and Thimble; maybe the underground tribes were no more. Quickly I put those worries aside.

"We need to move," Fade said. "If I know anything about those things, there will be more. They'll smell the blood and come, looking to eat."

Stalker gazed down at his fallen and shook his head as if apologizing for leaving them to become Freak food. I doubted they minded, now. *The strong survive, and the dead are past saving.*

"Tegan," I called. "Let's go."

She crawled out from under a table nearby, shaking from head to toe. "That was . . . the way you . . ."

"I grew up learning how to fight them," I said simply.

There was no reason for her to be ashamed of her fear. I was afraid of the sky and the sun, after all, and those things probably wouldn't hurt me. Not like the Freaks, though I was less than convinced the sun served any benevolent purpose.

"Where's Pearl?" Fade asked.

She'd called him Semyon. It sounded exotic to my ears, a hint of a past I would never share. I tried not to mind when he went looking for her. He'd chosen to stay with me when he could've remained in peace and comfort. A choked sound echoed, and I went to find him.

Fade stood over the body of a Freak. Pearl lay partly chewed between the shelves. She'd tried to run and had drawn the attention of a hungry monster. While the rest of us battled and talked, it had been eating her, quietly. These really were smarter than the rest. If it had been clever enough to slip away before we finished fighting, we never would've caught the thing.

"Come on," I said. "You can't help her now."

"She died because she let us look at her dad's maps."

That was true. We'd led Stalker to her door, and once we left, he had forced entry and taken her. So I had no words of comfort to offer.

We rejoined the others. I had no fears for Tegan anymore. Stalker had his hands full trying to get his lone Wolf out of the library before more Freaks showed up. Regardless of Fade's sadness, that had to be our priority too.

"The city's going to be overrun," I said quietly. "As more Freaks find the way out, they'll go looking for food."

"It's time to go," Tegan agreed.

I skirted the pile of bodies and still left a bloody trail of footprints as I headed for the door. She followed and after a few seconds, Fade got moving. Stalker caught up with us halfway down, more or less dragging his man.

"Go where?" he asked.

I didn't want to tell him, but he *had* helped us against the Freaks. "North. It's supposed to be better outside the ruins."

"Who says?"

"My dad," Fade said quietly.

"Was he some kind of holocaust expert?" Stalker's tone was mocking.

Fade shrugged. "He had a lot of books."

I wasn't about to let this disintegrate into an argument on the steps. We had a long way to go and no real idea where we were heading. "Which way is north?"

He tinkered with his watch and then pointed. "That way."

"Then let's walk until the sun comes up. Let the light mark our rest breaks." Stalker and his Wolf didn't need to know my fears.

Fade gave me a knowing glance but he nodded. "Moving."

"We're coming with you," Stalker said.

Tegan froze. "No. If you try, I swear I'll kill you in your sleep."

"What about your cubs?" I asked.

"They might be meat by now. If those things are swarming, then I can't help them by getting myself eaten on the way back."

"But why do you want to come with *us*?" Tegan demanded. "Just a little while ago, you wanted us dead!"

"Wanted. Not anymore. Those two"—he jerked his head at Fade and me—"seem to know how to fight these things. That means I need to stick with them if I want to survive." Then he fixed a pale gaze on her again. "I don't care what *you* do. You're useless to me."

Silk would find his attitude commendable. He embodied the Hunter tenet: "The strong survive." Part of me hated him for what he'd let the other Wolves do to Tegan, but the Huntress half of me wondered why she hadn't fought until she died. And I admired his ruthless skill with those blades that seemed an extension of his hands.

I glanced at Fade. "It's up to you."

"We can use another fighter," he said. "It's likely to be a tough journey." He glanced at the Wolf. "But I'm not sure he's going to make it."

He didn't state the obvious—that the bleeding wounds would draw more Freaks. If they could smell warm meat down in the stench of the tunnels, it would be like an invitation on the clean, crisp wind. I waited to see how Stalker replied, interested in how deep his pragmatism ran. He was ready to abandon his cubs. Would he leave his Wolf?

The question became unimportant when the boy in Stalker's arms gasped for breath. Blood bubbled up. We laid him down on the steps and when I peeled back his ragged shirt, I saw the wound was much worse than we'd originally thought. As a brat, I'd tended gut wounds in Hunters because nobody else wanted to, and they always died. Sometimes it took a long time but there was no coming back from the kind of damage I saw. The claws had torn into his belly, scrambling the flesh. Stalker whispered to him, and the boy gave a jerky nod. He ended things for him, and then we left him.

We walked along the dead streets in silence. None of us had the energy to do more. The vast wreckage around us weighed on me, as if I could hear echoes down the years from a time when these ruins were live and vibrant. Instead, there were only our footsteps, echoing in the dark.

Tegan hunched her shoulders, tension in the lines of her body. From the way she kept stealing glances, she seemed upset with Fade's decision. I suspected she would follow through on her threat to kill Stalker in his sleep. Or *try*, at least. I didn't think he would prove an easy target, even then. If he had fought his way to the top of the Wolves, then he qualified as strong.

As we walked, I kept my eyes down. I ignored the throbbing of my arm and the weight of the dark sky above. Sometimes I stole a look and the scope of it overwhelmed me. Fade had told me about the pricks of light above; he didn't know what they were, exactly. I imagined they were torches from a city built on high. It would take a bird to reach it, so maybe the people who lived up there had wings. They would be pale and beautiful with ivory feathers and starry hair.

We passed a dark pond with still water, where rainwater had pooled in the broken rock. It smelled stale, but I used it to wash the blood off. The others followed suit. Afterward, the chill made me draw my head covering up. Then we walked on until light showed on the far edge of the sky. It began in a gray that softened to pink and then gold. Before the sun came up fully, I could admit it was beautiful, the way it tinted the buildings and softened their ruined lines.

This far north, I saw no ganger markings. Stalker noticed it as well. "We learned how to survive close to home. We never went beyond our territories."

"Unless you were raiding for Breeders," Tegan said bitterly.

Stalker shrugged, as though her opinion didn't matter to him. *I understood,* I thought. He could respect Fade and me because we'd fought. Because she hadn't, Tegan might never gain full value in his eyes.

"Even then, we never came this far," Stalker said.

"Let's look for another shop," I said. "Maybe we can find more tinned food and water. I'd rather not build a fire before we leave the ruins."

The others agreed, so as we went on, the light starting to hurt me, we scouted for a likely place to rest.

Respite

topping at three different shops provided us with enough food for a few days, but we didn't like the way the places smelled. For me, it was more of a danger sense, cultivated during my days as a Huntress. So we kept moving, even through the daylight. By the time we found a building that looked solid and secure, apart from the broken window we crawled through, I was exhausted, and my skin tingled unpleasantly. I went inside first, and Stalker followed.

"You're red," he told me. "Haven't you ever seen the sun before?"

His attention didn't bother me. I had already proved I could defend myself.

"Not that much. I told you, I'm from an underground tribe." I used Tegan's word for us. "College enclave," I added, as if it would mean anything to him.

"You were serious?"

"Yes."

Tegan and Fade slid in. He came in first and helped her through. We stood in a hallway illuminated by rays of light that swam with dust. The floors were intriguing, a mix of green and white. I studied the pattern as if it held some clue about this place. It seemed almost like a hidden pathway.

Fade said, "We should split up and scout the place. I'll take Tegan."

Maybe he knew she wouldn't want to go off alone with Stalker whereas I could hold my own, even against his lightning blades. I moved out. The sign on the outside of the building had a number of missing letters, but I'd recognized the word "School." That was where brats went to learn. We'd had school underground too. The idea of a building this size devoted to teaching brats astonished me.

He fell into step with me, still thinking about what I'd said about coming from underground. "What was it like down there?"

"Dark. Smoky. There wasn't space like there is up here, so you got used to less. And I grew up knowing there were Freaks out in the tunnels, and that if I was brave enough and strong enough, I'd go out to fight them for the rest of the enclave."

"And did you?" he asked.

"For a while." I didn't want to talk about the exile, but I just knew he was going to ask.

Sure enough, he did. "So how did you wind up here?"

"Bad luck."

That sent the message clear enough. He subsided and took to searching the rooms across from the ones I picked. In silence, we patrolled the rest of the place. It was big with three levels, and lots of little spaces full of tiny tables and tiny chairs. They really *had* made this school just for the brats. In each room, there was only one big table and one big chair. Awed, I stepped in and saw a black wall with white dust on it. I could nearly make the faint impression of letters, but time had been too much. It was like almost glimpsing something in my own reflection that I wasn't meant to see. I touched my fingers to it and drew the first letter of my name. I didn't know how to spell the rest.

"What's that?" he asked.

"A *D*."

We moved on. Stalker moved different than Fade, less caution, more aggression. If there was anything in here, he meant to kill it before it threatened us. I found the contrast interesting, but he was still thorough and watchful.

"Seems safe enough," he said, once we'd walked our assigned levels.

I had to agree. There was nothing here but the signs of rats and birds, nothing larger or scarier. We passed into what I recognized as a kitchen from the pans, more than anything else. Copper had used similar objects for cooking down below.

Here, I found enormous tins of food. I'd never seen anything like it. "Too bad we can't carry these," I said. "We could eat for months."

"We should save the smaller ones for travel. Eat some of this stuff now."

"'Creamed corn,'" I read aloud.

His pale eyes flickered. "How do you know that?"

"I can read, some. Not as well as Fade."

Stalker stared at me, and then he asked, "What does that mean?"

How could he not know? And then I remembered how he'd come up, no Breeders to teach him anything at all. The only things he knew, he'd learned the hard way. Nobody like Stone had shown him *anything* or made sure he showed up for basic brat training. It was a wonder he could talk, let alone read.

"The letters here," I pointed. "They spell out what's inside the tin. I don't know what 'corn' is, but I'm hungry enough to eat almost anything."

I got out my tiny knife with all its funny blades. One of them punctured the tin, so I did it repeatedly, until I could pry the top off. I peered inside at the yellow goo. Stalker cocked his head and sniffed.

"Doesn't smell bad."

My fingers were clean enough from the pond that I dipped them in and tasted. Sweet. Not like the cherries, in a different way, but good. Following my example, he gave it a try too. I ate until I didn't want anymore and then got out some of the bottled water we'd found. So far I hadn't tried drinking it; I'd only washed off in it. But we didn't have any choice now. I cracked the bottle open and took a drink. It tasted funny, but not dirty. I made myself down half of it, then I offered it to him.

"It's not very good, but I think it's clean."

He took it, leveling a strange look on me. I realized he wasn't used to the idea of sharing. What he wanted, he took. But it didn't work like that, now. And he had to understand that.

I narrowed my eyes. "You realize, you're not in charge. You never will be. Fade thinks your blades will come in handy on the trip and he's probably right. But if you try to hurt any one of us, *especially* Tegan, it'll be the last thing you ever do."

His pale eyes narrowed, drawing up his scarred cheeks. "Don't threaten me."

"It's not a threat," Fade said, coming up behind me. "It's the truth."

Tegan growled low in her throat. "He can't change. We should just kill him."

"There's been enough killing." Fade put a hand on her arm. "Don't worry. I'll keep an eye on him. He won't hurt you."

Part of me didn't like the new additions to our group. I missed when it was just Fade and me against the world, even as I acknowledged we needed the help. There was no telling how far we had to go. He hadn't found any maps in the library, showing us the route. We only had his dad's stories and the hope we might get out of these ruins if we walked far enough. Right now it seemed impossible.

We lived in a dead world. The idea if we went far enough, we might find living people, who had fires and homes and food to eat—I might as well wish for those pale, lovely winged people to come down from the stars and take us there, as long as I was hoping for things beyond my reach. But giving up wasn't an option either. I'd put my faith in Fade's sire, and the fact that his stories must be true.

"Have some creamed corn." I passed the huge tin to her, and she smelled it, much as Stalker had done. It would doubtless make her mad to find out she had anything in common with him. "It's better than it looks."

If the water had been bad, I would know soon. Stomach pains, coupled with quick eruption, marked the dirty disease. *So far, so good.* I missed proper baths with soap, but the clumsy cleanup at the pond would have to do. All things considered, it was a small complaint.

Shouldering my bag, I found a dark corner and rolled up in my blanket. Tegan lay down on my other side; she still had my club, I noticed. She kept one hand on it even as she fell asleep. Fade put his body between Stalker and us. He didn't seem to care.

No harm came to us while we slept. I woke first, roused by the noise Tegan was making in her sleep. I put my hand on her shoulder and she came up swinging. She landed a solid punch to my face before she realized who I was. I rubbed my cheek and smiled at her.

"That'll teach me to wake you up."

"Sorry."

"Sounded like you were having a bad dream."

Her gaze cut over to Stalker. "You could say that."

"About him?"

"Well. No. But about what he let his Wolves do to me."

"I thought you said he took all females first."

"Not if someone else brought the girl in. He had the right to claim anyone he wanted, but he was usually generous." Her anger sizzled. "He made an exception to that rule when you showed up."

"You blame him for not helping you."

"Of course I do! He was in charge—they listened to him. If he'd asked them to stop or leave me alone, they would have."

"Can you fight?" Stalker demanded from the other side of Fade. I hadn't realized he was awake, but she wasn't being quiet, either. "Hunt? Can you make clothes or any other useful item?"

Tegan glared at him. "No!"

"Then as far as I can see, you're only good for breeding. My job was to keep the cubs together. Keep them hunting as a pack," Stalker said. He sat up and ran a hand through his fair hair. Like Pearl's it shone brighter when the sun hit it, and it stood in unruly spikes. "I *did* that. Better than anybody had before."

"And then you left them to die, because you were afraid to go back alone."

Stalker lunged for her then, but Fade slammed up an arm and gave him a shake. "Shut up, both of you."

I listened for signs there might be something coming for us.

But I heard only the moan of the wind through the halls. After pushing to my feet, I put away my blanket and took up my pack.

"This can go only one way," I said. "The two of you have to forget what came before." At Tegan's black scowl, I held up a hand. "If you don't, we won't make it. You think it's easy for me? I could be safe and warm right now in my own pallet in my own space with nothing more to worry about than following orders.

"Instead I'm here, where day by day, I don't know if I'll have food to eat or a place to sleep, if I'll wake up with something trying to kill me. It's *hard*. And it will get harder, the farther we get from known territory. We have no idea what's out there. *None*. And either you're ready to start over . . . or you're not. No more of this. If I didn't let go of what I've lost, I'd go crazy. I suggest you two do the same."

Angrily, I unfastened my shirt. I slipped my arm free of the sleeve and studied the bite. I should have tended it last night, but I'd just been so tired. The skin was purple around the wound, and the flesh was ragged and puffy. I couldn't tell how bad it might get. I dumped some water on it, smeared it off and then dug in my bag looking for the salve. It smelled no better than when Banner first gave it to me, still sticky and awful, and it burned like fire as it sank into my skin. I hissed, my eyes watering, and unaccountably, longing for home swept over me.

The Freaks might've taken College by now, if they'd refused to listen to our warnings. I'd never know what became of Stone and Thimble, and the uncertainty ate at me like the ointment on my wound. I didn't bother to wrap it, just pulled my sleeve back up. It hurt for a good long while, reminding me of Bonesaw's treatments. As Silk used to say, *What doesn't kill you, makes you stronger.* The Wordkeeper had a book of sayings like that, written by one man, a really wise one, I guess. I couldn't remember his name.

Sighing, I ate some more of the creamed corn and opened another tin. It smelled like meat, chopped up, with some other stuff in it. With a mental shrug, I ate some of that too. I drank some water and then passed the bottle around. The others were packing their things when I headed out of the kitchen toward the doors.

Darkness fell over me like a balm, cool wind carrying the hint of rain. I hoped it would hold off. I hadn't enjoyed our first night aboveground with the water lashing my skin in stinging needles. I felt a little warm still and my face hurt, not just from Tegan's punch. That would definitely bruise, though; she had a good solid swing.

Stalker caught up with me on the stairs. The shadows made him less fearsome, softening the scars and the paint. I noticed that hadn't worn off, despite washing, which intrigued me.

"I will if she will," he said.

"What?"

"Start over. I did what I had to with the Wolves. But things are different now. And I can accept that. I understand I'm not in charge."

I considered his words. In that way he was like me; he could flow as needed in order to survive. It was different from brute force, but I recognized it as strength.

"Nobody is, really. We have to work together."

He nodded and moved on, apparently considering the subject closed. "What do your scars mean?"

At first I didn't know how he'd seen them and then I realized. He must've watched me taking care of my arm. "They mean I used to be a Huntress." At his look, I added, "Remember how I said if I was strong enough or brave enough, I'd fight the Freaks for the rest of the enclave?" He nodded. *"That's* what they mean."

"So they're a sign you protect people," he said. "Fade has them too."

"He has more marks now." I spoke the words without accusation. Since I'd asked them to do it, I had to let the past go too.

"I guess he does."

I surprised myself by asking, "What do yours mean? And the paint?"

"It's not paint," he said. "It's ink."

"Like they used in books?" My brow furrowed.

"Kind of. We do it with needles along the line of the scar. It marks our rank."

I had been right about that much at least. "Did it hurt?"

"Yes. Did yours?"

I wasn't about to tell him that I'd cried when they put the white-hot blade to my skin. But I admitted, "A lot."

Before he could answer, the others joined us.

Fade cast a glance between us, as if wondering what we'd been talking about, but otherwise he was all business. "We should find the river again, and follow it north as long as we can. We'll need the water to boil and drink. There should be fish too, and we can hunt along the way when the tins run out."

That sounded like a good plan. I tugged the extra fabric up over my head as the wind kicked up. It carried a whisper of water, spattering us. The chill intensified. Though the days were warm, the nights were cold.

"Before we leave the ruins, we should look for warmer clothes," Tegan said.

I agreed. "I'm sure we'll pass more shops."

Fade hadn't talked to me much since yesterday. He was taking

Pearl's death hard, much as he had Banner's. It made me angry. He didn't understand the tenet: "The dead are past saving." You could miss someone, but it did no good to fixate on loss. I wished I had the ready words of a Breeder or the ability to comfort with a soft touch. I didn't. Instead I had daggers and determination.

That would have to do.

Trek

We traveled north along the river.

The ruins went on much farther than I could have ever imagined. They encompassed an incredible amount of territory. I could barely believe people once filled all that space. We stayed ahead of the Freaks, if there were any nearby. I watched for signs and sniffed the air, but the farther north we went, the less I saw any hint of habitation, human or otherwise.

At first, we set a good pace because we had some supplies left from the ruins. Once those ran out, the trip slowed because we had to find food, and boil water in the evenings to make sure we had some to drink the next day. Once we passed out of the ruins, we went longer without seeing any relics of days past. We still saw no indication anyone had survived the plague, other than the underground tribes and the gangers.

We had been walking for eight days when Stalker and Tegan complained about our hours. It was the first time they'd agreed on anything, though they were careful to keep the animosity silent and simmering. Neither of them let their past color our journey outwardly.

Stalker brought it up. "We can stop traveling at night. It's getting colder, and there's nothing much out here to avoid."

Apart from wild animals, I had to agree with him.

Tegan seconded. "I'd like to see the sun again."

Fade looked thoughtful. "We'd have to lay off travel for a day. Stay awake and gather supplies so we can shift to sleeping at night."

"It's not like we're going to be late." Tegan grinned at him.

I nodded. "It's fine."

Everyone had to make sacrifices, so it was my turn. But part of me couldn't help but fear what would happen. The sun was going to burn me to a cinder.

"Your skin will get used to it," Fade said softly. "Just stay covered up as much as you can during the adjustment period."

"Good thing it's cold anyway."

We'd picked up warmer clothing on the way out of the ruins, but it had been harder than I'd expected. Bugs had chewed a lot of fabric and mold and mildew had gotten a lot too. The slick fabric I wore now was the most resistant, so we'd started looking for heavier clothing made of the same stuff. Layers made sense, so we were all bundled against the bitter wind.

It was nearly dawn now, the first fingers of light tapping at the sky, and we needed to find a place to rest. Fade didn't like going too far from the river, so I scanned in both directions. I had the best eyesight in the dark, which balanced against the fact that the light hurt my eyes even through the glasses we'd scavenged. Stalker had the best day vision, by far, so once we started walking during the day, he would lead and scout for danger. I didn't know how I felt about that.

"I see something over there. Might be a building," I said.

"Can you tell how far?" Tegan asked.

I could tell by her posture that she was ready to drop. Of us all, she was least suited for a long trek like this. She wasn't strong; her life with the Wolves had prepared her to do one thing—and it wasn't walk all day long.

I shrugged. "Fifteen minutes, maybe? Can you do it?"

Otherwise, we had the prospect of rolling up in our blankets on the cold grass again. I didn't know about anyone else, but I could do with shelter, particularly if we had to stay awake through the day. Stalker and Fade nodded; they could do fifteen more minutes, no problem.

I set off in front because at this distance, nobody else could see what I saw. We'd walked half of that time before Fade said, "I see it."

As the sky lightened, the lines of the building came clear. Built of rough, irregular stones, it was very old, maybe the oldest thing we'd come across in our trek, but it had four walls and a roof. That was good enough for me.

The door had warped away from the frame, so it stood open as if in invitation. I shivered as the wind cut through my clothing. Inside, it was a little damp, and none too clean. Relics of days past gathered dust, and cobwebs trailed in the corners. Even with the dawn coming, there was no banishing the desolation from this place.

Broken furniture lay in piles in the first room, like someone had fought—and lost—here. It wasn't a big place, just four spaces. I recognized the kitchen from the basin and the rickety table. The chairs' legs had rotted away, built of lesser wood, and they lay tilted on their sides. There was an indoor waste closet and a room for sleeping, I thought, based on the lumpy pallet that had sunk into its wooden shelf.

In the waste closet, I pulled a handle down and was shocked

that the stool responded with a gurgle of water. I pushed another lever, and the basin spat water at me too. I squeaked in surprise. How was that possible?

Fade came to the door with an inquiring look. "Everything all right?"

"Look at this." I showed him what I'd found.

His expression reflected the same wonder I felt. On the far wall lay a bigger basin, one large enough to hold a person. He turned the lever there and more water spat out. It was a little brown at first, but then it ran clean, cold, but clean.

"If we boil a little water, we can add it to this and take a warm bath," he said.

It sounded like the best thing ever, better even than the prospect of being warm and dry for the first time in days. The first part of the day, we spent cleaning, and then we dragged all the dry wood into the fire pit in the main room. With a little help from Fade's lighter, we got a nice blaze going.

Indoors, the light didn't bother me as much, though I still wore my glasses. The pit actually had a metal device that looked suitable for hanging pots. I was eager to test the idea that we could bathe in the waste closet, so I filled a pan with water and heated it. I used about three of those along with a judicious amount of cold from the spout. Under the basin, I discovered what appeared to be soap. It crumbled when I opened the paper, but it lathered when I stepped into the water and dunked it.

I only had a little water to stand in, but it worked, far better than the cold, quick washes we'd been doing in the river. Afterward, I washed my clothes in the water and rinsed them in more cold. I put on the one outfit I had left from the enclave and tried not to think about how I'd feel when it wore out too.

After I succeeded in getting clean, Tegan took the next turn.

We were all filthy, after mucking out this place on top of all the days of hiking. But the fire felt fantastic as I settled down in front of it. I was tired and hungry still, but at least I was warm. I beat some of the dry dirt off my blanket, wrapped up in the clean side, and tried to comb some of the tangles out of my hair with my fingers.

A bit later, Stalker pushed through the front door on a cold wind. He let in both chill and brightness, an interesting contrast, I thought. In one hand, he carried a bloody something. On closer inspection I saw it was a bird. In the other, he held a furry animal.

"You may want to clean and gut those outside," I said. "I'll cook them if you do."

I'd watched Copper do it a hundred times. We had a fire, how hard could it be?

He raised a brow. "You're welcome."

"Thanks."

But he was already going back out. He pulled the door as far closed as he could, but it didn't shut all the way, even when you applied force. Stalker was quick with a knife, I'd give him that. Before too much longer, he came back in with the flesh skinned from the bone and pierced on sticks. That looked like a good idea.

He sat down beside me and kept one of them. We roasted the meat companionably. Watching him, I turned mine often to prevent it from burning. Pretty soon, the room smelled so good my mouth watered.

Fade came in shortly with more meat, animals I'd never seen before. They had funny back legs and long ears. I pointed at the door.

"No blood and guts in the house." It was an absolute rule.

He stood in the doorway, watching us for a moment while the wind swept through in a low moan. I couldn't read his expression. Then he went back outside.

By the time Tegan finished in the waste closet, we had more hot water for the next person. She took Stalker's place holding our food while he went to clean up. Once everyone had bathed, the meat was done; cutting it into smaller chunks helped with the speed of the cooking. Burning my fingers, I snatched a piece and blew on it until I thought it was safe to eat. It still stung my tongue a little, strong and gamy, but also juicy and delicious. We hadn't eaten well while we traveled, mostly fish we snagged out of the river.

Everything the guys had brought in, we ate. Maybe we should've saved some for later, but I think we were all too hungry to be cautious. Afterward, Tegan went into the kitchen to prowl around. I followed her, curious.

"There's more food in here!"

I peered over her shoulder and spotted tins like those we'd found in the ruins. She pulled them out while I examined the tins: mixed vegetables, tuna, something called "Spam," peas, and more creamed corn. All of it was sized to carry too, unlike what we'd found at the school. Divided up, this stuff wouldn't add significantly to our weight.

It was late afternoon by this time; I could tell by the angle of the light slanting through the dirty windows. My head ached with weariness, but we had to stay awake until dark. Then in the morning, I'd face my enemy the sun.

To occupy our time, Fade read to us from *The Day Boy and the Night Girl*. We were nearly to the end of the story, and I wanted to know how it ended, if they escaped from the witch, or whether she caught and killed them. Though I would never admit it, I felt their story had some connection to mine. Like Nycteris, I had grown in darkness and feared the light. In my heart I felt if she came to a good end, then I might also.

When dark finally fell, I felt weary enough to sleep without worrying about the future. But when we woke, the world had changed.

Snow

A white blanket lay across everything; it had appeared during the night and only the tiny paw prints dotting the surface gave me any assurance we weren't completely alone in the world. The sky hung heavy gray, and even the sun seemed dimmed, though it reflected brighter off the ground than it did up above. I pulled the door open, picked up a handful of the stuff, and then dropped it in amazement, rubbing my fingers against the cold. The others looked at me strangely, and I realized I was the only one who had never seen this before.

"What is it?" I asked with some resignation. There was no hiding my ignorance this time. They should be used to it by now.

"Snow," Tegan answered. "It's what happens when the rain freezes."

"It would be death to keep going north in this," Stalker said. "We're lucky we found shelter. We have water and food and the prospect of hunting more. This is a good place to wait out the storm."

"We should have a bit longer until true winter falls," Fade added.

"Winter." That was a new word. It sounded cold. I glanced at

Fade, whose face was closed and blank. If he wanted to keep going, I didn't know. These days, I didn't know much about him. He hadn't been the same since Pearl's death.

"The river's close by for fish too," I said, and then wondered if they froze to death when it got cold. Maybe there *were* no fish after the snow fell.

"What do you think?" Fade asked Tegan.

"I don't want to walk in the snow."

I glanced around, assessing its potential for comfort. We had no furniture, no rag pallets or so much as a stool or crate. Most of what we'd found, we would have to burn, and once that ran out—

"What can we use once the old wood is gone?"

Stalker went into the kitchen and came back with a tool that looked suitable for hacking things up. It made me uneasy seeing it in his hands. "I can cut more."

"You should do it before the snow gets any deeper," Fade said.

Their eyes met and clashed, a quiet dispute, and then Stalker turned with a shrug. "Fine. I'll be back soon."

To my surprise, Tegan got to her feet. "I'll go with you. I can help carry it."

Maybe she felt like she had something to prove, to herself, if nobody else. I could understand that. She didn't take a weapon as a point of pride. The club wouldn't do her any good against Stalker anyway; lack of training would betray her. Still, she had to establish that she didn't fear him and carve out her place in our group.

They went out together on a cold gust of wind. Afterward, I wedged the door shut as much as I could, digesting the idea that we weren't going anywhere for a while. I'd lost track of how long it had been since we left the underground, and I was a little surprised we were still alive.

"How long does this last?" I asked Fade, gazing out at the snow.

"Months, sometimes."

I shivered. "I'm glad we got out of the ruins before it hit."

"There probably won't be anything left alive, soon," he said quietly.

"Underground too?"

He shrugged. "The Freaks took Nassau, and College wouldn't prepare, so I doubt they'll fare any better." The sharp way he said the words, it was almost like he *wanted* to hurt me.

"Why are you so mad at me?" There was no point in ignoring it. I had hoped he'd get over the sadness or whatever had him acting this way, if I gave him time, but it didn't seem to be working.

"I'm not."

I swallowed the urge to call him a liar. "Then who are you mad at?"

"Myself."

"You feel bad about Pearl," I guessed.

"She managed to keep safe, after her dad died. I show up—and in one day, I get her killed."

Much as I wanted to, I couldn't deny our part in it. At this point, it didn't matter whether I'd liked her. I'd hardly known her, and in truth, neither did he. He only remembered the brat she used to be.

"Does it help anything for you to feel this way?"

"No. But I can't seem to stop either."

"Is there anything I can do?"

He stared at me for such a long time that I grew uneasy. And then he asked, "Are we still partners? I know Silk put us together, but would you choose me now?"

As before, I had the feeling he meant something different with the word. "I don't trust anyone like I do you."

By the way his face closed, it wasn't the response he wanted. I sensed I'd let him down somehow, but he didn't make it easy. He started poking at the fire, and the question weighed between us in the silence until the other two returned.

Waiting was tough. We divided up the work, marking the days by cutting wood, hunting, cooking, and turning our shelter into a decent nest. In trunks in the sleeping room, we found some fabrics we put to good use making proper rag pallets. I laid them before the fire, grateful for such small touches of home.

Tegan got stronger visibly. This work she handled better than walking all day. As for me, I missed patrolling. It was too cold for that to serve any purpose, though. Anything that might hurt us would get lost in the snow or freeze.

As the days rolled on, game got scarce and we ate canned goods some days. Spam turned out to be a hunk of slimy meat. That gave me pause, but once we sliced it, the stuff smelled and tasted fine. I concluded the goo must be to keep it fresh.

Fade fell deeper into himself, more like he'd been in the enclave before I got to know him. He had stopped reading the book to us, and I didn't have the heart to ask for the ending when he clearly had lost interest. I picked it up sometimes and touched the pages gently, marveling at its age.

To pass the time, I borrowed Tegan's letter book—the one her mom had used—and started teaching Stalker to read. He had a good head for learning. In just a few days, he memorized the alphabet, then the words followed swiftly. Sometimes I fell asleep listening to him murmur, "A is for Apple . . ."

Often I felt Fade's eyes on me as I sat with Stalker, but I didn't look up. If he didn't have the courage to say what was on his mind, I couldn't help with whatever was bothering him. The other two took to chopping wood during Stalker's lessons.

Eventually, I had to admit, "I think that's all I can teach you."

Fade could probably do more but he wasn't likely to offer to spend extra time with Stalker. He closed the book, stowed it, and stood. "Maybe I can return the favor."

"How?"

"Come on."

He led the way into the sleeping room, which was totally empty now. We'd burned or tossed out everything the former residents had left behind. That left us a good-sized space, though cold, compared with the front room.

"What are we doing?" I was no longer afraid of him. Whatever he had been in the ruins, he had sworn to start over clean, and so far, he was keeping his word. That was good enough for me. If anyone understood not wanting to be judged for past actions, I did. I'd always be haunted by the way I'd let them kill the blind brat, wrapped in fearful silence as the guards took him away.

"I thought I'd show you some moves. You're good, but predictable."

I brightened. It had been ages since I did any training, and sitting around would make me soft. "Don't use your blades. I'm not fast enough."

"I won't," he said. "Just hands and feet."

We practiced for a while, but I just couldn't get it. I was rusty and slow, and it made me angry. *Some Huntress.* He came around behind me to show me how to position my arms for the strike. My hands arced downward. Holding my daggers at the right angle, I'd slice a nice strip of someone's chest.

"What're you doing?" Fade asked from the doorway.

I turned. "Training. Want to go a round?"

He shook his head and slipped away.

That soon became our custom, and my fighting improved as I faced off against Stalker. Training made me feel better about our chances. I'd spent my life training to protect people; I couldn't just *stop*.

After one particularly tough bout, I sat panting, elbows on my knees. As I glanced up, I caught Stalker smiling at me. It was such a break from his usual expression, I tilted my head with a questioning look.

"You're good," he said. "Truly good, dove. I like fighting you."

The way he said *fighting*, it seemed to hold another layer. I raised a brow. "Dove?"

"It's a bird."

I pulled my knees up to my chest as he sat down beside me. "And why did you call me that?"

Stalker leaned back, resting on his arms. The room was cold, so his breath puffed out, curling before him. "I'd see them in the city, nesting in the broken buildings. They were small and fragile looking with their gray wings, but they could fly up where none of the other animals could hurt them."

"Not even a Wolf," I said softly.

I got the comparison. Though I *looked* weak, I had unexpected defenses. I couldn't mind being likened to a creature that soared so beautifully on the wind. I decided I wouldn't object to the nickname.

By the time the thaw came, we were all ready to move on. The little building had provided us shelter, and we were grateful. It was also small for the four of us when we had to stay near the fire pit for warmth.

The break had also given me a chance to get used to the sun without such burning heat. Now I felt ready to face it; I was used to staying awake during the day at least.

The morning we left, I took a long look at the place. We'd made it cozy and habitable, but unless we wanted to stay here, just the four of us, for the rest of our lives, we had to move on while the weather allowed. Since Fade didn't know how far we had to go, we might need a long time to get there.

The ground was wet beneath my feet, and everything smelled fresh and clean. A little bite lingered in the air, but through my layers of clothing, I hardly noticed. We set out early and cut back toward the river. It shone silver in the distance with tall trees beside it. I had spent a good portion of the winter months asking the names of things I didn't know, and they were all patient with me.

Now I could identify just about everything my eyes touched on as we walked. *It would be hard traveling, but we could eat some of the plants,* Tegan said. Fish leaped in the water, rippling the surface in telltale rings. Things could be worse.

We had been walking for five days, and that made our sixth, when the trees came into view around a turn in the river. I had seen a few here and there, but these lived in a village of their own. They clustered tight, throwing deep shadows across ground littered with fallen limbs and leaves. It gave off a rich, earthy smell, but better than dirt, and more rare.

I listened, enchanted, to the bird song. Bright flutters of color in red and blue among the green leaves made me cant my head in hope of seeing them fly free, burst upward, and soar on the wind. They didn't oblige me, but continued to sing from the branches. Other sounds lay over the top of the rushing river, chatter of animals and scrabbling claws. I had never heard anything so lovely.

"We'll find rabbits here," Fade said.

Thanks to constant review of the letter book with Stalker, I knew *R* was for rabbit, and the picture matched the animals we set snares for, more or less. I nodded. "Should we do a little hunting along the way?"

"Let's. Meet back here when you're done. Come on, Tegan." She gave me a puzzled glance as Fade strode deeper into the woods.

He had been doing that more and more lately, choosing her company over mine. At first, I thought it was because he didn't want her to be alone with Stalker, but we'd been together for a while. If she still feared him, there was no hope for her.

"Let's go get some meat for the pot, dove." Stalker angled in the opposite direction, still into the trees, but away from the path Fade had chosen.

Blissful coolness spread over my skin as I entered the green-cast shade. Everything hushed as if the trees filtered sound as well as light. I could hear my footsteps, though I prided myself on my stealth. But maybe that only applied underground. Out here, I cracked every branch I stepped on.

As we went, Stalker laid his portion of the snares we'd made from stuff we found back at the old building. Then he led me away because the rabbits wouldn't come running past if they smelled us close by. I didn't mind this part of hunting; it was similar to what we'd done in the tunnels, only we hadn't been catching rabbits.

He held up a hand when he thought we'd come far enough. I stood quiet, waiting for him to explain why I had to be silent.

And then he stepped into my space, pushed me flat against a tree, and put his mouth on mine. He didn't do it like Fade. His lips moved more and he pressed into me. I didn't know how I felt about it, so I shoved him back.

"I thought you wanted me to."

"Why?" I demanded.

"You taught me to read. And we spent all that time together training. I thought you knew it was an excuse to be close to you."

I thought of all the times he'd stood behind me, his head near mine, hands on mine as he positioned my body, and I understood. But for me, it had been practice. I had missed any other meaning in it. When I thought of him, I admired his speed with the blades and the power of his scars. I didn't know what else there might be. I'd never even considered it. He was my companion, like Tegan, but not like Fade. Nobody would ever be like Fade. That much, I knew.

"Why me? Why not Tegan?"

"I think Fade wants her," he said with a shrug.

The words cut into me. Was that the reason he sought her out so often? Not just protecting her from Stalker. Maybe it was more.

He went on, "And even if he doesn't, she's just a Breeder. She doesn't have anything else to offer. You, you're like me."

I didn't know if that was true, or whether I wanted it to be. "You mean a Hunter?"

"Yes. You're strong."

My marks said I was anyway. Some I'd received on my naming day, and others I'd received in battle, as a true Huntress would. Someday I might even have people to protect again, if this journey ever ended.

I reached up, tentative, and touched my fingertips to his scars. Almost since I first saw him, I'd been curious. From the texture of his skin, they hadn't used a hot blade to seal them. They had tasked him to heal them on his own. In its way, this was a kind of strength too.

"You don't mind?"

His eyes closed. "I never let anybody do that before."

"Why not?"

"It would look like weakness."

That was a very Hunter thing to say. I understood that from the inside out, even if we'd grown up in different worlds. If you wanted people to take you seriously, you couldn't let them think you were soft. You did whatever it took to prove you weren't.

When I dropped my hand, he caught it and used it to pull me closer. Warmth curled through me when he lifted me up and ran his lips down my jaw to my neck. The feeling shook me, so I put my hands on his shoulders. I intended to shove or kick, something to remind him he couldn't handle me this way. Instead, I found myself gazing down into his pale eyes. They didn't look cold to me anymore; instead they shone like the sun on snow. For an instant, I saw Fade in his place, smiling up at me. And the sensation split until I couldn't decide what I felt.

"We should—"

"Check the traps," he finished.

Stalker set me on my feet, and I led the way, swirling with confusion. The snares only had one rabbit, but it was enough. So I collected the rest of them and he stowed them in his bag. Tegan and Fade met us in the appointed place with a couple more.

"How'd you do?" Fade asked.

And my cheeks burned as if he could see what we'd been doing. But for all I knew, maybe he had been doing the same with Tegan. Maybe the flush in her cheeks didn't come from cold. They could've been pressed together in the shadow of the trees, whispering secrets. The idea didn't make me like her less, but I did feel sad and heavy, as if I'd lost something without ever knowing what it was.

Nightmare

Two weeks after we left the little building, we found something worse, worse than the big ruins by far.

The smell hit me first. I lifted my head, scenting, and then the river turned. A faded gray length of poured rock angled into the ruins. Compared with the others, these were small, but raddled with damage. Many had rotted away or crumbled to rubble.

And the place reeked of Freaks. It was the first time since heading north that we'd seen any signs of life. I'd started to wonder whether we were the only ones left. Scary thought. But this frightened me more.

Because it was nearly dark—time when we started looking for a place to rest—I could *see* them, shambling in the distance. That was their territory; I sensed it in my bones. I wasn't sure where we might be safe, but I was positive we shouldn't pass. "Let's not go through there."

Fade turned. "You smell it too?"

"We all do," Tegan muttered. "It's disgusting."

Stalker gazed into the distance, one hand shading his eyes. "If we cut east, we can go around it."

"That'll take us off course," Fade said. "But I think we'd better."

I didn't say so, but it wasn't like we *had* a course. Another path, overgrown with grass, led east. It had been made of that poured rock too, but time and rain had worn it down, so it was mostly broken, more dirt than anything else. It led away from the river, but maybe we could get back to it once we skirted the danger. Unless those ruins had a small human population, the Freaks must be preying on one another. That would make them more desperate and more feral than the ones we'd fought.

Or they could be hunting . . . like *we* did. The comparison worried me. I didn't want to find them like us in any fashion.

"I can't believe they're here too," I said.

"They're everywhere." Fade's voice was grim, his face cast in sharp relief by the rising moon. It silvered the world, making it soft and cool.

A grim thought—everywhere we went, we would be hiding from them, running, or fighting. Maybe we should've stayed at the little house by the river. At least there hadn't been any Freaks in the area, and we'd had food. But we'd all wanted to try to find the place Fade's sire talked about, where things were better. I was beginning to think it was hopeless.

Coming over the next rise, I froze. There were ten Freaks, and at first they seemed as surprised as we were. Still hideous, still terrible, but they looked healthier than the ones we'd left behind. The Freak hunting party raced toward us; they dropped their kills—animals, as I'd guessed—and snarled in vicious anticipation of bigger, sweeter meat. I whipped out my daggers.

"Get behind us," I called to Tegan, but she had my club and she took a position beside me with fierce determination.

"I've been practicing with Fade," she said.

There was no place for her to hide here anyway. It hurt a bit when Fade and I didn't go back-to-back like we used to, but I had other things to worry about. Stalker fell in on my other side, blades in place on his hands. The Freaks surrounded us, no doubt expecting an easy win. They couldn't be used to prey that fought back.

These weren't as hungry as others we'd encountered, so they attacked with their claws first, teeth second. I used my elbows to block like Stalker had taught me while going for the quick slashes against their torsos. I didn't have his speed, but I managed to avoid most of the hits and protect my chest. We each needed to take down two, and then split the difference.

Beside me, Tegan swung wide and hard; I gave her plenty of room. She drove them off while I caught them in the recoil. The world narrowed to the stab and punch, kick and thrust. Blood spattered. I swiped it from my eyes and kept fighting. I had no time to look at anyone else, now. These Freaks weren't going down as fast as the others.

Kill them, Silk whispered in my head. *Kill them all.*

My Huntress nature emerged, sharp and clean, like a new knife rising from the hissing steam. These were smart. I saw in their eyes, as they tried to learn my tactics and lunged to test my reflexes. My daggers flashed in the moonlight, blood on silver, and my heart sang with each spin, each press of the attack. I hardly felt the wounds I took. I didn't know how bad they were. I lost sight of everything until the last Freak fell. Fade killed it with a clean slash of its throat. Beneath the stars, on the grass, it showed dark as the night sky. The gurgling, choking breaths slowed, then stilled.

My breath came in hungry gulps. "Everyone all right?"

"Few cuts," Stalker said. "Nothing serious."

Fade smeared some blood off his palms and onto his shirt. "I'm fine."

I turned to Tegan just as she crumpled. Fade caught her as she hit the ground. She dangled in his arms, pale and wan. Her eyes looked big and scared.

"Where are you hurt?" he demanded.

"Her leg," I said softly. The fabric of her pants had torn, revealing a long gash on her upper thigh.

With my dagger, I cut the bottom of her pants into strips and Fade tied off the wound. It helped with the bleeding, but she didn't look good. *That won't heal on its own,* I thought. The claws had rent her flesh deep.

The pain of having the slash tended put her out, or maybe it was the sight of her own blood. I'd seen people react that way before. Whatever the reason, she went limp in Fade's arms.

"Let's get out of here," Stalker said.

I paused and glanced at Fade. "Can you carry her?"

A sense of having been here before came over me. I remembered asking him that about the blind brat—and look at how that turned out. His face went tight. "I can. We need to find a place to rest and see if we can do something for her."

No arguments there. Since I had the best night vision, I set the pace and scouted ahead for more Freak patrols. The farther we got from their ruins, the more I hoped their numbers would be sparse. I couldn't count on us finding a safe spot to rest soon, though. I had to assume they were all around us. My one comfort—that I'd smell them before I saw them, even with my good sight.

We walked through the night with Fade and Stalker taking turns carrying Tegan. She woke up eventually and asked us to let her walk. I just shook my head and kept moving. I hadn't been this exhausted in a long time. Living aboveground had made me soft in some ways. As if from a distant dream, I remembered our run to Nassau and how only willpower kept me going. I called on it now to keep moving—and I wasn't even helping with Tegan.

I felt like I had to offer. "If you want me to take a turn with her—"

"We need your eyes," Fade said. "At least until it gets light."

"Do you think we're far enough to stop?" I sniffed the air experimentally and it smelled clean, only the crisp scent I associated with trees and plants, mingled with a hint of musk from some animal that had marked the bark, and a trace of rotting leaves. I also got the tang of blood from Tegan's wound, so anything hungry in the area would scent her too. *Bad situation.* The Huntress in me suggested we should leave her behind, too much dead weight. I silenced that voice with an angry clench of my teeth. It wasn't a choice I could make; maybe I did have part of a Breeder's heart, and that possibility didn't shame me anymore.

Stalker answered, "Best to keep going until daybreak, at least."

Tegan just whimpered and Fade shouldered her again, taking her from Stalker. I didn't have the watch or any sense of where we were going now, so I simply followed the road and watched ahead for trouble.

Just before dawn, I smelled it.

More Freaks—their rot carried on the wind. I spun in all directions, scanning for them. They came from behind this time, which meant they were tracking us. *Worse and worse.* Dark words boiled up, full of fear and dread, but I swallowed them and kept my report practical.

"Put her someplace safe. We have another fight coming."

Fade carried her off toward the trees and laid her down gently. "Stay here. *Don't* move. I'll make sure they don't go for you, and if they do, I'll stop them. Understand?"

She nodded, flattened herself against the ground, and went still. Playing dead? It might work as long as we occupied their attention. This time, we had twelve incoming and we were down one fighter. Not that Tegan was great on her best day, but she'd been deft enough at swatting them back. It kept them busy long enough for the rest of us to slice the monsters up.

"Four each," Stalker said.

I nodded and planted my feet, despite the aching exhaustion that coursed through me. It would have to be daggers this time. Though I could use my club—Tegan didn't need it—I no longer had the strength or stamina. The odds of winning were steeper this time, and the potential consequences of loss more grave.

As the Freaks charged us, I braced for the first wave. I didn't expect to survive the fight, but the steel Silk had instilled in me wouldn't let me roll over. I wheeled and cut one open. Its guts spilled out, slicking the ground. I danced backward, dodging an attack and leaping away from a snarling bite. These Freaks were angry—I saw it in their bloody eyes; they *knew* we'd killed their kin.

I caught a claw in the side. The pain astonished me, but before the Freak could fully rip into me, I stabbed it through the hand, and it wrenched back, worsening my wound. But not as bad it could've been. I still had my guts in place. I ignored the pain and sank my other knife deep into its chest. Punch and pull, as Silk had taught me. The monster fell, but two more took its place.

Tiring, I fell back, slipping in the blood and guts. They came at me from both sides, and I took them with twin downward slashes, just as Stalker had taught me. I had no doubt the extra training saved my life. I turned to see how they were faring, only to watch Stalker and Fade drop the last Freak, cutting into it in unison. They were fierce, beautiful, and oddly complementary, like the moon in the night sky. For a moment, I studied Fade's darkness and the fair gleam of Stalker's hair, and I *ached*.

I covered my injury with one hand as we stumbled toward Tegan's hiding place. She sat up, her face tight with pain. "Did we make it?"

"Yes," Fade said. "I don't think another tracking party can catch up to us."

I wasn't so sure, especially now that we were all covered in blood, and two of us wounded. To make matters worse, we all desperately needed a rest, and if we stopped here, now, they'd pounce on us while we slept. But I recognized that Tegan needed reassurance. I let the lie stand, but when Fade's eyes met mine, I called him on it silently. He lifted his shoulders in a quiet shrug of acknowledgment.

As the sky lightened, I dug in my bag for my sunglasses. I still couldn't see as well as the others during the daytime; maybe I never would. I'd do my best to compensate with hearing and smell. My bloody fingers left smears on the sidepieces, and my hands trembled as they fell. I pressed the right one to my side again, hoping it wasn't as bad as it felt. I remembered how the Wolf had died on the steps of the library. I didn't want a quick and merciful death—what was more, I didn't want to see how easy it would be for Stalker to do it.

Keep moving, I told myself. *Just like the tunnels.*

Stalker took the lead this time, and Fade swung Tegan into his arms. I stumbled after him, knowing both of us needed our wounds tended, but there was nothing but this dusty, silent road, leading endlessly into the distance. The fields around it

Despair

S talker found us shelter in the overhang of a ravine. Despite the bandage, Tegan passed out, her skin taking on a pale and sickly sheen. When I checked the wound, I saw she had been bleeding; the fabric was soaked. If we didn't get it stopped, she would die, no question. Bonesaw would've taken a needle and thread to it, but we had none. So I knew of only one thing we could do.

"Get some wood," I told Stalker. "And build a fire."

Though he must've been exhausted too, he rose and went to do as I asked, gathering the scrubby grasses, leaves, and fallen twigs he could find first, and then he ran off toward a distant tree. Breaking limbs would create a smoky blaze, but it couldn't be helped.

Fade sat with her quietly, her head in his lap. I recognized in his nature the Hunter instinct; it drove him to be fierce and protective of those weaker than him. Maybe that was why she drew him. She needed that part of him because she had no matching instincts. In that sense Stalker was right; she *was* a Breeder, but I no longer thought that was a bad thing. If not for them, our world would not go on, even in its limping way.

I scraped one dagger clean as best I could. The flames would do the rest.

"You think this will work?" Fade asked. He knew what I was planning, of course.

"Don't know. But if we don't seal that wound—"

"I know."

Before long, Stalker returned with his arms full of wood. I arranged it and then we started the fire, using the twigs and leaves first, and encouraged the green wood to burn. It caught slowly, but with continual attention it stoked up. The smoke would signal any Freaks in the area to our location, but sometimes you had to make the hard choice.

I cut away the fabric from Tegan's thigh. "Water."

Since we'd been traveling along the river until this point, we didn't have a lot to spare. I used it lightly, wiping away the worst of the blood, so I could see how deep it went, and where the ragged flesh opened up. It was bad, maybe crippling. If she walked again—if she *lived*—she'd limp far worse than Thimble. I rinsed off my hands as best as I could, and then I coated them with Banner's salve. I applied that liberally to the injury, then put my dagger blade in the fire. I held it there until it glowed. Stalker watched me in silence. I glanced at Fade.

"Want me to cover her mouth?" he asked.

I nodded. Even if she was out, she still might scream. With one hand, I sealed the edges of the torn skin; with the other, I branded her. It was all we could do. We didn't even have Bonesaw's limited supplies.

She did cry out, a terrible wail of pain that ended in Fade's hand. Tegan bit him hard, fighting to get away, but I didn't stop until I could see it had worked. I pulled the knife away then, and put it back in the fire to burn it clean. The wound could still get infected; her leg might swell. If she took a fever, well, I'd never seen anyone recover from that down in the tunnels.

My hands shook. I closed my eyes for a long moment and dropped my head back against the rock-and-dirt wall behind me.

"You did your best for her," Fade said softly. "That's all we can do."

Stalker's expression said he'd just leave her. He wouldn't have cared much about the brat, either. He embodied the Hunter tenet about strength and survival. Sometimes I admired that about him. Not right now. Tegan was my friend, even if she'd come between Fade and me. It wasn't her fault he found her softness more appealing.

"I need someone to do me now," I said, lifting my shirt.

Fade's breath came in a hiss when he saw what I'd been hiding. I couldn't actually see where the claws raked me, but by their expressions, it looked ugly. I glanced between the two, waiting to see who would reach for my dagger. It had to be sealed. I ran the same risks as Tegan: infection and fever. Freak claws weren't clean.

Stalker said, "I will," and plunged the knife in the fire.

He copied what I had done with our precious water and then applied the ointment. On my raw torn flesh, it burned like nothing ever had before, like fire before the white-hot knife. In a way it prepared me for what came after. I closed my eyes, clenched my teeth, and said, "Do it. Don't give me any warning."

He didn't. The dagger seared me, felt like it cut nearly to the bone, so far past my pain threshold that I bit my lip until it bled. I choked my screams, clinging fiercely to my Huntress mettle. *Don't let them see you weak,* Silk ordered me. *I taught you better than that. You were my best, Deuce. Don't you ever forget that.*

Now I knew I was dreaming. Silk never said anything like that to me. She didn't praise; she gave cuffs upside the head, orders and backhanded compliments, like, *You might be decent, if you weren't so stupid.*

When I finally opened my eyes, I found myself somewhere else. The fire was gone. Fade was gone. No Stalker, no Tegan. Everything was black and white, like one of the pictures I'd seen in the ancient, yellow papers at the library.

And Silk stood there, waiting.

"You're not dead," she said.

She'd always been good at reading my expressions. I half smiled because it was good to see her, even if it meant my mind had finally snapped. She looked the same: small, imperious, and confident.

"But *I* am," she went on.

The loss hit me hard. Could it be true? Was the entire enclave gone? If so, I was alone as I never had been. I thought of Thimble, Stone, and Girl26. I remembered Twist and ached to know his ending. I wanted to remember them all—each lost face, every crooked smile and funny gesture.

"Are the Burrowers gone too?" I whispered.

"I don't know. But you're the last of us, Deuce. Only you can tell our story."

"There's Fade."

She shook her head. "He was never one of us. He's a hybrid thing, and still doesn't like the fit of his own skin, despite my training."

"He just needs to find his place."

Silk ignored that, her face quiet and grave. "I came to say good-bye, and to tell you to keep the fire burning."

"What does that mean?"

I heard Silk again, whispering, *Keep the fire burning*. I opened my eyes, reaching for her. *So much to ask.* I grabbed ahold of Fade instead. For a minute, the two realities blurred, the black and white and the too-bright day. Then the dream went away, leaving me with that aching echo.

I'm the last Huntress.

"The enclave is gone," I said shakily.

"You passed out for a bit," Stalker said, kneeling beside me. "But I think you'll be all right. You're a tough one, dove."

"Get *away* from her," Fade snarled. "And *stop* calling her that."

I could feel the tension in his body. He held me in his arms, as if he'd been rocking me. I must've scared him when I passed out; such weakness was humiliating.

Stalker didn't back off. His scars pulled to the side as his mouth curled. "Deuce can make up her own mind."

Were they going to fight *now*? I felt far too sick at my stomach to deal with this. I shoved away from Fade; the shift sent a lance of fierce fiery heat through my belly. Concern got the better of both of them; they put aside the quarrel at least.

I decided not to tell either of them I had seen Silk. They probably wouldn't believe me anyway.

"How's Tegan?" I demanded.

"You weren't out long. No change," Fade reassured me.

A relieved sigh slipped out. Gradually, I eased back against the packed dirt. My stomach burned with a steady heat, but I could bear it. I had to.

"Get more wood for the fire?" I asked Stalker. "We're going to need it."

I didn't explain that request either. Fade pushed to his feet. "I'll go see about getting a couple of birds for dinner."

He was wicked quick with a rock. Often he could stun one

with a throw and then snap its neck while it lay helpless. After the long day, I had no taste for food—I only wanted to sleep, but I couldn't leave Tegan unguarded. Maybe I wouldn't be much protection in my condition, but she was still unconscious.

Before they left, I made sure my knives sat within easy reach. I wasn't sure I could get up if my life depended on it, but cutting the muscle behind the knee would do a lot of damage and bring the attacker down to my level. I watched the approach through the smoky filter over my eyes; it gave the world a peculiar green haze.

By the time Stalker returned, I felt light-headed. He bent to stoke the fire, and I grabbed his forearms in both hands. "Don't let that go out. Promise me."

"I'll watch it."

"No, *promise* me you'll keep it burning."

From his expression, he thought the wound had driven me a little crazy. But he said, "I swear. I'll go back for more wood as often as I have to."

That was all I needed. Darkness swept me away, deep as a night-kissed river.

When I woke, night had fallen. Tegan thrashed in a feverish sleep, and I felt none too healthy myself. The smell of roasting meat filled the air. That was welcome.

"Feeling better?" Fade asked. "Here."

He passed me the water bottle, and I could see how little we had left. With the rise of the moon and stars, the air cooled as well. The fire banished some of the chill. I drank a little, taking care with it. There was no telling how far we'd come, or where we would find the next clean water.

"Hungry?" Stalker sliced some meat for me and held it on the tip of his blade until it cooled.

I ate it in two bites and wished for more, but I could see there wasn't much. "Has Tegan woken?"

Fade shook his head. "Not once. She keeps asking for her mom."

"We should get moving," Stalker said, starting to kick dust in the fire to damp it.

"No!" I half pushed to my feet and staggered, astounded at how much I still hurt. I clutched my side, nausea rising. I hoped I wouldn't lose my food. I needed it.

"You want to stay here through the night?" Fade asked.

Not just through the night. I couldn't explain my irrational certainty, but Silk had been telling me something, something important, with the fire. We had to stay here and tend it. I just knew if we went roaming off, we were going to die, and nobody would *ever* hear our story, none of it.

But I couldn't put my conviction in any terms that made sense, so I just said, "Yes. Maybe she'll be stronger by morning."

But she wasn't.

At dawn, Tegan burned hot as the fire I insisted on tending. I bathed her with the last of the water and tried to get her to drink some. She thrashed and moaned and cried. Tears ran down her cheeks until she didn't have any left.

Glancing up, I saw the suggestion in Stalker's eyes. *We can spare her this. End it now and move on, before we're too weak.* If I had been going solely on my Huntress instincts, I would've agreed with him. But I had more, now.

"Give her until nightfall," I said softly. "The two of you go see if you can find any water. Get more wood."

Stalker raised his brows. "You're obsessed with that fire."

Yes, I was. *Keep the fire burning,* Silk had said. It was a promise we would survive, as long as we did. I wouldn't fail her.

"I'll go hunting again," Fade said. "I'll do better today."

"Thanks." Food wasn't my primary concern today, though. Water and wood, those we couldn't live without.

Once they had gone, I whispered to her. Little things the Breeders had said to me over the years, and then I read to her from the ABC book. "A is for Apple . . ."

Sometimes she cried. Sometimes she smiled. Once, she opened her eyes and tried to sit up but she didn't see me. I pushed her sweaty hair off her forehead and knew the most awful fear—that I'd lose her, before I got to tell her how much she mattered.

"Don't die," I said. "You're my only friend."

She was different; she didn't *demand* anything. There were no confusing layers with Tegan. I could talk to her—and that was all I meant by it, though it might've hurt Fade if he heard me. I didn't care.

Maybe now I knew how Fade had felt about Banner and Pearl. I'd never lost friends like this. I hadn't seen their bodies. I suspected Thimble and Stone were gone, like the rest of the enclave. He was right; it was different, and I understood him more. I wished I could go back and offer all the little kindnesses and comforts I'd withheld without realizing he needed them.

"Don't leave," she whispered.

"I'm not going anywhere. I'll stay with you."

"I don't like it when you leave, Mama." She clutched my arms with weak fingers, but she saw someone else imposed upon my skin. I imagined her mother, sneaking out for food, and leaving Tegan by herself. In the enclave, I'd never been alone.

There were different kinds of strength. I knew that now. It didn't always come from a knife or a willingness to fight. Sometimes it came from endurance, where the well ran deep and quiet. Sometimes it came from compassion and forgiveness.

The guys were gone a long time, and Tegan finally quieted, but it wasn't a good rest, like when a fever breaks. It was more that she had exhausted all her energy fighting, and now she would just die.

This time, Fade came back first, bearing several birds and a rabbit. He also had water for us to boil in the pot we'd taken from our winter home. "I found a pond. It was pretty shallow and muddy, but . . ." He shrugged.

At this point, we couldn't be picky. Heat would kill most of the bad things in it, but it took time to cool. By that point, Tegan's lips were dry and cracked. I tipped it down her throat and she swallowed, but I had no hope it was a long-term cure. When I checked her wound, it had started to swell. *Oh, no.*

Fade's face went grim, but he set to work on the birds and rabbits, skinning and deboning far enough away that the entrails wouldn't attract scavengers while we slept.

Later, Stalker returned with an armload of wood. He must've ranged farther this time.

He confirmed my guess by saying, "I did a patrol around the area. Seems quiet enough."

"Good to hear." We didn't need more Freaks.

He sat down beside me and touched his fingers to my forehead. "You're burning up, dove. Have you had anything to drink today?"

"I was saving it for Tegan."

"Why?" he asked, genuinely puzzled. "She's not getting better. You might."

Fade passed me a bottle, now refilled with the lukewarm water. I drank some slowly, conscious of how sore my throat had become. I did feel warm, now that Stalker had pointed it out. I'd assumed it was the proximity to the fire.

"Because she's one of us," I said finally. "And I'm tired of giving up."

Stalker shook his head. "Accepting the inevitable is not like giving up."

Fade gave a bitter half-smile. "Yes, it is."

"Well, she can't walk, and I'm not carrying her this time."

"I will." Fade started cooking.

I knew Stalker would want to leave as soon as we'd eaten. With every part of me, I knew we couldn't. We had to stay *here*. We had to keep the fire burning. Maybe it was the fever talking. Maybe I hadn't seen Silk at all.

But I couldn't believe that, or I'd have to accept Tegan was dying, nothing we could do would save her, and there was nothing better out there. Just more Freaks and empty land and silent despair. Before I realized it, tears streamed down my cheeks.

"The whole *world* is like Whitewall's razors," I burst out. "It cuts us, and we bleed but there's no purpose to it."

My fists clenched at my sides as I tried to get myself in hand. *A Huntress wouldn't act like this,* I told myself. But this time, it was only my voice in my head, not Silk's and I felt she had finally left me—that her good-bye had been real. And I wasn't a Huntress, not truly. I had been exiled, even before my whole tribe died. As I'd thought, so long ago, I was only a girl with six scars.

I did as you asked. It's not fair. I kept the fire burning.

Fade passed the roasting meat to Stalker, and then for the first time since I didn't remember when, he sat down beside me. He put his arm around me, and leaned his head against mine, as he'd done so long ago in the tunnels, when we had only darkness and each other. The tears fell harder; I couldn't will them away.

"We'll get through this," he promised, as I had, long ago, when we set off to Nassau with no hope of coming home again.

"Will we?" I asked, glancing at Tegan. "How?"

And then a strange voice, a new voice, called out from the darkness, "Whozere? I seen your smoke. If you're friendly, I'd appreciate a reply. If not, I'll be moving on 'fore y'can catch me."

I gazed up at the column of smoke swirling toward the dark sky, made more visible from the green wood, and I whispered to Silk, *Thank you.*

Salvation

I scrambled to my feet, biting back a moan of pain, and gazed up, for the voice had most certainly come from above us. For a moment, I saw nothing, which made me fear my fever had gotten worse, and then a shadow sharpened into a man-shape. He was tall, and he was most definitely *there,* staring down at me. In one hand, he held a lamp, like the one Fade and I had used in the relic room underground, so long ago now.

The man shone the light on us, studying us. Surprise cracked his voice when he said, "You're naught but young'uns. What're you doin' so far from safety?"

I strangled a laugh. In my world, there was no such thing. "We're lost, and we have an injured girl."

He eased cautiously forward to verify my claim, and he saw Tegan below. "Well, let's get moving. We don't want to linger."

Using my hands as best I could, I climbed up the slope. It was a fairly steep drop with a good overhang; that was why we'd chosen to stop there. He gave me a hand up. Up close, I could see he was bigger than Fade—and *old,* but not like Whitewall. This was a different kind of age, a version I'd never seen before. He had sloped shoulders and he wore something on his head, but it didn't hide the silver hair. I gazed at him in silent amazement.

"You're a long way off the trade road. D'you hail from Appleton?"

If I hadn't been mute with shock, I might've come up with a sensible reply. I kept my hand pressed to my side and my left on my dagger, just in case. Stalker came up behind me, and he too drew up short. But he had the presence of mind to say, "We came from the city."

The man raised his brows. "You funnin' me? Nobody lives in the cities anymore."

Our savior had granted those words the kind of conviction I'd once offered the elders. But his ideas were no truer than mine had been. His people didn't know about mine. This wasn't the time to argue with him, however, or to convince him Stalker spoke the truth.

"Tegan's pretty bad off," I got out. "Her leg's all slashed up."

"Ran into the Muties, did you? No wonder, out here. I never go anywhere without Old Girl." He raised a long black thing that I identified as a weapon, even before he made it pump and click. "I'm Karl, but folks call me Longshot."

"Why?" Stalker asked.

"Because every time I live through a trade run, it's a long shot. Been doin' it nigh on twenty years."

That couldn't be possible. In the underground tribes, in the ruins, people barely lived that long, let alone held the same job for that amount of time.

"How old are you?" I asked.

I knew the question had to be rude, but his answer was crucial. Because his very existence shattered and remade my picture of the world.

"Forty-two."

He *had* to a live in a better place, where people didn't shrivel up and die so young. With every part of me, I wanted a glimpse of it. Maybe it wasn't too late for me, despite my years below the earth. Maybe it wasn't too late for any us. I clung to that hope, fiercely exultant.

"I don't believe it," Stalker breathed.

But the old man didn't hear him. "Lessee about getting your friend up here. I can't leave the mules standing long."

"I've got her," Fade called.

Stalker went down to help him. I waited up top because it had been all I could do to get myself up the incline with the hot knife in my side. I didn't want to show weakness more than I had to. Silk might have sent this character; she might not. The boys gathered our gear, put out the fire, and then scrambled up. But when the old man got a look at Tegan he recoiled.

"That's fever," he said, backing off. "She plague-ridden?"

I shook my head, forgetting he probably couldn't see me in this light. "No, I swear. It's an injury. Let me show you." I lifted her leg so he could see where we'd sealed the wound, and how her limb was swelling up.

"Y'did some backcountry doctoring. Right brave, that was. But her thigh looks bad, and we're a day out of Salvation. Let's get loaded up."

He led the way back toward the road. I fell a little behind the others because the movement sent pain lancing through me. It was farther than it looked, and I was panting by the time I reached the wagon. I'd seen smaller versions, usually rusted and painted red. His was giant in comparison, and had two animals tied to the front of it. Mules, I seemed to recall him saying. They seemed placid enough as we approached.

"With all the supplies I'm hauling to trade, you'll have to squeeze in back there. One of you can ride up front with me."

"I will," Stalker said, and vaulted up.

The old man hadn't been kidding when he said it would be a tight fit. I climbed in first, swallowing another groan, and then I helped Fade get Tegan settled. The back was piled high with bags and boxes; luckily some gave when we leaned on them, and they weren't all hard-edged awful.

"You set?" the man called.

"Ready," I answered.

With a shout of "yah," he snapped the lines he had tied to the mules and we jolted into motion. Once I found a corner to curl up in, it wasn't so bad. Tegan lay across my lap and Fade's. Every now and then, I gave her a little water. She had gotten too weak to swallow it unless I rubbed her throat.

I ached as I looked at her. Fever chills wracked me too. One minute, I felt like I was burning up, and the next, cold as ice. Fade put his arm around me and I put my head on his shoulder, not thinking about the future. Nothing we could do about it. We'd given this trip everything and then some.

"You knew somebody was coming," he whispered. "Didn't you?"

"Kind of."

"How?"

At that point, I was too far gone to care if he believed me. "Silk told me."

He fell quiet, either worried about my mind or pondering what I meant. It was all the same to me. I slipped into a sleep full of whispers, as if I listened through running water. *Don't leave me, Deuce. I need you. I want it to be like it was, before the others came. I never had the chance to say it*—it *sounded* like Fade, but he'd never speak these words. Never whisper with such raw emotion. Did he just say—

I love you?

I *had* to be dreaming. The next thing I knew, daylight blazed against my eyelids. My whole body was stiff and sore; my legs had gone to sleep from Tegan's weight. I couldn't feel them.

I bent down, frantic, until Fade stopped me with a hand on my shoulder. "She's hanging on. It's all right."

"Nearly there?"

"I think so."

A slow exhalation pushed out of me. "Could you do me a favor?"

He almost smiled. "If it's in my power."

"Tell me the end of the book?"

Fade didn't ask why. He just dug into his pack, found it for me, and opened it to the page where we'd left off, before Stalker and Tegan came between us, before his sadness closed him against me like a heavy door. Softly, he began to read:

They were married that very day. And the next day they went together to the king and told him the whole story. But whom should they find at the court but the father and mother of Photogen, both in high favor with the king and queen. Aurora nearly died with joy, and told them all how Watho had lied and made her believe her child was dead.

No one knew anything of the father or mother of Nycteris; but when Aurora saw in the lovely girl her own azure eyes shining through night and its clouds, it made her think strange things, and wonder how even the wicked themselves may be a link to join together the good. Through Watho, the mothers, who had never seen each other, had changed eyes in their children.

The king gave them the castle and lands of Watho, and

there they lived and taught each other for many years that were not long. But hardly had one of them passed, before Nycteris had come to love the day best, because it was the clothing and crown of Photogen, and she saw that the day was greater than the night, and the sun more lordly than the moon; and Photogen had come to love the night best, because it was the mother and home of Nycteris.

Though some of the words were strange, hope sprang up in me. It felt like the right ending, the day boy marrying the night girl. In their triumph I found faith.

Just then the wagon jolted to a stop.

"We're here," Longshot said to us, and then he yelled, "Trade caravan! Open up!"

Easing Tegan away, I pushed up on my knees so I could see, and my breath caught. Tall wooden walls surrounded an aboveground enclave. Men stood on top of the gate with weapons like the one Longshot carried. They gazed down at us with hard faces and scrutinized the old man, his cargo, and us before waving us through. Most were younger than Longshot, but older than us. I had little way of knowing more.

As my heart lightened, someone opened the gates, so the mules could trudge inside. They moved like they were tired, and no wonder, hauling us all through the night. I put the book away and drank in the sight of Salvation.

The place was *wondrous*. The buildings were all new, built of wood and clay, maybe, and some even had fresh white paint. *People* walked the streets openly and none them appeared to be armed. They were clean and well fed.

"This is the place," Fade said. "My dad was right."

Once the wagon stopped, I climbed down, ignoring the pain

in my side. My fever had broken, leaving me more or less clear-headed.

"Let me take you to see Doc Tuttle," Longshot said. "Bring the girl. If she can be saved, he's the man for the job, and if not, he'll say some kind words for her soul."

"Soul" was a new word, one I didn't know, but instinctively I connected it to the trace of Silk I'd felt with me, long after I knew the Freaks must've eaten her.

"Thanks," I said.

Fade carried Tegan every step of the way. His back had to be aching, but he never faltered. After collecting our gear, Stalker paused every now and then to gaze around; I knew just how he felt.

People showed equal interest in us. We were wild looking and filthy, I had no doubt. The wall went all the way around the enclave, and people I took to be Hunters stood at every vulnerable point, guarding the safety of those who lived within. Here, there must be Breeders, who made sure the new generation could carry on, and the Builders, who made the things folks needed. It wasn't so different from what I'd known, after all. But everything was bright and clean, and the air smelled sweet.

"Here we are. Bring her on in. Doc!" Longshot shouted. "Got business for you."

"Did one of those mules bite you—oh." The man who came into the front room was short and wide with a bald head. Like Longshot, he wasn't young. I'd never imagined such a place, where people grew to look like this, instead of withered from the wasting that took us underground.

Longshot said, "Poor girl tangled with a Mutie. Hope you can help her. Anyway, I best get tending my goods before people take a mind to help themselves."

"Did you cauterize this wound?" the man called Doc Tuttle demanded.

I shared a look with the boys and then said, "We put a hot knife on it to seal it up. It was bleeding buckets and we were in Freak territory."

"That's what I meant. Oh, you've made a mess of things. Get out of here now." When we hesitated, he scowled at us fiercely, bushy brows drawn. "Get!"

"We'd like a minute with her," I said firmly.

His frown didn't vanish, but it softened. "Very well. I'll go get my things ready."

She wasn't conscious, but it didn't stop me from cupping her cheek in my hand, bending and kissing her forehead. "You'll be all right. We'll be back soon, Tegan."

"We will." Fade brushed her hair back and studied her, a muscle flexing in his jaw. I could see the idea of leaving her hurt him. But it hurt me too.

To my surprise, Stalker stepped forward and joined us at her side. He didn't reach out, but I saw something new in his face. "You're stronger than I knew, maybe stronger than *you* knew. So fight hard."

"You should stay," Fade said. "You're injured too."

I shook my head. "She's more important."

"You done in here?" Doc Tuttle came back with a tray of supplies, most of which I didn't recognize.

Since none of us wanted to risk Tegan's health by angering the man who could fix her, I nodded. And we left. I was afraid he might be cut from the same cloth as Bonesaw and would just make it worse, but we'd done all we could for her. I could only be glad we hadn't given up on her. Beyond that, I could do no more.

Gazing around, I read the signs on the buildings. SHOES. RE-
PAIR. CLOTHING. GROCER. BUTCHER. I knew shoes. Mine had worn
clean through during the long hike, and I'd lined them with fabric to keep from walking my feet bloody. I could use new shoes,
but I doubted I had anything anybody wanted to trade. What
was more, I didn't know any of the rules here, or where we
should go.

The guys stared around, for once in complete agreement.
They clearly didn't know what we should do next. But . . . maybe
I did.

"Longshot might help us," I said. "He did once before."

I led the way over to the wagon, half the length of the enclave. Longshot stood watch while men unloaded. He glanced
over at us with a friendly air. Through my glasses, I noticed the
lines on his face in the daylight more. He had a long, droopy
bunch of hair on top of his mouth, and I'd never seen that on
anyone before, either.

"Something else I can do you for?" he asked.

I nodded. "Is there anywhere we can stay while we wait for
news of our friend?"

In truth, we needed a permanent place because we'd find a
way to fit in here. There was nothing better out there; we already knew it. But one step at a time. Given our dirt, we'd sure
need his help in securing shelter.

Longshot thought and then said, "Momma Oaks will take
you in. She has a couple of spare rooms now. Lost one boy to
Muties, and the other's married." He paused, looked us over, and
added, "Say I sent you." He went on to describe the house and
how we could find it.

"I can't thank you enough." Then I realized I could help in

turn. "We saw Freaks—that is, *Muties*—not too far from here. They're smart too. You need to be prepared to fight."

Unlike Silk he didn't dismiss the warning. Instead he hefted the weapon he'd called Old Girl. "We're always ready."

I followed his gaze to the Hunters on the walls. "Do you get many attacks?"

"Less than we used to," he answered. "But we haven't gotten comfortable. Seen too many outposts pay the price."

I relaxed a little, seeing tragedy wouldn't repeat itself here. They were alert and wary. With a nod, I went to collect our belongings. It wasn't much, but the few things I had in my bag—that was all that remained of the College enclave—the underground tribes, as Stalker called us. Longshot gave us a wave and then went back to supervising the work.

Stalker roved ahead of us, taking in the sights; local girls paused and gazed at him wide-eyed. He returned their looks with a wolfish grin. Fade walked more slowly, head down, sorrow in the set of his shoulders.

I touched him on the arm. "Don't worry. Tegan will get better."

He looked at me with his black eyes and nodded, but I wasn't sure if he believed me. We'd lost a lot of people along the road. I thought maybe he looked at Tegan, and saw Banner and Pearl. I had to trust Doc Tuttle could save her. Any other outcome would break my heart.

This time, Fade led the way; this settlement wasn't too big, but it was so bright and lovely that it hurt me a little to look around, not just from the sun. I wished the brats could see all the marvels, particularly 26. She'd like it here.

We found the place easily. It was bigger than some of the

other buildings in town, taller too, and it had been coated with white paint that made it shine in the sun. Dark wood offered a pretty contrast, and there were even plants out front, blooming pink and red and yellow.

I slicked back my hair nervously and then drummed my knuckles on the door. The woman who opened it had to be as old as Longshot. I couldn't get over the shock of it, no matter how many of these faces I saw. She drew back at the sight of us, and probably the smell as well. Her eyes widened when she noticed Stalker's ink and his scars. Wisely, the boys left the talking to me.

"What do you want?" Her tone wasn't friendly.

"Longshot sent us over. He said you might let us sleep in your spare rooms."

"And why would I do that? You lot are filthy."

This wasn't going well, so I dredged up my best manners, learned through trying to appease the elders—and Silk, of course. "Please, sir. We'll clean up outside and we can help with work if you tell us what needs doing. We've come a very long ways."

"Oh?" That piqued her interest. "From where? Appleton?"

At first I couldn't remember the name of the ruins. I'd seen it, I thought, at the library. I squeezed my mind tight, trying to dig it out, and then I had it. I said the name out loud, though probably wrong.

Her face paled. "You lie. *Nobody* lives there anymore. Not since the evacuations."

"It's not a lie," Stalker growled.

I put up a hand, not wanting him to scare her. She was already upset with us. If she thought he was dangerous, she'd shut the door, and then where would we be?

"Show her the book," Fade said softly.

I smiled, dug into my battered bag, and pulled out our copy of *The Day Boy and the Night Girl*. She took it with reverent hands, examining the age of it, and then she opened it and flipped to the back. An old yellow card was stuck there, stamped with the letters PROPERTY OF THE NY PUBLIC LIBRARY.

Her eyes lifted and met mine. "You *do* come from the city. I must tell the town council at once. Edmund!" she called to someone out of sight. "Listen, there are people living to the south in Gotham."

"Are there?" a man asked.

I heard movement and then he stood beside his wife, peering at us. He, too, was old in a way that lightened my heart. His face spoke of years lived, not lost to the withering sickness. Maybe living here could grant us that health.

Momma Oaks murmured, "Come in. You must tell me your story, child."

I almost said, *I'm not a child, I'm a Huntress—the very last,* but then I looked on her kindly face and knew the truth would scar her in ways she might not be able to bear. When she opened the door to us fully, we went inside.

Author's Note

It's hard to envision the end of the world or predict what it might be like. Most of my research indicated that if some apocalypse occurred—disease, famine, or zombie scourge—society as we know it would likely break down within a hundred years. I read a number of articles, including this one: http://news.bbc.co.uk/2/hi/science/nature/8206280.stm. Full study details are available here: www.mathstat.uottawa.ca/~rsmith/Zombies.pdf.

In the nebulous future described in *Enclave*, biological weapons and manufactured plagues were to blame for the swift deterioration of modern life. I pulled my projections of what the cities might be like from what occurred in New Orleans, after Hurricane Katrina. Thus, the poor remain in these wrecked, abandoned cities, still devoid of hope or resources, taking their rage out on one another. Therefore, the gangers are violent, vicious, and patriarchal. I tried to imagine what such life would be like, both above- and belowground. To aid in that depiction, I watched *Life After People*, an informative and entertaining show on the History Channel.

I also investigated what products might still be functional after such a calamity, what scavengers might be able to pluck from the wreckage of a lost world. Plastic has a long, long shelf life—one article I read said certain plastics will never break down in a landfill—so the buckets, bottles, and sunglasses make sense in that context. I also determined that such a catastrophe would preclude the use of motor vehicles, so nothing more advanced than a bicycle can be found in *Enclave*.

I also came across fascinating information regarding the longevity of canned goods. One anecdote relates that a can of veal, which was more than a hundred years old and had gone on an Arctic expedition with William Parry in 1820, was opened in 1938 and fed to a cat, who enjoyed his meal and had no complaints. In a similar case, the steamboat *Bertrand* sank in the Missouri River in 1865 due to excessive weight of its provisions. It was recovered north of Omaha, Nebraska, in 1968. Among the goods were cans of brandied peaches, oysters, plum tomatoes, honey, and mixed vegetables. Chemists analyzed the food for spoilage and nutrition; though it wasn't fresh anymore, it was still all as safe to eat as when it was canned. More information can be found here: www.internet-grocer.net/how-long.htm.

Finally, the inspiration for the heroine's underground tribe stems from my fascination with the folks who dropped out of modern society and developed their own counterculture, right below New York. You can read more in this fantastic book, *The Mole People: Life in the Tunnels Beneath New York City* by Jennifer Toth.

Hope you enjoyed the apocalypse.

Acknowledgments

Without my agent, Laura Bradford, and my friend, Shannon Delany, this book would not exist. I extend heartfelt gratitude to them both. Early on, Sharon Shinn gave me the courage to continue through her lovely response to the first pages. I will always appreciate her kindness. Thanks also to Liz Szabla for being such a joy to work with and for making *Enclave* better through her insights. She was the perfect editor for this project, and I thank my lucky stars she took a chance on me. I must also thank the amazing team at Feiwel and Friends for doing such a beautiful job, especially my copyeditor, Anne Heausler. I'm so grateful to have such a fantastic group behind me. Finally, thanks to all my readers; I am nothing without you.